T hank you for choosing this book. If you enjoy it, please consider leaving a review on Amazon (and even Goodreads). Sign up for my newsletter for updates, sneak previews, and so that you don't miss the next book, A Reign of Heavenly Fire, coming soon!

# Twelve blades in contempt

## The Epic of Egaisha
## Book One

Jorden Darrett

# Red Leaf Press

**Cover artist: Giaphox** (https://www.reddit.com/user/giaphox?sort=top&t=all)

**Map designer: Strigunart** (https://www.facebook.com/Strigunart/)

**Interior art design: Prognosis** (https://www.reddit.com/user/ResortMuch9109/)

To all the family members who were angry I dedicated the First Edition to the dogs, who are basically my daughters. I dedicate this to the dogs too, of course.

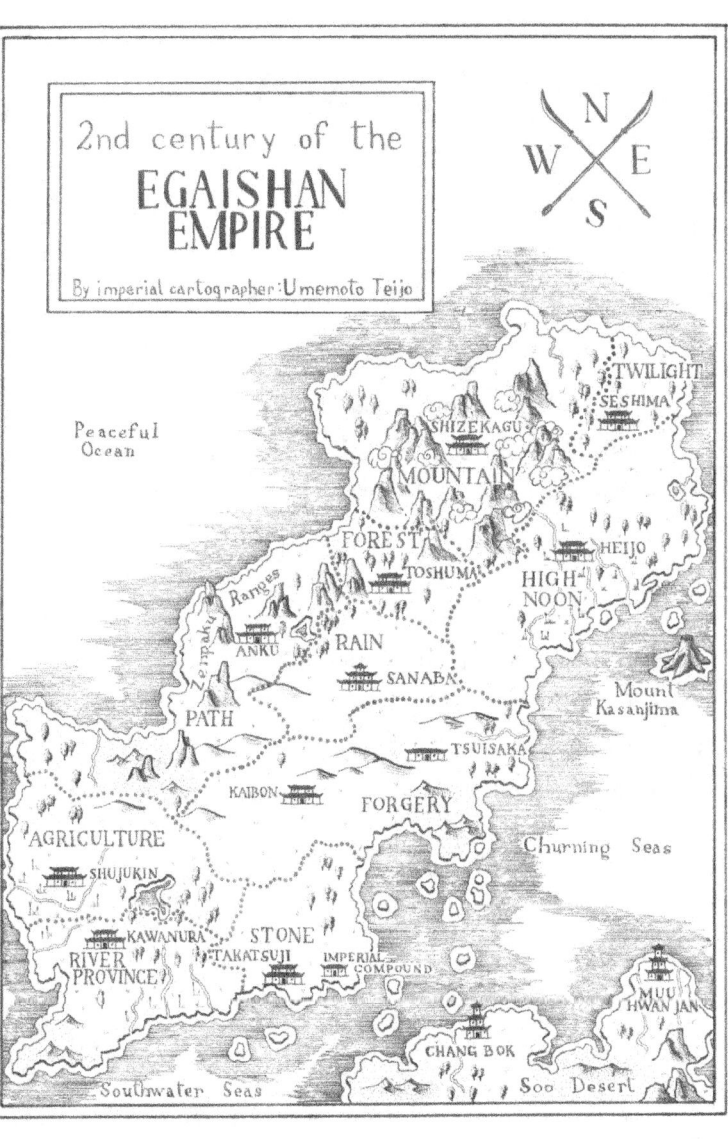

2nd century of the
## EGAISHAN EMPIRE
By imperial cartographer: Umemoto Teijo

N
W
E
S

TWILIGHT
SESHIMA

Peaceful
Ocean

SHIZEKAGU

MOUNTAIN

FOREST

HEIJO

TOSHUMA

HIGH
NOON

Ranges

ANKU

RAIN

SANABA

Mount
Kasanjima

PATH

TSUISAKA

KAIBON

FORGERY

Churning Seas

AGRICULTURE

SHUJUKIN

KAWANURA

STONE

RIVER
PROVINCE

TAKATSUJI

IMPERIAL
COMPOUND

MUU
HWAN JAN

CHANG BOK

Southwater Seas

Soo Desert

# Glossary

**Spring Months:** Toma, Saka, Rama,
**Summer Months:** Jun, Joku, Jkoku,
**Fall Months:** Hanam, Oban, Eman,
**Winter Months:** Yin, Won, Fenn

**Erru:** A person descended from the Egaishan tribes. Their people are spread throughout the continent of Egaisha

**Kotonese:** A person of southern Egaishan descent. A small population.

**Tarshan:** A continent south of Egaisha, mysterious to most Erru.

*"Why do you flee? Why do you abandon me?"*

*The night asks of the moon.*

*"Am I not your child?"*

*"I am left to be transfigured by the light."*

# Contents

# Silencing

Takasa Aiya gripped the Silencing Daggers, one under her chin in her left hand and the other still poised at her side. Each was a foot of honed silver embedded within a chiseled blue hilt, slick with sweat and rain. She huffed. It had been three storms since anyone had been silenced with either blade, but tonight was not like most nights. Tonight, she would wield them as she had in the past, strike down her clan's enemies, and feed the earth with their blood.

"I can't strike them all, not before my damn time limit is up," she told her brother.

Takasa Koji stood cross-armed to her side in the training grounds. Beads of evening skywater dripped down his face and robes, illuminated by shielded lanterns dangling from stone posts throughout the courtyard. The cool air was filled with an ominous breeze. Eight fish-headed wood totems, each ten feet high, gazed down at them in a circle. About two feet in diameter, each was equally spaced from the others, bearing slash marks in chaotic patterns. She could see judgment in her brother's watchful eyes as Koji spoke those dreaded words for the dozenth time.

"Try again."

She almost denied him, almost asserted that it was pointless, that she'd been hacking and cutting for nearly an hour with no progress. Shozhu would come for their departure any moment now. No, she wouldn't allow that. For too long she'd subjected herself to these futile attempts at manifesting her full abilities, even if reluctantly. She was not one to give in, however humiliating. Life was an accumulation of accomplishments–so too was her honor.

She wiped long strands of black hair from her face, sleeve adjusting to reveal the river tattoo on the side of her wrist. Three parallel flowing lines. Coming here had been a last-minute decision on Koji's part, with no time to prepare. Thus, the two wore bright blue robes with billowed sleeves, as was custom of the Takasa clan.

The courtyard sprawled around them, walled in by pink leafed ash trees and the looming Takasa estate. Their deity's altar, a wide stream, burbled softly through the yard. Crickets chirped, and there was a damp-earthy scent, bending around gardens, wood benches, fountains.

Aiya closed her eyes and altered her mind.

When she opened them, a deep blue like the ocean had pooled over the usual dark brown of her irises, her pupils black islands. With sudden energy, she burst from the ground and landed against the side of the pole in front of her, crouching on its surface. She pulled her dagger across it, then pushed off to one across from her.

Landing with a smack against wet wood, her dagger sliced here too, cutting deep into the totem before gliding off its slick surface. Not a moment later she was gone, already landed to mark her third. As silver cut into the target, there bubbled that familiar sensation: an instant of uneasiness and fear coupled with a break in her focus.

Then, she saw it.

Aiya failed to shake the numbness from her body in time, pushing off the totem at only half her normal strength. She flew halfway across the training ring and tumbled to the ground, hands clawing for grass as she rolled to a still. She was glad for the cushioned fall provided by the soft field. The robustness in her frame faded away.

A light drizzle fell from the dark sky, freshly coating her with dampness. The light blue silk robes adorning her were grass-stained, likely beyond repair, but at this point she didn't care. Nothing bothered her except for the frustration of her repeated failure. Her gaze moved to the towering totems. From this angle, they appeared like predators who had finally succeeded in tiring out a rather tenacious prey.

Koji took shape above her, offering his hand. He was two years her senior, twenty and towering a full head above her when he stood at her side. He kept his expression neutral and chose his next words carefully, steeling himself against the urge to reprimand her. Aiya perceived the concern showing in his eyes as dark as the rolling clouds. When it came to training, hers most of all, he was solicitous.

His offered hand remained. "Is that all?"

Aiya took it and got to her feet. Save for the purling stream, the central courtyard felt quiet now. There was not even the soft rustling of leaves in the backdrop. Even the chilled air held still in anticipation, awaiting what fateful turn of events would come.

"Try again," Koji told her.

"Brother, it's no use, I can't align myself for long enough without—"

"Cease your grumbling and get back up there."

His tone was stern but his eyes were sincere. He hated seeing her like this.

"It's a stone's throw for you," she muttered. For him, maintaining alignment with River's deity was child's play. She ought to have attained his adeptness years ago, but it was when she displayed her power in full that she began to falter. Koji's anxiety for her own safety tonight was understandable, but that made it no less a burden on herself. Her face went hot with shame. Koji hadn't been hard on her up till now, yet she was sure she sensed his patience thinning. It wasn't long before their lives would depend on their adeptness.

Resigned, Aiya stood, arms hanging at her sides and eyes closed, her breaths becoming deep and rhythmic.

She concentrated on her deity.

Her proximity to the "river" made it easy. There in the background, the gurgling stream existed as an altar to the deity, the imitation of a river. It was no longer a necessary aid for her mediation, although it made slipping into this state of mind much easier, like the coalescence of water, leaving absent the mental strain of separating her mind from tangible reality.

Tension released from her muscles and her mind softened, allowing her thoughts to flow freely before they settled on the one and only other thing in existence. The river engulfed her consciousness, not a mere thought of the physical land feature, but of all its spiritual and metaphysical meaning. Meanings she had spent years pondering and studying. The river was strength, a natural substance molded into a force possessing its greatest potential. It freed itself from the natural prisons of water, the great mountains and the unyielding earth below them, and carved its path to the sea. It was speed and it was hungry power, drowning any land creature who dared overstep its boundaries.

But above all it was life. Through the river, civilizations arose and fell. It was clean drinking water, bathing water, a trading route and irrigation for crops. It was far more than gleaned the eyes at first glance, a deity whose glory lay incomprehensible. Incomprehensible, to a disorienting degree, was how it felt as Aiya gazed across the infinite well of power it offered and could only fathom a small part of it. Above her flared spiritual orbs of light as numerous as the stars.

She sank deeper into the trance until she could hear every lap and current of the river, as if she were leaning over it with an ear above its surface, or as if she had become the surface. All other senses dissipated and she was left floating, watching water ripple in her mind. She and the river became one. Her deity was as much a part of her as she was a part of it. She directed that sacred power inwards and felt a surge of energy and strength. Before even realizing she had opened her eyes, she was flying through the air, propelled by legs that could crack the ground beneath her.

She landed on a totem, slashed it, then swung herself to the next, curving the blade upwards as it slid off the wood. The same 'v' shaped pattern they always used. That made it more difficult, taking longer to properly mark all the totems. She chose this strategy years ago for herself, without instruction from Shozhu, before it caught on with her siblings. She would not give herself the easy way out, no matter the exhaustion nor frustration. This she had sworn to herself. She hated failure, but cheating herself was a far greater disgrace.

She was determined to get her ten marks this time.

Aiya leaped from pole to pole, furiously slashing then moving onto a different target. At this speed, landing with any sort of balance was impossible, so upon reaching the small surface she immediately pushed off to avoid falling. A haze of water and splinters sprayed with each mark.

There was her sixth. A tie for her personal best.

She kept her mind with the flow of the river, running forcefully, hindered by nothing. She wouldn't think of what was coming. Such was the only way to prevent it.

*I've got this. It won't happen this time*, she thought. Power sang and emanated through her frame, offering endless vitality. She was a blur, like the swift glide of a hornet stinging victim after victim. Seven. Eight. Raw power filled inward. She would accomplish her goal this time. Then she would do more. Fifteen marks was her personal goal. She could do at least that much. Ten marks came first. She still had yet to reach ten.

Nine.

Her alignment with her deity wavered. An all-too-familiar fear bubbled up in its place, and despite her best efforts her concentration faltered for only a second.

A span of time just long enough for that malformed thing to bleed into her vision.

Her eyes widened, and she saw it. That gross, decaying body, like a corpse dissolving at the bottom of the river. A sickly green-black color of rotting skin, the deformed jaw revealing decaying gums, devoid of any teeth. Its sunken features were forever curled into a smile, ghastly and malicious, a wide taunting grin that possessed Aiya's dreams as a child. Why she couldn't force it away like her brothers, Aiya didn't know. She only knew that it was here in front of her, arms spread out to catch her mid-flight, bobbing as if submerged under water. Her periphery sank into blackness, leaving the bloating corpse to consume her vision. A wisp of breath barely escaped her lips as her stomach went plummeting down her abdomen. It was here, really here in front of her, because she could smell its putrid odor, hear its ragged breaths, feel the tendrils of cold seeping from the tears in its skin. Blood froze and left her body rigid.

*It's not real!*

The thing never lost its effect on her. Lucidity came slowly gnawing at the fear that had briefly frozen her in place. She had failed to overcome this terror countless times. She wouldn't let it continue to paralyze her. Clearing her mind, Aiya squeezed her eyes shut. *It's just an image, Aiya, conjured by your brain which can't possibly comprehend the power of the river!* She opened them again. She would not look at the thing itself, much less its eyes. Much less those fattened sockets of pure hatred.

She focused on the dark nothingness at the corners, bringing her thoughts back to the river. The river was all that mattered, all that existed, and in it her fears did not. In it was complete power, peace and tranquility.

Slowly, the blackness began to fade.

It was already too late.

As the figure vanished, a totem pole materialized in its place and caught her forehead. Hard. Her head smacked off of it and her body tumbled to the ground. She sat up feeling her forehead, groaning in pain. It had already started to swell. She knew she was being pathetic. All that determination had only led to another failure.

Koji appeared at her side. "It happened again?"

Aiya said coldly, "What do you think? We've been at this for an hour! I've been at this for years! I still can't get myself under control."

"You're near a breakthrough, I can feel it. You're bound to figure it out eventually."

She scoffed. "Empress' soul. For all the admiration Shozhu gives you, you sure are naive. I'm just not as good as you."

"Wrong. You're surprisingly good for the short amount of time you have access to the river. You just need to extend your alignment longer."

"Well, shit, Koji, thanks for telling me something I didn't know."

She regretted the harshness of her tone, set on by her rumbling frustration that couldn't be stopped. No, it wasn't frustration, but anger. Anger stewed from long years of disappointment. Koji insisted they test themselves as much as possible in the last hour before they slipped through the Hebi Lord's defenses and massacred the traitorous clan. While the more casual use of her power was simple, he knew she'd always had trouble exerting herself for more than thirty seconds.

"You need to remain calm, Aiya. Getting worked up only-"

"Hinders my growth, I know Koji. Did you notice that repeatedly following your advice has gotten me nowhere?"

"It works when you take it as a whole and not in pieces," he said, irritation creeping into his voice. "You get angry every time you slip. Frustration like that interferes with your progress."

"Why don't you just admit that I'm not where I need to be, that I'm disappointing? Father does, Shozhu too. I could handle it coming from you."

"They don't know what they're talking *about*." The words came out sharp, cutting away the next retort forming in Aiya's mind. He exhaled with closed eyes, letting his shoulders relax and taking a moment to gather himself before giving her a sincere look. "Don't talk like that. You know I don't see you like the others do. I...You and me, Aiya, we're really family. I won't pull statements like that out of my ass for you if I don't mean them. You're...I'm sorry for making us come out here tonight. I thought it might make a difference, but...damn, it seems our time is up."

It wasn't just the two of them anymore. She spun to face an approaching Takasa Shozhu, his oversized noble robes trailing down the stone steps leading into the training circle. He was a heavy, pudgy man. He appeared strong, assured, possessing an upright posture and sagely beard combed to his chest. There was, however, a slight limp to his step, some injury sustained in battle, or perhaps caused by long years of the deity's weakening effect on the body.

"I trust the two of you to be ready?" came his gruff voice, almost a growl. Everything from the man's mouth sounded growling and hostile to Aiya.

"Master Shozhu!"

They hurried to bow to their uncle.

"We are clear and confident about tonight's task, I hope."

"Of course, master," said Aiya. Their time was up. Their mission tonight was simple but twofold: confront a noble traitor and kill him, as well as any hindrances, and to burn down the estate after the fact.

"Remember," Shozhu demanded, face serious, "You are to simply go in, massacre, set the entire place ablaze, and get out. Leave no one alive and nothing unburned. Return as soon as possible, and be sure to bring the weasel's head back with you."

It was a nasty duty, a silencing duty. It was, however, necessary.

An avowed duty of the Ginju; unsuspected nobles by day, powerful, supernatural forces like Wailstorms by night. Sweeping and indiscriminating, creeping through households and over borders, descendants of their High Clan whose abilities few had ever witnessed. Few ever knew them personally, but all Erru knew of them. They knew the stories of well-guarded lords of the past, considered invulnerable one night and unrecognizable or headless the next, done in by what could only be Ginju, never heard, and seen only by their acts. They were imagined as beastly, as Erru exaggerated to monstrous effect.

"Understood," the two Ginju replied in unison.

Tonight, the rumors would prove true. There would be a monstrous display of might, and, come morning, they'd have another dead lord for the history books.

# Escape

The two teen girls raced past the rice fields, having escaped the town of Kun and leaving it in the low dust behind them. There was no one around them; even while running in the breeze the night felt still and open. Kun was a sleepy town of old farmers and family artisans, a town of people who slept early and woke earlier. Now the two girls ran freely, existing as if they alone were the only souls awake within a half-day's walking distance.

Sanabaji Tara, bounding at nearly six feet at seventeen years of age, maintained a good distance ahead of the other girl. Yohari trailed her down the dusty road that ran parallel to the terraced fields. She was six inches shorter but fast as a scurrying rabbit. How could they *not* have snuck out here for the night to escape the redundancy of their farming lives? The night was still young in their eyes, bringing with it a full moon that lured them towards a handsome view at the top of the town hill.

Her braided red hair swaying, Tara rounded a bend where the road steepened and the town of Kun receded from her view as the Hebi estate came into it. In the rice fields, pale moonlight glinted off the waterlogged bays. The petrichor was still strong in the air, the ground still soggy. Not much was visible in these windswept black plains. Tara liked it that way. Just her and Yohari.

It was in these fields they spent their entire lives working. Their hometown was supported by the rice trade and owned by the Hebi clan. Her father loved and feared the clan, never short of praise for how 'considerate' Lord Owa could be. It wasn't the work, but the boredom that numbed Tara's mind. Sow and harvest all year, reap their portion, and repeat.

Yohari was from a family of equal devotion. They worked on opposite fields, and planting had been particularly rough the past few months. The two seldom had any time for each other throughout their days, leaving them only the nights. Tara soaked in the musky air on her cheeks, feeling more alive than she'd been in days. She'd been scheming to get Yohari out here for the longest, for time spent with just the two of them. Time where she could smell Yohari's short black hair that cupped her ears, grip her waist closely and brush her mouth against her lips, appreciating everything about her with nothing in the way. This was her chance.

Tara's lover slammed into her from behind and they both tumbled to the ground, laughing.

"Your long legs don't mean you can outrun me," Yohari said. She always spoke in a bubbling tone, excited and full of young energy.

"Haven't I been outrunning you my whole life?" Tara said in reply, brushing Yohari's hair aside from her face. She could smell her from this distance, faint but fresh, like tea leaves, and appreciate the silhouette of her face. "Because of my father, I've kept a distance between us. I haven't allowed us to bond."

"Don't be coy, you've come onto me more times than I have you." Yohari's smile gleamed brighter than the moon. She adjusted a bit of Tara's robe to the side and Tara beamed like hot embers.

"Is that so?"

Yohari leaned in closer. "Yes. You know what else?"

Tara's heart sprung. She and Yohari were finally alone, with no one to interrupt. All day long, she'd anticipated this moment. The two of them stared into the other's eyes, knowing nothing would interfere. Yohari leaned in so that their noses were almost touching.

There was a rustle, then splashing sounds. Someone behind them.

"Who's that?" Yohari asked, alarmed.

Tara propped her elbows on the dirt path and flipped around to see two black figures sprinting through the water-logged fields. Her heart sank in sudden terror as the figures made their way past them.

The black shapes burst forth, moving towards the Hebi estate at inhuman speeds. *By the spirits....*

Wind like a hurricane blasted against their faces. They squeezed their eyes shut and screamed.

"What was that?" Tara said, keeping her crazed voice hushed as her hand flew over her mouth.

"Spirits?" asked Yohari.

Whatever they were, they were heading straight for the Hebi estate.

Aiya and Koji made for Lord Owa's abode. At this speed, the rice fields around and under them were a blur. Two stagnant bodies, likely commoners, flew by. Little did they know.

Tight clothing covered them from head to toe, black silks allowing for agility while keeping them unseen. Only a cut-out across their face left their eyes uncovered. The breeze aided in masking the sound of their movement, rustling the grass. Commoners were of no concern, however, and so Aiya focused her gaze on the Hebi estate ahead. There slept the man who owned these fields and the town of Kun across from it. It was much smaller than Kawanura, but then, it wasn't the capital city. Only a sleepy town about half an hour out by horse. She was faster than horses.

She couldn't keep it up for long. The night grew blacker around her vision and was forced to slow as her balance faltered. Koji slowed pace too, if clumsily. She couldn't guess at whether there was frustration in his eyes, but she felt awkward regardless.

When her alignment began to slip, she was forced to let go of the river, slowing for a span of seconds before regaining her speed. *It's not far now. Concentrate...*

"How are you feeling?" Koji kept his face forward.

"Grateful Ira isn't here." She thought she heard him scoff.

"It's not right for you to think he needs sheltering."

Aiya lost her footing, stumbling and catching her fall with her hands. She tumbled, then kicked herself up off the slick grass only to slam into Koji's chest as he seized both her arms. "You alright?"

Aiya wiggled free, face flushed. "You know it's this I don't want him to see." Without waiting for him, she ran. *Finish our mission or be damned.*

Even Ira couldn't say whether it was right what they were doing or not. Even so, he certainly wished for his own part in this back at home, to not be cooped up with their unblessed siblings at home who, unlike himself, were destined for statecraft, and to perhaps murder each other when the time came for a new clan heir.

The thought of them slaughtering themselves in a contest to be named next High Lord was sickening, though it couldn't be helped. The ranks of the nobility were like a large web entangled in the wilderness. It was bewildering in its complexity, and brutal in its competitiveness. That was why, after all these years of taming that wilderness, it was a mystery that Aiya could still be so bothered by the blood on her hands.

Her first Silencing was four years ago. Her father was entertaining a rival lord over dinner, a veil to discuss private matters with his rival: the head of the Hyuki clan, a man who sat on the council of judges which was composed of high-ranking noble families directly under the Takasa. Takasa Arusuke considered his life forfeit, having discovered his conspiracies against his clan with a few other mid-ranking lords, which meant at least a few dead military land governors. One of them had been a rat, and was rewarded handsomely for it.

Aiya and Koji crept behind the private dining room door. Ira was often claimed by his illness, absent while being cared for in bed by their servant Kisane. There was a slapping of feet behind them, accompanied by short titters. The two of them spun in alarm to the sight of Asaya waddling towards them.

Aiya's entire frame froze.

"Little bird!" she exclaimed in hushed tones, bringing a stiff finger to her lips. Koji moved, grabbing her and placing his hand over her mouth.

"It's okay, shenshen," he said, turning her around. "We'll play later. Go all the way upstairs, back to Kisane." Sadness welled in her eyes, but it didn't take more to convince her. She tottered back the way she came. Lucky for them, she was smart for a three year-old.

Aiya watched her go, eyes alert, then faced the door again. She could no longer concentrate on the conversation inside, the voices from behind the door sounding muddy. The fact that a child had nearly walked in on a murder had given Aiya a disturbing amount of clarity to her situation. *We're officially trained killers.*

Her heart felt like it had blown up three times its size and was now pounding against her chest, ready to burst. She noticed the dagger shaking in her palm. Suddenly, she wasn't sure if she could do this. She'd trained her entire life, seemingly for this moment. Now her first test presented itself in front of her. Would she stand and uphold the Takasa name as High Clan of River? Or be disgraced under pressure and cowardice?

There was the signal: Two loud claps, followed by a hacking cough. Her legs sank like lead, but one look at Koji was all she needed. He'd already leapt forward without a moment's delay. Despite herself, she followed. He swung the screen door open, inviting a smell that might have wafted jovially into Aiya's senses. Plates of fish and buns and dipping sauce and bowls of Yama noodles were spread between her father and the startled man, a competition of annoyance and fright in his expression. Now the room smelled of fear, and murderous intent.

The noble lord stumbled trying to rise from his knees, uttering unintelligible phrases of surprise as he spat out his half-chewed meal onto the floor. He had quick wits, making way for his escape, but Koji was already advancing to block his path towards the opposite wall doors. The man must have suspected seconds before their interruption that this was a trap. Their father had let it slip, knowing his doom here was inevitable.

Aiya lunged at him, Silencing Dagger held forward like the tongue of a viper, and she could see in his eyes preparation for its fatal bite. He was large and should have been able to easily crush her with his hairy fists, possibly escaping into estate gardens to be intercepted by Jodai. There was no escape from a Ginju.

It was over before it had really gotten started. The lord doubled over, letting out gargled cries of pain as his blood spread down his stomach, legs, onto the floor. The room was suddenly filled with a stench of blood and shit. Aiya didn't see herself eating here again for quite some time, if ever.

The lord looked up at her in confusion, fury, and behind them both, despair. As if this were treason beyond sanity. Try as she might, Aiya could not look away. Her grip remained on the stained dagger, and she stood as if possessed.

"Your conspirators ratted you out, Ren-shen. It's what happens when you go messing with the natural order of things. Now calmly join the storms." Arusuke walked over to them, head high, and spirits higher. A few helpings of sake showed in the red tinge of his cheeks. He stood a few feet away with his arms crossed, his expression stern, looking down on the man dying at Aiya's feet, whose blood had begun losing its warmth, like a starving orphan caught in a Wailstorm. The same expression he always gave his blessed children, forever stuck in a state of disappointment and agitation, as if ashamed of them. A temperament he played at to remind them of his station. He was a petty man, bitter she and her brothers wielded power he could never hold, a crime unforgivable in his egotistical vision of the world. He nodded at Aiya, a simple acknowledgement of a task well done that he knew would still leave her wanting, then trained his eyes on Hyuki Ren. "Join the storms."

"But, Aru-, I..." The lord trembled as he spoke, with barely the strength to muster a sentence. Aiya looked down on him and felt a sort of kinship, particularly, because they shared the same fate; to exist under the heel of this prideful man.

There was a slight pity in her stomach. He was no different than the other nobility, just in a worse predicament. He'd have done the same in their father's position. It was a dog-eat-dog world. This was the world the Empress herself had created by ordaining them as the High Clan. This was a just rule. Then why did her midsection churn as her fingers kept a desperate hold on her daggers? She pulled in her stomach, flexing the muscles. For her family, she'd do what was deemed necessary, even if she'd come to gradually despise them over the years. That was honorable.

Still, she'd never gotten disrespect from him or other clans. None would openly disrespect a Takasa, even without knowing her place as a Ginju within the clan. But he'd stepped out of line and would have her dead if the opportunity came. Her heart still pounded with a fright while her senses pulsed, heightened to a crest she'd never known till now. Tears welled in her eyes....

*I'm sorry.*

She raised her dagger to put out his misery.

"Let him *die*." Arusuke gripped her hand closed in the air. It was a weak grip, though he surely commanded all his strength. How easy it would be to break free, for him to be next.

But there was Ira. Bedridden, she couldn't imagine the horror on his face finding their dead father upon gaining his strength. Koji and Kisane would hardly approve. She would never forgive herself, while burning with shame for the rest of her days. She took hold of herself. Their father completed their clan. He was family. Even if her clan didn't treat her as such, they were bound together in a way that could not be so easily broken. What a terrible thing to give herself over to impulse.

Arusuke lowered her hand and released her, Koji brisking over on one knee and bowing. Aiya assumed a matching position.

"That was good work. Quick work," said her father. A rare show of praise. "Remember this day, because there will be more like it to come. What you were made to do was harsh, but necessary, and you have honored yourself by it. Clean this swine from my floor. The Hyuki clan should recognize him whole."

The entire province would recognize Owa's murder as that which only the swift justice a Ginju could bring about. Reaching the bottom of the terraced field directly under the estate, they climbed up the hill on their hands and knees. Aiya kept even pace with her brother, scowling as she failed to keep her breaths the same. She felt Koji's eyes dragging against her. "I really would make a great addition to your sketch book."

"Something tells me there'll be more resistance than normal. I need you to gather as much of the river as possible."

"You don't need to tell me."

Whatever burn Aiya should have felt from the climb was replaced by an excitement of nerves, a dreadful apprehension of duty. At the top, the Hebi castle sprang high into unyielding blackness.

It was a slim white walled keep on elevated terrain, accompanied by a few dozen trees. It lacked the fortification of a proper keep, and a guard on duty was busy relieving himself on the side of a tree. His back was turned. The only other guard rested still as a rock at the base of the stair entrance, an angry red torch flickering beside him. She watched Koji scan the darkness for extra guards, in case anyone had heard or spotted them. Her eyes moved with his. There was only the whisper of wind, and her own stale breath trapped by black cloth.

Aiya breathed in, let go of her thoughts and let them flow down the desired path. A rush like adrenaline shot through her. She jumped onto a low tree branch, landing more loudly than she wanted. Fleeting uses of her power like this were easy, a stone's throw, but often less graceful.

"Hu...what's that?" the pissing guard exclaimed, as if coming out of a trance.

Aiya was still, hand around the chiseled blue hilt of her sword. A Riverblade. It was pristine, a treasured possession reflecting the greatest craftsmanship. Two identical blades, possessed by her brothers, made up the three in existence. She gripped the four feet of folded steel lying dormant in its sheath. Koji would take them out swiftly as she scaled the top floors of the castle looking for a way in, while he went through the main entrance.

"Hey! You heard that, Bafi?" The guard fumbled with his britches.

"I thought I did," the other Jodai replied, apparently wide awake. "But then I remembered it's always around this time your good for shit-all cousin stumbles across these parts in his nightly drinking habits."

"Come now, Bafi, there's something in the trees! Or *some-one*."

This one had good instincts. The other guard made a noise like grumbling, and silence followed. There was the sound of impact, feet scuffing against dirt. Her head swiveled, but even she couldn't spot Koji.

"There, surely I'm not hallucinating, Bafi!" the guard shouted, this time half-hysterical. "Footsteps. I know you heard it too!"

"Who's there?" Bafi called out. He held out his torch. "A servant? Kishi? Goten? Shout if you're there! Let us know it's just you!"

Instead, Aiya disappeared up the tree as Koji took care of the now alert men. She heard their dying shouts as she flew through the branches, air blasting her face as she reached the treetop. The world looked expansive below, yet the castle rooftop was still high above. The castle stood three stories, each floor separated by an extended roof on the outside. The curved, overhanging roofs were guarded by small statues of divine spirits, or Kiru, posted at each of their four corners.

Aiya let out a breath she hadn't realized she'd been holding. The distance from where she held firm to the thinning trunk and the castle rooftop had to be at least twenty feet, and the fall surely longer. She pressed her lips together. *Sure could use a drink about now.*

She couldn't imagine making impact with anything other than a thud loud enough to be heard by at least half the patrolling bodies below. At least she'd make a proper entrance.

"Heavens damn it." She breathed in, out, and jumped. Her body flew up through moist air in an arc, giving her an all-encompassing view of the grounds below. Even for her, seeing it from this height was dizzying. She saw torches beginning to flood the premises, Koji having garnered the entire household's attention. Aiya reached the top roof of the keep and smacked against it, rolling then skidding to a halt. She lay motionless, listening. Shouts from below. Cries of agony and anger. She peeked over the ledge.

*Empress' soul, that's a lot of manpower*, Aiya thought. What looked like twenty or thirty Jodai had come running out of the keep, swords ready and bows bared. So, Lord Owa was keeping himself on guard at all times, knowing what his insurrectionist ramblings would incur. Koji spared none.

She took off to the other side of the building, stopping as soon as she felt her alignment falter, settling her mind back in place. Sweat beaded on her forehead as she tore her eyes away from the moon above and focused on meditating. The river became one with her soul, filling her with strength.

Aiya imagined the guards heard what they thought to be some vengeful spirit come to terrorize them. It was common for Erru to blame spirits for things, even for Ginju. Especially after dark. They'd terrified her as a child, like so many children. She and her blessed siblings in particular had never grown out of that fear. Spirits, or at least the idea of spirits, as she'd never actually seen one, had an insidious quality about them that seemed too familiar.

Creeping down the wall opposite from where they came, she dropped to the third floor roof and made her way to a window. Aiya found herself wishing she could simply slip through the walls and be invisible like the local spirits of legend, but there was no need.

There were three windows on each floor, cut into each of the four castle walls, covered by blinds made of thin, overlapping strips of wood. A survey of one of the rooms revealed a mostly empty space other than a couple of floor mattresses. Her eyes darted around her before she moved on to the next window.

Two figures sat in this one, illuminated by a dimly lit oil lamp. One of them spoke every once in a while, muttering something about the commotion outside. Scrolls piled up on a desk in the middle, some fallen onto the floor. Local administrators no doubt. They sat unmoving, still. Too still. She sensed the fear that enwreathed them, even out in the night. Aiya burst through one of the windows and sent wood clattering everywhere.

The two men cursed and drew their swords. Aiya didn't give them time to use them. She lunged and, with quick jabs to their necks, took both their lives. The men fell, leaving their seat-cushions lifeless. Her hands were suddenly wet, but she didn't slow. She bolted out the doors and down the narrow hallway which led to a staircase. She guessed the two men before were told to stay put and keep calm, while Hebi Owa himself fled downstairs towards the backdoor. Or perhaps...

She came face to face with two Jodai guards running up the stairs. They boasted deep blue lamellar armor, their blades thin and deadly steel. Jodai warriors, men who made up the military forces of each province with a reputation of fearlessness and brutality. Each came from noble birth, mostly second-class clans. Common Erru were, in most cases, forbidden from carrying weapons, being relegated to the position of farmers, fishermen, merchants or artisans; These were noble men who'd trained their entire lives for combat.

She raised her own sword.

The guard in front received first honors, his sword swinging in a wide arc, flying straight for her neck. She sidestepped, opening up his sides. He shrieked as she grabbed his neck and sent him hurling into the other. They crashed down the stairs, armor not doing them much good. She was on the second floor now, another hallway, this time wider, with sliding doors barring each room.

Three more guards stood, weapons bared, while four smaller bodies–Lord Owa's children she assumed–made for their escape down the final staircase behind them. Watching the children's backs as they disappeared, she caught a whiff of burning wood and smoke. Suddenly her posture wasn't so sure, her stance in a perpetual state of uncertainty.

Those children would die. Their deaths would undeniably be her doing. She couldn't count the number of clan enemies she and her siblings had brought an end to, yet none of them included children.

She was a Ginju, a tool ordained to be used by her father. This is what it meant to protect her clan, to protect her brothers. The kings of old would not hesitate a second to secure their own families. Her heart sank. For them, anything went.

Her reserves were empty, so she steeled herself, and began drawing more of the river. There was that creeping fear again. Darkness evaded her vision and her alignment slipped, reserves still empty. *No!*

Noticing her faltering, the guards engaged.

The hairs on the back of her neck bristled. There was a presence approaching from behind her, and she jerked sideways, barely managing to dodge a stab for her heart. The Jodai man who would have had her life stumbled forth and nearly fell, clumsily rounding on her again with surprising speed for his age. There was fire in his eyes.

He managed to drag his blade across her left bicep. Splitting pain. Cursing, she resisted the urge to nurse the wound. Instead, she scampered backwards and altered her mind. He came for the kill.

Her foot connected with his jaw, sending him back into a wall. She spun to face the other guards who were on her, slicing her Riverblade upwards through limbs, torsos, faces. It was a fight as unfair as could be, like a warrior striking down a frail mob of elderly cripples. Cutting them down, she dashed to the bottom floor.

The sight before her was grisly. The rest of the guards were dead, corpses littering the red-stained floor like ragdolls. Koji had trapped the Hebi clan lord, along with his four children. His wife, Hutani, was nowhere to be found. Strange. The flames had already begun their work, licking at the walls and creating a thick haze of smoke throughout the large floor. The heat rapidly became sweltering.

Lord Owa was left helpless with his children. He gripped the shoulders of the oldest, Shinhou, from behind. At fifteen, he'd spent a number of parties and public events in Aiya's vicinity. She'd conversed with him, spoken as equals with his mother and father.

They dared not move, no sound except for the heavy breathing and whimpering of the three younger children. The oldest son trembled, eyes hard, welcoming whatever came next. Lord Owa was her father's age, hair tied back over a face as calculating as any other. Now, he simply smiled, an uncharacteristic crazed smile that spread a little too wide.

"What's the meaning of this?" Owa asked, hand hovering at his hip.

Koji spoke firmly, though his voice wavered slightly. "You threatened the Takasa clan."

"I only spoke for the people!"

"You were aware it would come to this eventually," Aiya said, swallowing any last bit of hesitation. A blade would not do. She sheathed her sword and pulled out the Silencing Dagger, as was custom. "A friend turned foe always stumbles into justice."

Owa pulled out a glinting dagger of his own. His grin wasn't one of mirth, but of deep anger, a rabid dog forced on its last leg. His eyebrows furled as he held it in front of his son's face, pointing it back and forth between her and Koji. "Bastards, who do you think you are?"

"Your High Clan," Koji answered. "Ordained by the Empress herself, come to take your life and destroy your legacy. None stand in the way of the Takasa."

Owa watched him for a long moment, his dagger pointed out like nothing more than a pitiful stick. Finally, he said, "I see that bastard Arusuke truly is unable to give up his place, even making his own children his dogs."

Koji started, stepping forward. Aiya instinctively jumped back, eyes flying wide. An alarmed cry lodged itself in her windpipe as Hebi Owa cut his own throat.

# Clan

Takasa Shozhu was the last clan member of his generation. Of course, save for that smug bastard, Arusuke, who lagged five years behind him at age thirty-nine, clinging on to his last year of youth with not yet a hint of gray stubble. Shozhu's own ungraciously long life was not at all a blessing, but a curse. He still got urges to spit at his brother's feet when he showed deference.

The unblessed of his siblings had fought for the title of heir barely out of their teen years, while their father lied on the cusp of passing. Arusuke, perhaps the most cut-throat of any of them, naturally triumphed. The two others of Shozhu's ilk had perished nearly fifteen years ago. Naturally. One had to accept that the increased strain placed on their bodies would lead to declining health.

He supposed the fact that none of them tried to stab each other through their youth could be considered a miracle.

The castle room in which he waited patiently was barren and lit by a single candle, its shadowy silhouette prancing across the floor. In the air, there was incense freshly burned, bringing him back to his days as a youth. The world had been a better place back then, simpler. The youth had been stronger. More resilient. Any youth he knew today would not have survived in his era. Least of all Arusuke's brat, Kitani.

None of the youth back then had been complacent. One had to be hungry. That hunger he carried with him for decades still ate at him from the inside. There was an appetite in him that could *never* be satiated. Most days it ached.

The sliding screen across from where he sat rattled. They'd arrived.

"You may enter," Shozhu said.

The two young rodents he called his students stepped in and took to their knees. He regarded Aiya. A pretty girl, silky black hair and symmetrical features, with a kind yet sincere face that made her appear studious, sensible, strong. Were she not his brother, she'd make good arm candy at Kitani's side, and an excellent First Lady of the clan. A shame her Ginju status meant she'd never marry, and an even bigger shame her proficiency with the river lacked in comparison to her brothers.

Koji. That one possessed a greater air of authority, yet appeared more amiable than was proper for a member of a High Clan. Worse was his indulgence in an unbecoming habit, his secret fascination for writing romantic poetry, an odd trait for a warrior. Ira was a failure by default, a cursed sickly child. All three shared inadequacy, yet were so dissimilar in appearance, as sometimes occurred with *siblings*. How naive these two were. That Arusuke could be as spiteful as Shozhu himself.

Aiya held a beige sack, dropping it to the ground, eyes forward. "For his lordship, an enemy delivered, for the Takasa clan, and then for River."

"Well done," Shozhu said, stroking at his long beard. "I trust your own eyesight to be better than mine."

He grabbed the sack and began to unwrap it. Not as wet as he expected it to be. They'd taken time to let the blood deplete after chopping away his neck. He removed the head. That disgusting face, cold, pale and dead. Owa had finally gotten his turn of chaos, silenced. Satisfied, Shozhu pushed it back into the sack. "Survivors?"

Aiya kept her eyes forward. "None."

There was darkened cloth around her arm.

Shozhu nodded. Aiya and Koji released themselves from their position, sitting on their heels a few feet away from him. There was something to be said of the smell of death, of spilled blood, so strong it seeped into his nostrils through the smoky incense. It kept the spirit hardened. His soul never tired of it.

"Well done. Your father will be pleased when he wakes in the morning. That cleared, his lordship had an unexpected surprise for us this morning. An hour past noon, there will be a public meeting held in the square. We're to attend the grounds for diplomatic relations with Forgery. I wish I'd foreseen the short notice, but I myself was just told this morning. Apparently, Lord Arusuke and Forgery have been engaged in secret discussions until now."

Surprise marked their faces, which quickly morphed into suspicion. Koji spoke. "Master, if I recall, Forgery has been involved in civil conflict for the past four months now."

"You'd be right to suspect the meeting will concern requested aid," Shozhu replied. He set the sack to the side. "But we shall see soon enough. Owa's demise will simply send more shockwaves through the nobility than previous assassinations. Like always, other families will be wary of us, especially second-class clans. Act as if nothing has changed. We want a healthy fear for our name, not the impression of merciless tyrants."

"Understood," Koji replied, "we'll get Ira ready."

Shozhu made a sour face at his mention. "Hmph. Off you go then."

Lord Takasa Arusuke breathed light and stared at the ceiling of his bedroom. His body felt heavy in the futon he shared with his wife, where he'd been woken by the feathers of dawn falling through the window. It was amazing how soundly he slept on nights like the one just passed. Nights in which his clan silenced those who would oppose him. He supposed he slept so soundly because he had succeeded in silencing them so many times, no matter their relation to him. Arusuke took whatever he wanted, as great men did, to the scorn of the weak. It was why he was here now, carrying on his father's legacy.

Sometimes he wondered if this province was all he was ever meant to rule.

As he slipped from his sheets, the rustle of Uaya's movement stole his attention. "Does something trouble you, my dear?"

She was a worrier, Uaya, ever since he'd snatched her from the Kayumi clan nearly two decades ago. She worried that Yuuki or Ari might one day be caught in a Wailstorm if they weren't careful, worried about the quality of plays being produced at the Oto theater, and lost sleep over a gnat's wing.

The High Lord often wondered how a man of ambition like himself ended up with a woman so fretful, and yet at the same time so devoted and strong-willed, so juxtaposed. She'd worried incessantly about her mortality before giving birth, convinced she would not have the strength to bear his strong, noble heir. It was part of the reason he'd not given her a child for the first seven years after their consummation, though that was not the half of it. He wanted blessed children of age, Ginju, first and foremost. It was tradition that they begin commitment towards their deity at the age of seven. Arusuke refused to rely on the likes of Ippei and Toyozo, who'd manage to drunkenly kill each other over a small feud in the courtyard when Koji had been only three, though the older Ginju had shared his disdain while alive; the old fools, including that miserable Shozhu, would not be so willing to do their High Lord's bidding once he could raise dogs of his own. As the young new ruler of River province, that left him with only the empty threat of Ginju for his enemies. Though the fear Ginju inspired was never forgotten, their last deployment against the subjugated clans rested in the days of his father's early rule; he'd killed his way onto the throne by the Empress' ordination, which was long enough ago that fear could distort into contempt, and contempt into grandiose aspirations of treachery.

"Not at all, my love. I'm off to celebrate." He pressed his lips to hers reassuringly before departing.

*No substitute for a celebratory drink on a morning like this.* A morning of enemies vanquished. He left the room and came to another two doors down the hallway. His private study. When he opened the door, Aiya was waiting for him near the only table. She sat on her knees in tight black silks, facing the tall vessel of sake perched on the table's opposite side. Their eyes met.

She wouldn't dare speak before he did, so he said, "Shozhu must have cracked his other leg and fallen to bowel sickness."

"Father, forgive my impertinence...what you asked has been done. The Hebi clan is no more."

"I assume so, otherwise you'd have the dignity not to show yourself."

His daughter looked as if she was fighting something with her tongue, lips held tight in suspense. "There were children."

He didn't expect her to share his disposition towards swift castigation, and it was better she didn't. Still, to be so affected as to bother him like this....

"He sacrificed them without a fight," she continued, quieter.

Arusuke poured sake himself in a small cup, then took it in one gulp. Its warmth immediately filled his chest. For himself, a cup was more refreshing than a cool stream of water in his throat on a summer's day. Slipping into displeasure became less grating, and he became resolute, more adamant, his wit replaced with an eagerness to reprimand any heads raised too high, and for any failure of duty. It was as a High Lord should be.

He scowled. Even Koji would probably not do as his eldest daughter did now; he likely couldn't. Not without losing his face and dishonoring himself by lashing out with disrespect. That one sometimes lacked control over his temper, often through vicious subtlety. Of course, to go against their father, their High Lord, even as Ginju, would be to go against the Empress herself, to damn their souls to the storms. Threats of the afterlife were never enough to control the actions of the Erru, or any man for that matter, but even slight deterrents should not be overestimated.

More important was to cultivate the personality of a tough father figure, for kin and nonkin alike. Family was honor, and honor the adherence to family. Words from the Old Kingdom. His father's words.

"That's to be expected from such a clan. I'd have fought tooth and nail for Kitani, or Yuuki or Ari." Her exclusion was cruel, but they were best kept at an arm's distance. Part of him relished it. "You've done well."

Her hand went over the tear on her bicep, grisly red flesh mangled with the black fabric. He hadn't noticed it until now. How had that happened? For all their power, they were quick to show weakness, cowardice. Had only Arusuke been blessed as a newborn by the Empress, been taught their ferocious art by his father's brothers, he'd inspire fear in his enemies such that none would think to challenge him in a thousand generations.

"I was a year less than Koji when I became High Lord," he reminded her. "Do you think excessive generosity afforded you those nice silks, held this estate to our name? Leave me be, for today is a day of celebration. Later we will engage in a more peaceful discourse with a lordling of Forgery, if Shozhu has not already told you."

She got up to remove herself, and no sooner did the door slide open again, only for Uesaka Sano to enter with an obligatory bow. A man his own age with a tense face, small eyes set lightly in their sockets, eyes that had delicately watched his clan's investments for so long. They passed over Aiya, who glanced at him with a guarded posture, holding her head high before excusing herself from the room. Arusuke beamed. Far better. Someone not prone to spoil the day's events.

"Even I can admit it is right to be drinking on such a morning," said Arusuke's closest retainer, "though your wife would have me say otherwise. She was disappointed all those years ago to discover your love for rice wine."

"Familiarity breeds contempt, and children." He took another swig. The vessel weighed lighter than it should have. A shame. "She was no stranger to it herself when we first met. But I'd rather focus on the prospects of the future."

"By that you do not mean some alliance with the lordling."

Now that Owa's voice was quelled, he could exercise Takasa clan authority more smoothly. Sano knew him well.

"What provincial matter do you bring to me?"

A former Jodai and current seat on the council of judges, Sano brought those concerning and most widespread issues to him directly. "This silencing won't quell the rebellion down south."

Predictable. For all his astuteness, Sano could sometimes display an unhealthy obsession with Kotonese, neglecting the far more immediate menace of the highborn.

Before Owa's extinction, the River High Lord was understandably crossed. Imperial tax collectors from Rain came to bleed River dry, year by year. Commoners, naturally, carried the tax burden, namely those in the fishing trade as River's largest industry. Arusuke's father had been ordained High Lord, and it was more accurate to say the burden of taxes rested on the nobility, for it was they who were at risk of being thrown into a storm come summer. *If the quota isn't reached, we'll be the ones to freeze.*

The past year presented a record low yield of fish, not helped by filthy mobs of protesting Kotonese fishermen. Suffice to say, profits were inadequate. Lord Arusuke would have nobles pay the difference. Coin would come quicker that way. Lord Hebi Owa, a military land governor, vocalized his disdain for raised taxes. Considering his wealth and Jodai forces were nearly equal to half the council of judges together, Lord Arusuke decided the man had breathed long enough.

"The kots are indecent, but they are a 'soulful people', as King Tsae once noted. Valuable too. I won't press them just yet. Generosity is a virtue, after all."

Sano cracked a heartfelt laugh. "Wasn't it you who told me that religion is for the weak who refuse to take power?"

"The Oshidai's teachings prove useful for all men in some measure. Even I can admit that."

"Of course, my lord. You are a man of vision who knows how to read the currents and direct them where you please. You're a good heir to your father, it's why I respected you far more than your sisters and brothers. May you reign for many years to come."

Koji stepped in front of the screen to Irashida's room, Aiya at his back. The two were freshly bathed standing on the cool floor, rectangular mats of tightly woven fibers fitted into an interlocking pattern. The walls were white rice paper, and the ceiling ten feet high, with translucent folding screens leading into another room across from them. Simple artwork graced many of the screens, from paintings of sunsets to cool colored meadows. He'd sketch that as his next cover up. Outside, a staircase at the hall's end led down to the castle's first story, ceramic flower vases placed at its base. Past the lavish gardens surrounding the estate were the streets of Kawanura, capital of River province. A hub of economic activity, full of merchants and artisans. Firetaming and puppet shows were popular attractions, drawing in thousands of nobility and commoners alike from the surrounding countryside each month. The Takasa estate was situated at its center, surrounded by storehouses, towers, barracks and living quarters for lords, retainers, and their garrison. A reminder to the common Erru of noble wealth and prestige. More importantly, it reminded the lower nobility who really held dominion and authority.

The sun had begun to rise, warming the house with its rays. Koji adjusted his robe's billowed sleeves then refastened the silk belt around his waist. The light blue silk, sown with inconspicuous wavy patterns, was soft enough that it was barely felt throughout the day.

He slid open the door. "Oversleeping again? I thought we ordered this sloth out weeks ago."

Irashida sat up from his bed, his mouth curving into a smirk. He had a beaming, affectionate smile, one that complimented the soft curvature of his narrow face. It was that same honest smile that pulled all the way to his eyes and touched his dark hairs. Ira was strong like the elk, affable like a deer, and passionate like the wolves, yet gentle as a doe.

"It would seem his affliction of laziness has spread," Aiya said, brisking over to his bedside.

"Don't go on acting like mother again," said Ira as his sister placed a hand over his forehead. "I'm glad to see you two unharmed. How was...last night?"

"Well enough, for us. Not so well for the Hebi," Koji answered. Owa was perhaps a man no better than their father, though were they any better for punishing the entire clan indiscriminately? Could they be sure that all were complicit? Could his children be held accountable? Koji pushed the guilt aside, only for it to be replaced by another. Ira didn't know Aiya still struggled, and he'd just lied by omission. Would it be better for his brother to worry?

"Well, I suppose it was for the better. Good riddance to the traitor."

Only two servants currently occupied the austere room, burning incense. Koji observed them, so peaceful as they contemplated the smoke rise and billow, restoring the house with its aromas. He noticed from time to time how their lives were like the steady, predictable burning of the incense sticks, in contrast to the lives of nobility, which were like the chaotic patterns of smoke rising, swelling, until it expanded so much as to snuff itself from existence. To carry out their duties was all it required to earn sustenance and a roof to enjoy it under. Safe from the political strain placed on higher noble backs, the constant social warfare between the lower noble houses vying for prestige, and never considered a mere weapon from birth to house the power of a deity. They knew their place in the world.

He felt for his book and pen tied under his garments at his waist. Now that was a poetic line. "They know their place in this world, like a gentle kiss," he muttered. He'd save that one for later.

Aiya and Ira shot him puzzled looks.

"You've returned! Thank the Empress," a voice from behind them called out. Hitsune Kisane drifted into the room and bowed.

Koji smiled and pulled her to her feet, embracing her. "You know we hate it when you do that."

"You look beautiful, Kisane," Aiya said, brushing past Koji. He caught a hint of alcohol on her breath as she did. They embraced each other, and Koji frowned as his sister grimaced in pain. She pulled back her shoulder, a slight shift from where Kisane's arm had brushed her left bicep. Had she been hurt during last night's excursion? *Was that why she was hiding her left side from me?*

Koji steeled himself from the irritation welling inside him. She hid things like this from him, anything that might set him off, and perhaps this was the exact reason. To avoid his 'parental tirades', his siblings had dubbed it. Koji couldn't help it. Stuck abrasively at the back of his mind, since a child, was the morbid realization that death was real and random.

He'd spent many nights tending to Ira after his brother had fallen sick. He comforted Aiya in her night terrors, explaining that to keep alignment with one's deity, the spiritual harmony for maintaining access to its power, the deity's servant was to overcome their own mind. Also known as their 'lower selves', as Shozhu put it, which revealed itself through a grotesque form during alignment. Once thought to be an interfering evil spirit, it was considered the mind's natural defense against the effect one's deity had on them. The mind, unable to comprehend the deities, would dredge up some horrifying illusion in response. Perhaps the mind comprehended the deities as an invasive threat. Something sinister and vastly powerful, too frightening to behold, akin to the evil god of the Tarshani religion.

But the deities weren't gods, as gods didn't exist. At least not in the way most thought of them. The deities made up the remnants of beings of the natural world. Great, mysterious reserves of power attainable if one took the time to seek them out through meditation. Of course, this was a secret reserved for only a select few of noble blood. He often worried if his siblings were not capable of progressing with him, considered unworthy by the heavens and cursed, unable to wield the power of their deity. He worried more that their lives might someday be taken from them, by sword or by sickness, and then he would be alone.

Koji reverted his eyes to Kisane. Warmth spread into the house servant's dimpled grin that only aged mothers possessed. Kisane was short and thin, a middle-aged woman whose hair always smelled sweet like roses and ash leaves. More of a mother to the three of them than their birth mother ever was, yet today, her characteristic cheery expression was absent from her face. "Everything alright?"

"I told Asaya you two were going on a trip, and she missed you. I just put her back to sleep. She said she dreamt the three of you were being attacked by a hound on the road while protecting our family."

Aiya looked concerned. Kisane's adopted child of seven had finally hit the age where one understood that the worst fear wasn't knowing, but not knowing what tomorrow would bring about. "Empress' soul, we should show her that we're alright."

"She sleeps now, my lady." She looked to Ira. "Ira has been in my care, and he's improving quickly."

"No rain this morning. Even the sun comes out to sing its praises," Ira said, throwing off his blanket and sliding on his feet.

Koji eyed Ira, an endless longing in him. His sickness usually kept him bedridden six or seven days out of a month. He'd randomly become dizzy, weak, and confused, forced to be cared for while he recovered. The physicians knew nothing of his condition nor its origin. "Well," Koji said, "Just in time, because it looks like you won't be missing out today. We've all been summoned by father. It's an urgent meeting with an heir of Forgery province."

# Plea

B ustling bodies filled the streets of Kawanura. The nobility boasted robes of heavy silk with all manner of color and designs. Commoners slipped around them, content with their duller, more modest attire. Though only specks of clouds drifted above, a considerable number of Erru held up raincatchers, not chancing the prospect of a full day without skywater. Aromas of noodles, fresh produce, and cider swirled through Aiya's nostrils, and the hypnotic rhythm of violins in the background was so melodic that she at times felt as if she had begun floating. There were gobi fish displayed in overlapping stacks in the stand next to them, its stench a fraction of the offense coastal towns and port cities offered. It was a warm start for winter, Third Day on the second week of Yin.

Aiya, Ira, Shozhu, and Koji lagged far behind the rest of the Takasa family, perpetually sidetracked to every attraction along the way. It was on noon days like these that Aiya imagined the four of them as a pack, paroling through the city with prowling eyes, daring any of delicate flesh around them to make one false move, or else whisper the wrong thing. In times of tension, even nobility were better off keeping their guard up, lest they be subject to the

High Lord's wrath. A malicious thought, one that made her question how much she aligned with her father, but was it not steeped in truth? Even so, the question, along with an unceasing whirlpool of guilt, combined with the sense that she was floating through the days, weeks, years, internally adrift, lingered at the back of her mind. The rice wine was failing to wash away the resentment she felt towards her father. Roaming the city atmosphere with Koji and Ira did its part to ease her, though she could do without Shozhu.

"How many clans do you think will dedicate soldiers to this heir's cause if father agrees to an alliance with him?"

"You really reckon there's a possibility that we'll hand over our manpower, Aiya? I'd say he's come at the worst possible time. Do tell, what's in it for us?" Koji asked, though the question came off as more an accusation.

Ira lunged to her defense. "Forgery is one giant smithery, the largest in the empire. The only thing we can offer is manpower. You're dismissing that they are a more central province, so a deeper relationship with them can only improve our standing within the empire."

Shozhu waved for them, sauntering on with his slight limp. The pudgy man freed himself from the lure of a street musician by dropping a few coin bits in his basket. The musician nodded once, eyes still lowered as his fingers worked furiously upon his flute. Like Aiya, Shozhu shared a particular appreciation for the melodic arts. "Let's press on, young ferrets. His lordship must already be at the meeting grounds."

Aiya dodged a serious-looking noble man, whose cloud-patterned navy blue robes seemed a size too small. He did a double take after noticing who she was and stopped to profusely apologize.

"My lady, forgive my indifference! I failed to notice you."

"A small thing, Lord Ona," Aiya said, putting on a smile. She only barely remembered him from his stiff posture paired with a wobbly tone. She knew nothing of his trade, only that he'd proposed his three sons to her on a number of occasions, swearing their eternal servitude. Though she'd declined, she'd seen kindness in each of their eyes, and did so with grace. "You may be on your way." They briskly separated, the man complaining something to the merchant as they walked away.

No one recognized the four of them as Ginju. Of course, very few knew who, or even what, the Ginju were. To the Erru, they were men just short of monsters, hidden or perhaps locked deep away in the High Lord's dungeons, waiting to be unleashed and wreak havoc. But here they walked now, free as doves, enjoying the festive atmosphere the meeting had brought upon the city. The morning announcement proved a shock to the masses in Kawanura, and the streets were soon flooded with anticipation. Children laughed, adults droned or chattered in excitement, and Aiya couldn't help but be intoxicated by the thrill, a much needed respite from the events of the previous night.

The four Ginju went through shops, long-ribboned women spinning to the hum of stringed instruments. Crowds gathered around firetaming performers. Unable to resist, they found themselves pulled into a crowd standing outside a caravan and waiting for the beginning of a story. Aiya squinted her eyes at the sight in front of her, vision a bit shaky from one too many helpings of sake. "Why is Ari lagging behind the rest like a lost pup?"

Ira shook his head. "Yeah, I thought that was our job."

She noticed their approach, turning nonchalantly in her spot among the gathering crowd. A blue dyed orchid complimented her slim Takasa robes, tucked into her hair bun. A flower for the unwed and the innocent. She was just fourteen after all.

Aiya closed in and snatched it from her sister's head with as much drunken grace as she could summon. There was no reason to handle her like Kitani, but there was also no reason for her to be here, ready to ruin their stroll with some sly quip she'd no doubt already formed as soon as they'd met eyes. She didn't need words, though–she could say everything with a look–remind Aiya of her servitude to a woman four years her junior. The disdain between their two parties was destined to go on and on, perhaps till the end of their days. "You shouldn't go off on your own, defying father."

"I'm not, you brute." She stuck out an open hand with a defiant expression.

Sometimes, Aiya coveted her younger sister, and she found that weird. As the middle child, she was more grounded than Kitani and less emotionally volatile than Yuuki. Father and mother would have her as first pick for heir, were it not for optics. Aiya couldn't deny her some respect. Still, the orchid remained pinched between her fingers.

"You've been drinking like the adults?" Ari asked.

Aiya tensed as Ira and Koji's presence behind her sent pressure in her cheeks. How to keep them from questioning her decisions? "It's the proper thing for adults to do when we celebrate. Makes us happy."

Ari only studied her. "Father's a real asshole when he drinks."

"Good thing I'm not him," Aiya replied, and tossed the orchid back. She turned to the sight of tall figures at their side, not seeing if Ari had caught it.

A number of Kotonese sidled among the walking throng. Her eyes darted from one to another with slight aversion. Unlike the tawny Erru, they were a terracotta skinned people whose features appeared scrunched at the upper half of their faces. Men and women alike avoided eye contact, avoiding the attention of the Erru in any way, the lank of their limbs kept rigid at their sides. They didn't look sad, or scared, but simply observant of what lay ahead of them.

Kotonese represented nearly half the population of southern fishermen. They'd occupied Egaisha a long time, perhaps the most stagnant group of people on the continent. Despite their majority population in some southern towns, the sight of them was enough to evoke feelings of revulsion. Even common Erru thought of them as low, an unmotivated and mischievous race. The mental image conjured up by their mere mention was a base person simple in their ways, groveling, wretched, undignified. A scowl skipped across Aiya's face before diverting her gaze.

"Apparently a diet of just salmon makes you lazy. That's why they don't want to fish anymore. That's why they can't learn to do anything else." Ari began walking ahead, but turned and faced Aiya again. "You're just like them."

"What's that supposed to mean, you wide-nosed pig?" Ira demanded, but she'd already stalked off.

"Let the little brat go," Koji said. "Looks like it's about to begin."

A pair of Ushin in dirty white burlap robes strode together in front of their view, sporting wide brimmed straw hats atop their heads. Aiya trailed them with her eyes. Ushin warriors, dubbed snidely as the poor man's Jodai, made their living as mercenary soldiers for hire against bandits and thugs. They might police the streets of a countryside, or save city shop owners being robbed, or act as escorts to a caravan traveling through dangerous roads. Unlike Jodai, they were of low birth and far from military grade.

Even they could be organizing treason against the High Clan.

*Enough of that.* Aiya shook her duties from her mind, concentrating on the story that was about to unfold at the gathering's center. A dull excitement rose in her. This was the true highlight of any city-wide festival. At the very least, she would enjoy herself for the duration of it.

The crowd's energy dissipated into an excited hum. A storymaster in mauveine robes of exaggerated length and beard hairs woven into a thick braid exited the caravan's door and began to speak, a solemn but lively spark in the wrinkle of his eyes.

"Before River, we were a people of the Kingdom of Nirogawa. Before Nirogawa, we were only men, whose main pastime was strife, as much as it is today. Before men, there was only the Empress." The storymaster cast his voice, settling like a blanket over the audience. His hands moved in hugely exaggerated gestures, inciting awe in his present audience. "The Erru have always been a squabbling people. Hundreds of years before even the earliest era of the empire, we fought against one another among innumerable tribes. It was a far more treacherous time then. Spirits and monsters roamed from place to place, and much of the land suffered an endless torrent of freezing rain.

"Times grew unbearable as war turned into necessity. Across this same land of mist and rain, starvation, plague, and despair took the lives of many. However, there would come a savior. A woman in robes of lavender whose porcelain skin radiated like the rising sun. The woman was said to be the daughter of the Shinti, an immortal who walked the earth, watching over each creature, all the same. As part human, she felt responsible for her half-kin. She witnessed the carnage throughout the lands, as tribes turned on tribes, father on son and mother on daughter. Thousands of men lay torn to pieces in the Valley of Zakura, where demons feasted on them from First to Seventh Day.

"The woman was not to interfere with the Shinti's creation, but finally her desire for order took the better of her. The great warlord, Kozuku of the Uchiname tribe, came to the woman to request her aid in exchange for his eternal servitude.

"'None under the heavens can ever be eternal in body apart from me,' the woman answered. 'But in name, your honorable words today will make you so.'

"Thus, she became his head, and he her vassal. She banished the monsters and spirits from the physical realm to the spirit realm, where most hide today, lurking with resentment and fear. She and Kozuku conquered all his enemies, until they stood united under one banner. Thus, the immortal woman became Empress, sovereign over her people.

"Many would submit in fear at the first sight of her, but there were those who would stop at nothing to nourish the greed in their hearts. Many a tribe came together as her armies rampaged across their borders. Her Sovereign was untroubled, and demanded her troops stand aside. Ten times ten thousand men with spears and swords and clubs charged doggedly before her. But there was no intimidation in any part of her.

"With a simple gesture, she conjured up storms of lightning and mists and wind. These were no ordinary storms, but storms of spells, causing those inside to shrivel into frozen husks of themselves. They screamed, cried out, and more quickly than any other army had before, died. It was a gruesome sight to behold, one that was never forgotten. That is why, to this day, the Empress causes Wailstorms, and the frostsickle they inflict. They are a mere display of her power, their wails serving in remembrance as the last cries of her enemies brought to justice by the storms."

His tale had drawn the audience into a sort of trance, so that Aiya didn't even notice Shozhu before he had to pull them onwards. She'd heard the tale before, but its grandeur performed with such zeal never failed to leave her spellbound. It was a story of ancient and mythic quality, indeterminable in authenticity yet cautionary in its profound plausibility.

Koji and Ira went ahead as Shozhu took her arm and stopped her. "I won't let you go through today believing your blunder has gone unnoticed. Look perplexed as you wish, I have seen the injury on your arm that you've been trying to hide."

Aiya flinched at his mention of it, pain returning to the gash along her bicep. Somehow his judging stare was worse. "You sure never asked if I was okay."

"The music, these festivities, they nourish the soul, don't they? Your father doesn't share our appreciation of these fine arts. The bastard is simply a dullard. However, seeing you like this, I'd rather fill my time in his presence over yours on any occasion. Dull as he may be, he is simply a true Takasa. He and I spoke shortly before our departure. He noticed it too. He believes such an injury calls into question your dedication, your resolve and character. I share his sentiment. Look around you. The clans, they do not respect you for who you are, as intimidating as you think you may be. They respect you for what you are. They fear the Takasa blood within you. Koji has thus far proven himself, in my eyes. Ira, disappointing as he is...at least there's a reason for his incompetence."

Aiya's innards sunk as Shozhu's bearded scowl turned away. The notes in the air no longer invigorated her, but passed through her, empty, as she followed her hobbling uncle to their destination. For once, she'd believed she'd done everything right, carried out her task in a way above reproach. Perhaps she was incapable of even that.

Off in the distance were the meeting grounds, an expansive circle of cobbled stone surrounded by wooden fencing. Inside the fence, there were already a number of noble families gathered around a central tower. Commoners congregated outside it.

The crowd parted, making way for the late-arrivals. As they made it into the inner circle of the meeting grounds, Aiya watched her family standing on a stage encompassing the entire base of the tower. Below them, lower River clans stared reverently.

Lord Arusuke perked up as a Jodai guard approached him from the opposite side of the circular stage. Arusuke wore the same light blue Takasa robes, except for a white gobi fish patched onto his chest. Lady Uaya wore matching robes, and together, they represented High Lord and First Lady of River.

The two made the perfect duo, each on the cusp of forty, Arusuke two heads taller with an ever present distinguished look on his face. Uaya sat contently, pretty with red lipstick and an alluring smile. From a more intimate point of view, however, one discovered Arusuke's strong face took on an irritable and self-centered quality, and Uaya's smile became a simple facade to hide a personality as reserved yet fiery as a viper. Aiya was not much closer with her younger siblings, Yuuki and Ari, the unblessed of the River lord's daughters. Even at fourteen and twelve they were crass and simple-minded. Kitani, eldest unblessed son, was a year older than Ari, a selfish brat that reminded Aiya of a yellow-back monkey, with his long limbs, knobish build and his habitual outbursts over trivial matters.

The Jodai whispered something into Arusuke's ear, deep blue lamellar armor glinting in the sunlight. He was a servant of Arusuke, as were all Jodai in River, noble men of every class trained in the sword since the age of two. The title of general granted authority closest to that of the High Lord himself, though this man was likely only a high-ranked footsoldier, marked by the absence of an officer's finned helm.

Aiya had always seen Jodai as tall, straight-backed warriors with an appetite for ruthlessness. Though she hadn't the experience of participating in the midst of battle, her interactions with them proved true. They were among the most honorable and dignified men in person, but when facing opposition, they fought like ravenous wolves and stole the heads of their enemies as trophies. Disregarding internal strife, River had remained on good terms with neighboring provinces since the establishment of Takasa rule over forty years ago. She'd seen the aftermath of their craft in the history books, leaving her to wonder just how true these men around her could be to their historical image.

Arusuke held up a hand and the crowd hushed.

"Hold on," Shozhu demanded. They were at the front of the crowd and facing the stage, stopping so as not to disrupt the ceremony. They'd watch from afar, keeping their ears open for any dissenting noble opinions. Not far from them, the crowd was making way for three Forgery caravans, large wooden carriages marked by bold and exotic colors. A tingling levitated in Aiya's chest, uplifting her spirits as she looked excitedly on the beginning of the festival's main event. The caravans came not twenty feet from the crowd as guardsmen hopped around to escort the passengers out.

Aiya picked up harsh whispering behind her: "I can't take this. When will we receive our own caravans to parade around the city?"

Aiya turned to see a wispy haired, solemn faced old man violently nudging a younger looking one. "Lord Takasa protects us, watch your tongue and mind your blessing!"

The young man noticed Aiya, eyes timidly falling to his feet as he reluctantly piped down. She turned her attention back to the caravan, noting the bold red painted wood complimenting matching red wheels. The doors were opened, and out stepped an orange robed man with hair so long it fell to his shoulders. He had a determined expression to him, clean shaven with strong features. He was also surprisingly...young. Young and unexpectedly handsome.

The Forgery heir walked on stage, men from the other two caravans stepping out to follow suit. He waited for the rest of them to stand behind him, presumably his trusted subjects and counselors. He was a spectacle, standing opposite the Takasa family, facing the crowd with those closest behind him. He opened his mouth to speak with a rich voice of conviction that suggested he'd spent more years on the earth than at first glance.

"My name is Lord Yomenuura Sen, heir and soon-to-be highest lord of Forgery province. And you, colleagues of River, are an honor to stand before. Underestimate not my gratefulness for the opportunity. Upon my return from these doors, I hope to consider you more than colleagues, and to secure an alliance that may aid us both. May the Empress shine her favor on River."

He turned from the crowd to Arusuke. The short speech seemed slightly rehearsed, but still the crowd watched in anticipation. Lord Sen and his retainers were led into the tower first by blue armored Jodai. Soon, Arusuke and his family followed in silence, a jittery buzz returning to the crowd.

"Let's go," Shozhu said, stepping forward, as Aiya focused on keeping her balance. The doors remained open for them, and as they walked through, a chill ran down her spine. The events of the day's unfolding had finally begun to weigh on her, as she realized the conversation in this room could very well alter the course of River. Such an opportunity would provide her clan a pocket of power outside their province borders, furthering the scope of their influence, and at the same time, their enemies.

The inside was modest, nothing but the polished floor and ashwood walls, filled with a foreboding quiet. Jodai guards stood off to the sides. She recognized the goateed man sitting next to her father as General Yun, whom in the past, she had limited interaction with. Unlike his soldiers, he wore a black robe, though he still kept a sword tucked at one side. His gray hair was pulled back, just long enough to form a tail.

They sat behind their father in a line with the rest of the River lord's family, while Uesaka Sano and a couple of high ranking lords took their spots behind them. Aiya waited for one of the lords to speak. Ira fidgeted as she resisted the urge to sniff. The young Forgery lord, strong-jawed and handsome indeed, cleared his throat.

"We thank River for this welcoming occasion. Lord Arusuke has been gracious to us, and we wish to make the most of our meeting today. Your time today shall not be in vain." He dipped his head, touching together two fists. His next words were spoken with more conviction. "As you understand, the relationship between my clan and I has been less than ideal as of late. The conflict concerning my sister has continued for too long. Through our own persistence, we've managed to hold back her advances. However, our resources have been dwindling, and not all who fight under my banner remain faithful. Therefore, I come today to humbly and formally request an alliance between River and Forgery."

He looked up with hard eyes boring straight into Arusuke. "I understand River has experienced dwindling relations with Agriculture, especially as of late. With the joining of our forces, my last living rival would be pincered between us, overpowered and forced to give up her conquest for the throne. We would be forever in your debt."

Moments passed before Lord Arusuke's answer. "Interesting. You speak more of your own province's interests than you ascertain mine. Who's to say you'll keep your word if we do lend you aid?"

*Quite direct of you*, Aiya thought. She was no stranger to statecraft and had sat through a fair number of diplomatic negotiations with lesser officials from outside provinces. Such suspicions were usually brought about with more tact that kept both parties in good faith, leveling the ground until a more clear opportunity to position oneself higher arose. Though River was already on higher ground, such blunt accusations on the Forgery lord's character were surely unnecessary.

"Your lord, with respect, such an act would not only be foolish, but selfish."

"Yes," Arusuke mused, "and possibly advantageous. You're young, not only inconsiderate, but also inexperienced. I expected a speech of more character. Something revealing intelligence."

Sen twitched at this. Some of the men around him moved uncomfortably.

"Lord Arusuke, perhaps I was not clear enough about your own benefit from our allegiance. I understand we do not come from a place of close companionship, and your own misgivings are of a more personal nature. Yet we serve the same Empress, and are both served by our respective people. We possess resources you lack. The conquest for Tarshan grows more heated by the day. You are second closest in proximity to those raging seas. You may soon want a cheap way of garnering arms to prepare yourselves, in case the Empress deems your shores fit for a second vantage point in the war. We could supply you greatly in high quality steel, of course."

Arusuke eyed the Forgery lord. "I suggest you think before you speak, boy. For what sensible purpose would we expend bodies in your own power struggle with no guarantee of a return on investment? We have enough soldiers taxed out of us each year. I suppose next you'll suggest we stoop as low as to draft commoners. This was supposed to be a negotiation, instead you offer a half-assed plea!"

"Pardon if I speak out of turn," said a large white-haired man next to Sen, adorned in robes of crisp white, "but Lord Sen is fully accustomed to court politics, and his presence demands respect."

Arusuke paid none of it. "He's barely more than my eldest son. If he's to be the next High Lord, the future of Forgery does not look bright."

Aiya grinded her teeth in agitation. The discussion was not progressing how she'd hoped. Were an agreement met, it would further cement the firm rule of Takasa, and that might mean less midnight excursions to murder insurgent clans. She ignored the burning ache in her bicep, reminded of the consequences of those who tested her father. Aiya could think of no reason for his rudeness and unwillingness to engage other than foolish pride.

If she prodded gently, she might sway things...

*No, that's the sake in you.* That wasn't true. She was in control, even if her head had begun spinning and spilling with pent up anger, discontent. She was here to look out for her clan's best interests. She could set the meeting on a proper path. She unfurled her fists, red from her own grip.

"Father," she began, with a voice more faint than she knew she possessed, "it may be..."

"SILENCE!" She didn't meet his face even as she jolted at his demand. Her eyes stuck to the mats below her, her beating heart almost knocked from its place. *Fool,* she thought. *Idiot.* He'd taken great offense to her interruption, his reaction untempered; perhaps she would be excluded from the rest of this *diplomatic* discussion. She'd not shame herself further by lifting her head for all to see. She waited for his correction.

When nothing further was said, she raised her head to the opposing party, no longer seeing through a drunken haze.

Sen now looked angry. "I assure your lordship I've enough experience to not come to you as ignorant as you presume."

"You are nothing," the River lord responded flatly.

The white-haired man grew bolder. "I refuse to listen while my lord is mocked and his accomplishments undermined!"

"Surely the boy can speak for himself," Arusuke said, not caring for the offense being given, "I'm simply helping him understand his place: an innocent pup pretending to be one among the wolves. He's yet to even grow a wisp of hair on his chin."

Sen glared at Arusuke, a dangerous look in his eyes. "Your careless threats might prove reckless and dangerous. I advise you to show some of the respect you so readily expect for yourself."

"Oh, the pup attempts to growl," Arusuke said, challenging. "But will he actually bare his teeth?"

The man shot up from his sitting position. He was surprisingly bulky for a man his age, somewhere in his mid-fifties. He was at least a head taller than every other person in the room, with an appearance like that of an ape. "Lord Sen will receive his due reverence! I won't take anymore from this River scum!"

"Down, Juso," Sen said. The man hesitated. Finally, he sat with reluctance.

"I am greatly dismayed at our conversation so far, Lord Arusuke. It seems it was a mistake to have been so optimistic for this talk between us. For some foolish reason, I assumed you'd be more reasonable."

Arusuke chuckled. "What would a child understand about reason?"

Aiya was appalled by the malice in Arusuke's words and actions. Even for him, she'd expected a more civilized performance of statecraft. He had no intention of bringing this anywhere. He was purposefully antagonistic, emphasizing Sen's reliance on him more than he relied upon Sen.

The man named Juso bounced to his feet again. "I'll have no more of this!"

"You've no choice but to." This time the words came from General Yun, who still sat coolly on the floor. "What Lord Arusuke says is true, whether or not you accept it. This was agreed to as a meeting between lords, not dogs, and any further interruption will force my own involvement."

Juso took a step forward. "I hope you understand what you are suggesting could unwittingly cost you your life." His hand went to his sword hilt. "An honorable duel with me is not likely to end well."

Yun merely smiled. "*Hmph.* If that's what it will take to silence your barking, then so be it."

"Stand back, Juso!" Sen commanded, but Juso ignored him.

"I humbly apologize, my lord, but I must uphold your honor above all else." He unsheathed his blade. "I, General Juso of Forgery under Lord Sen, accept an honorable duel between me and the River official scum before me."

Aiya's eyes darted from Juso to Yun. The escalation between the two parties had occurred so quickly, she could scarcely believe what she was witnessing.

General Yun stood, a whole two heads beneath Juso, unsheathing his own sword. His blade sung softly as it slid against the metal scabbard.

# Honor

The two generals posed on opposite sides of the cleared room. Yun was much shorter than his opponent, though Aiya could see by the fit of his robes that he wasn't lacking in strength. Yun's amused face only served to work up General Juso's rage. Juso held out his blade with a meaty hand over his right shoulder, the curved tip pointing downwards. Yun had his blade at his hips, his double-hand grip seeming more relaxed. It was a scene out of a painting, suspended warriors posed against the other, awaiting the perfect striking moment.

None of the bystanders dared to make a sound. During an honorable duel, only the clash of weapons and the men that held them spoke. Lord Sen and Arusuke stood far behind their respective fighters. They both watched closely, Sen's apprehension visible in the stretch of his eyes and downward tug of his lips. Aiya stood off to the side with the rest of the nobles and armored Jodai, praying that Yun's provocation proved wise.

Juso's face twisted into disgust. "Your head will roll." He charged.

Juso brought his sword down. Yun easily parried, only moving his arms in the process. The clash of blades rang through the air, startling Aiya despite herself. Yun grunted as he took the blow, almost thrown off balance. With his free hand, Juso formed a fist like a boulder and launched it at his opponent's face.

Yun backstepped, evading the wide swing as Juso's knuckles narrowly missed his nose. Juso kept to the offensive, giving chase. Yun met Juso's blade again, throwing him off and scurrying around to Juso's weak side. Juso kept pace, hacking at Yun while shuffling forward with each strike. He tried cutting Yun with a strike to his shoulder, exposed torso turned sideways to prevent an easy counterattack by the River general, but Yun dodged it from below and retreated. He knew to use his height to his advantage.

Juso looked and fought like a maddened gorilla, relentless with his vicious attacks. Aiya imagined him snarling to reveal a pair of hidden fangs. Yun by contrast, was like a smaller but more agile monkey, intellectual and skilled beyond his years.

Juso eased back a bit, Yun having made it clear his tactics would not work.

Yun went for the other man's torso, opting for a close-range attack. Juso feigned an attack, then released a hand from his hilt and lunged at Yun, grabbing at him. He inched to the side, avoiding Yun's blade and catching the smaller man by the throat.

Time seemed to slow almost imperceptibly.

Juso raised his sword fiercely as Yun's own weapon nearly flew from his fingers. Yun caught the hilt in his grip, then plunged it into Juso's side. Aiya blinked and saw ribbons of blood soaking the white of his robes.

Juso grunted in pain, dropped Yun while cursing the man, then stumbled backwards, his opponent closely following. The Forgery general heaved, eyes wide with pain. He moved to retaliate, but Yun withdrew his blade and made him double over. Juso gave a pitiful groan of pain and took two shaky steps back, toppling over onto his side. His eyes squeezed shut as he gritted his teeth, bright blood staining them red.

The Forgery officials protested, hands fidgeting over their hilts, fighting the urge to draw their own weapons.

Both Lord Arusuke and Sen observed, betraying nothing. The duel had been decided. The Forgery general had been unable to bear the offense taken by his lord and gotten himself killed. Now Juso said nothing but laid gasping for air, unable to climb to his feet.

Yun breathed in and out, catching his breath. Then he charged. Sen jerked, astonished.

"Wha—" was all Juso managed to get out before Yun was on him, sword poised above his neck, his other arm pinning the dying man to the ground.

"Stop!" were the cries of Forgery. In the end, they did nothing. Juso let out a loud, gargled croak, Yun's blade already working viciously. He kept at it until he pulled the head from the thoroughly severed neck. He stood in triumph, holding Juso high like a trophy, blood dripping at his feet.

# Omens

Silent awe emanated through the meeting tower. It grew heavier and heavier, culminating in the volcanic eruption of screams and drawing of blades. Several Forgery officials in robes of red and orange stomped forward, cursing with bloodlust. River Jodai were quick to meet their demands, preparing to draw their own weapons and growling taunts with equal contempt. Lord Arusuke's lips tugged up in a satisfied smile.

"Enough! Sheath your weapons at once! Your lord commands you!" Sen motioned his orders to the guards on each side of him. The officials were almost driven mad with rage. A couple stepped forward, shaking, eyes darting ferociously from Yun to the shouting Jodai behind him, as if unable to decide who should be the first to die in Juso's name.

"I said stand down! This was an honorable duel, and it will not devolve into a bloodbath. Listen to your orders!"

Aiya was amazed at their submission. Their weapons shook in their hands, then finally they began unarming themselves one by one. Still, they stood their ground holding crazed looks on their faces.

"There was nothing honorable about what was just done, my lord," answered one of the men, but he backed off anyway without taking his eyes off Yun.

The Forgery men behind Sen cursed Yun and Arusuke, some falling to their knees, distraught. Sen stood himself now, hands balled into fists at his side. He spoke directly to Yun. "The general was already defeated, lying on the ground. What possessed you to end him so savagely and deny him a final moment with his lord?"

Yun still held the head high as blood ran down his robes. His words were calm and cool. "If you mean to ask why I took his life, it was because he never asked for mercy, as any reasonable man would have done. The duel was to continue until his death, and so I rightfully brought it. Don't worry about his head. This," he said, lowering it, "should be kept as a souvenir, and as a reminder, to exemplify what happens to pricks who step in River's household without paying the proper respect." He tossed it at them, its mushy, sickening roll leaving a trail of blood.

"River bastard, we should have your head!" a skinny, long-haired official shouted from the side. Another retrieved it while two others gathered the body, wrapping them in a variety of spare drab colored robes.

Arusuke smirked. "You've come to my lands without a proper proposal for our unification, and then you threaten my subject who only acted within the bounds of reason against your own general's hostility. I suggest you all remove yourselves from my sight, if you wish to see another sunrise."

Aiya churned in disgust, not from the carnage in front of her, but by the sick manner her father flipped the situation onto Forgery, as if this procession of events were some-how their doing. Needlessly, he'd made enemies of a sizable portion of an entire province and was too busy gloating to realize it.

Sen stared at him for a long time. His face was tight, lips working as if unable to remain open or shut. It seemed the young lord would lose control of himself and order an attack. Finally, he said, "You'll come to regret this day, Lord Arusuke. Your callous words and actions will not be forgotten."

"I look forward to the day your promise holds true."

With that, Sen ordered his men to their feet and the Forgery officials escorted him out. Their faces contorted all the way out the door, the animosity in their eyes so strong it might have crushed an opponent of less conviction. The doors parted and soon the room was empty of any other than those of the River. No sooner than they closed did the Jodai begin cheering amongst each other, the tense atmosphere finally dissipated. The release of tension cracked a nervous smile on Aiya's face as she looked to her siblings.

"Well, that ended better than expected," Shozhu said, adjusting his robe. His forehead glistened.

"I wasn't fully prepared to witness that," Uaya declared. A tinge of distaste seemed to have touched her powdered complexion. She held tightly to the napes of Ari and Yuuki who'd huddled at her sides, then turned sharply to Aiya. "You three, watch your mouths!"

When it came to her mother, never were any one of them scolded without the other. When it came to Uaya, Aiya's chest swelled with a modicum of defiance. *You could never stand up to him. This family could be trapped and burning in our estate, and you'd stand there screaming for father to do something.*

The satisfaction on Arusuke's face beamed brighter than that of anyone else. His children seemed disturbed by what they had seen, even Kitani, sitting solitary, stiff and quiet as he took in the reactions around him.

"You've done a good service today, Yun. I am well pleased."

Yun kept his face straight and bowed, walking over to his men to change out his soaked robes.

"We'll take our leave then. Hold your heads high," Arusuke commanded.

Outside, the fresh air was rejuvenating, and Aiya felt lighter as they stood behind Arusuke on the stage.

Arusuke raised a fist in the air before the murmuring crowd. "Long live the Takasa clan. Long live our people, for we stand solitary, and as one. Long live the River!" He bellowed the words, and the crowd exploded into cheers. A festive flute melody began in the background as the commoners and noble families were dismissed. Arusuke turned to Shozhu, pleased with the day's events. "Shozhu, my brother, I wish to see a smile on your face as well. I'll be spending the rest of the day with my wife and children celebrating. I suggest you do the same with the rest of the pups."

*Pups*, Aiya thought. The days were far and few inbetween that he acknowledged them as his own offspring. Most Erru who knew them from the legends feared them, but for Arusuke, there was only contempt.

"Thank you, my lord. Events of late have greatly increased my confidence in our hold over River."

"Forgive me, father, if I speak out of turn," Koji interjected, assuming a bow, "but was it really wise to be so hostile towards another potential High Lord?"

Arusuke turned, unfazed. "Nonsense. The young man had to be put in his place. He came to me in desperation with not a hair yet grown on his jewels and still barks when I point out the fact? His downfall is certain no matter which way you choose to look at it." He left them, family close behind.

Now it was only the four of them left, making their way out of the cobblestone grounds. The Forgery caravans were out of sight, making their way out Kawanura now, where they might be jeered the whole way. Lord Sen had made it sound as if he were in quite the desperate situation, and Aiya mused that his misfortune of losing a well-respected officer, and over such trivial matters at that, could not bode well for him. Under his strong frame, he'd seemed a kind and reasonable man. She could not help but bear pity for the young man, and bitter regret for her father's own actions.

Ira cursed angrily to himself. "Damned fool...."

"That is your legacy." Shozhu smirked, an occurrence Aiya did not often see. "That is who you will be following and what you will become. I admit, I hope you don't grow to be as old as me."

"I can see why we have such a long history of fighting each other," Koji said. "The Erru celebrate violence and pettiness as much as honor."

"Not in the Old Kingdom," Ira responded. "Not under King Tsae. The tribes and kingdoms of the south were united back then. Even if the world were infested with demons and creatures of darkness before the Empress' time, we fought together."

The Old Kingdom was long gone, stolen. The Empress was responsible for that, but there was no point in reminiscing at this moment. Aiya sighed. "Perhaps we made a difference. The war in Forgery's been hindering the Empress from sending troops through to the shores of Tarshan. The sooner the fighting stops, the better."

Shozhu kept his pace, eyes forward. "It's unlikely Sen would pluck one of his most valuable generals from the battlefield while they're in such a tight knot. I suspect he was of middling caliber in terms of tactical strategy. Aiya is correct, regardless. Delays are not convenient to the Empress' purpose. An empire is only as strong as its weakest link." Shozhu stopped them. "You're all free to spend the rest of the day how you please. I'll be at the temple seeking the Oshidai for guidance."

He changed directions and walked off without another word.

Aiya stretched out her arms wide and yawned, feigning boredom and ignoring the simmering discomfort paired with tight unease in her frame. "Well, I've had plenty of surprises for two days. Time to see what else the heavens have in store."

"That reminds me, there's something I have to do," Ira said, slipping away, leaving his two siblings to their own devices.

Alone, Shozhu traversed a random path through the throbbing crowds with nothing on his mind, headed nowhere in particular. At least, he had to appear that way.

Much had transpired in just the past twenty-four hours, but the most important moment was yet to come. The sun was sliding from its pinnacle in the clear firmament, but the festival around him carried on. He caught a whiff of something sour, a dirty musk like unwashed bodies. Others around him were doing the same and glaring as a particularly wild Ushin warrior passed by, his burlap robe ripped in places and his skin full of grime. His hair was a knotty mess, arranged into a tousled ponytail. His face, not entirely dissimilar to a weasel, scanned around as if looking for something, or someone.

His gaze landed on Shozhu just before they passed and he clapped his hands together and bowed in a gesture so quickly that Shozhu nearly stumbled back.

"My lord!" the man cried. "Your humble servant sees you are traveling in solitary among these ravenous crowds. If I may, might you accept the escort of your humble servant? Or perhaps you have a service at hand you wish to be performed?"

"Hmm," Shozhu mused. "I'm making my way to the forest shrine. Your services are welcome, but keep ten paces ahead of me. You smell like roadkill."

The Ushin man bowed and led him away. They walked for a minute before coming to a wheat bun stand, and Shozhu told the man to wait. He ordered two wheat buns, since eating usually distracted him from the pain in his leg. Chewing on the soft bread, they came across the Engo temple located on the far east side of the city near its walls. It was a massive building. Spread throughout the temple were rusted copper statues turned green, carved out into legendary spirits, known as the Kiru, or earthly spirits. They set an uneasiness in his heart. To the furthest side was a multitude of statues carved from a single block of stone, ferocious men who seemed bred from beasts snarling menacingly in all directions. The Ginju, or at least, what most Erru thought of them. It was always a bit amusing walking amongst a crowd who believed him a monster. If only they realized those fearsome creatures walked with them side by side every day.

At the top of the temple's steps was a statue of the Oshidai, the Engo monk figure sitting peacefully and holding his arms to his sides, hands on his lap. Engo postured as the religion of enlightenment, its founder sitting there as the highest of all. The stark contrast to the bloodlusting statues below created an odd sense of beauty. It occurred to Shozhu that these entities were to him, save for the false image of the Ginju, a lot like he was to most others. He believed in the spirits, yet his eyes had never chanced upon one. It was said the spirits preferred keeping themselves hidden from the physical world. In contrast to mankind, they were much more in the image of their creators, the Shinti, while far less powerful. The beings were also said to be individualistic, and usually kept to themselves, some benevolent and willing to help the odd traveler beating his feet on a road, while others might be malevolent and terrorize a house or field. The Erru prayed to them at times, but it was risky. One never knew if a spirit could be trusted.

The Erru hoped their prayers would be answered in compassion, but Shozhu did not believe much in the virtue, which was why he did not pray to the spirits nor the Oshidai, and was, in fact, not limping his way towards the shrine for this purpose. He passed under the great stone archway of the ironwood eastern gates, his impromptu guardian close in front, but far enough to keep away his unpleasant odor. The forest immediately welcomed him, oak and ash trees abutting the wide stone walls.

Shozhu's eyes glazed over a smear of bloodstains on the walls next to the gate. A noble family, one of little note, as well as a handful of commoners had been executed here. Three summers ago, an imperial taxman's grand entry into the city had come to a humiliating halt upon falling from his carriage and planting face first into the morning's muddy road. An unforeseen rock had caught his carriage wheel and toppled it over. The fool had been riding too fast, but regardless, he'd had his imperial soldiers take out his rage on the nearest bystanders. Shozhu made it a point that the city officials keep the main road pristine within twenty leagues of the city-at all times.

Finally, they came to a bridge leading across a dry creek barely satiated by a thin stream, which led to the local shrine. There were many shrines placed out in the forests. The heavens and the spirits were said to be more accessible in these 'cities of nature', and he, of course, was praying to the Oshidai. Or at least, that was his story.

The Ushin led him through the thin brush and path made by many wandering feet, music fading through rustling leaves. Shozhu was up the path about fifty feet in. The shrine was placed in a massive clearing, four red archways combined to make an open cube like structure, with a gold life sized statue of the Oshidai in the center.

"Here," Shozhu said, and the Ushin stopped in his tracks. The man turned around. "That will be all, my lord?"

Shozhu fished a small bag of coins from the insides of his robes. Thirty pennies, enough to keep him fed and clothed for the next six months. The Ushin man took it, with a pointed measure of control, and went on gracefully to distract anyone coming too close.

"Three doves, one feather. Fallen sun, gray weather," said Shozhu almost to himself, but just loud enough for anyone nearby to hear. There was a rustle as a man came from behind a tree and through the bushes. An Agriculture province messenger, the man named Yosuke.

He wore a striped robe of green and gray, and strapped across his brow and cheek was an eyepatch, his youthful face serious as usual. "Smart thinking, hiring a common thug."

"The task is complete," Shozhu said. "Now for you to do your part."

He began to hand the Agriculture nobleman a paper he pulled from the same pocket the money pouch had been. "Guard this with your life."

"What is it?"

"A message. One too sensitive to possibly be intercepted. I'd rather deliver it myself. You've remained under cover?"

Yosuke nodded and tied the rolled parchment onto his upper arm, then rolled his sleeve back down over it. "I hope to see you-"

He abruptly stopped. Shozhu immediately scanned the area around them. There was rustling in the branches and a note of scuffed footsteps.

"I heard a voice," Yosuke said, turning to face the direction of the sound.

Whoever was coming would have no reason to be suspicious, but still the idea they might have been heard kept them frozen in place.

The suspense was upended by a figure revealing itself from behind a tree, pushing past brush that jutted onto the path. Out came Irashida, alone.

"What the hell are you doing here?" Shozhu demanded, shocked. Why was this child disrupting him at such a moment?

"Taking a stroll through the woods. Why so alarmed?" There was a clear indication on his face, a slight diversion in the eyes and shift of the lips. It said that he knew he'd been doing something Shozhu shouldn't know about, though he did his best to hide it.

"This is a private fellowship," Yosuke said. "We hired an Ushin warrior to keep the premises clear, but I'm guessing you had already been over there."

"Taking my usual scenic roundabout to this lovely shrine," Irashida said, going around them. "But I know where I'm not wanted, I'll take my leave. Apologies."

With that, he made his way out the direction Shozhu had come in. His master's gaze did not leave Irashida until the boy disappeared behind the trees. When Shozhu finally turned away, his heart had not yet ceased thumping in his chest.

# Rise

The months of Yin and Won passed by in relative quickness. Relative to the unbearably warm summer months and the only marginally cooler fall weather. The River clans operated with caution under the Takasa, ensuring there were no longer disgruntled murmurs proliferating the high social circles. Each clan scraped together their due taxes, and nothing more. The tear in Aiya's bicep healed remarkably fast with the care of physicians and a helping of Kisane's scolding. She could now move it freely without pain and found herself enjoying more time with her Ginju brothers, Kisane and her adopted rascal. Koji spent long hours playing games of Maton with Ira as Aiya read books of classic tales to Asaya. Kisane brought them tea from time to time, much to the jealousy of Kitani. Aiya formed a habit of discreetly taking hers with a side of sake. Even a temporary buzz could help even out the day.

This was her true family. In their presence, the strenuous relationship she and her brothers' shared with the rest of the Takasa became less grating and more bearable.

The three Ginju kept to themselves as much as possible. When she did interact with the others, it was usually protecting Kisane from Kitani's harassment, who often singled her out and berated her over the minutest things, from dropping a goblet to forgetting to prepare his baths at the proper temperature. Aiya had more shouting matches with him than she cared for, though she suspected he was enjoying them more than he let on. She dreaded the day she might swear oaths to him, when he became High Lord. Their own father and mother expected it, and for all their condescension casually thrown about, Yuuki and Ari were far too passive to desire such a burden.

*I will never swear oaths to a turd flinger like him*, Aiya swore to herself. Kitani wasn't strong in the head like their father, and he certainly wasn't more benevolent of character. As much as she respected the familial hierarchy, there were some responsibilities that simply couldn't be followed through.

Lord Arusuke and Lady Uaya hushed their quarreling over preparations for the Year-End's gathering, as the month entered into Fenn. It was in this final month of the year that they began celebrating their harvests up until the start of the new year, usually marked by ever more frequent Wailstorms. It was this wave of storms the Erru considered to be the arrival of a new period, a violent tempest to signify caution for the new year, that they be grateful for the occurrences of the past and carry their newfound wisdom into the future. This year the celebration was to be held at the meeting grounds of Kawanura, where a party was hosted every Third Night by a different noble family, for Arusuke reasoned that distributing hosting privileges among the clans would breed a sense of inclusion, and thus quell any festering dissatisfaction.

Immersing herself in the library for a night of pleasant reading was far more enticing than attending the Year-End's Festival, but her duties came first.

Aiya closed an artbook of vibrant landscapes accompanied by poems from the Old Kingdom. They were consistently heroic and dreamy, praising the vast southern kingdoms and tribes, before the rule of the Empress, and exalting the traditions of Nirogawa under King Tsae, who ruled the land before it became known as River.

"That drawing reminds me of the field I saw in my dream," said Asaya, watching the book as Aiya paused her flip of the page halfway. "Except it was bigger, and the sky was dark."

The two sat on a wooden bench next to each other in the gardens, the weather far too perfect to be spent indoors. Kisane was somewhere trimming grass and foliage about ten feet away. It was up to Aiya to immerse the seven year old in the tradition of the old texts. Asaya was bored of having Ira read them to her, bluntly remarking his lack of enthusiasm when doing so, sometimes even spacing out in the middle of the sentences as if in deep thought. Koji, for some reason, preferred to indulge in the texts alone, opting to spend their time on some activity or taking her to theater.

Aiya studied the wheat-colored strokes illustrating the grasslands, noting the yellow sun emanating red rays of heat onto the field and through black ink characters that spelled the closing of the tale of the Sun Dragon. "What dream?"

Asaya paused, then fidgeted. "Read the story about the little wolf. The one that barks more than the big ones, even though they're small."

Aiya frowned sympathetically, closing the book. "Little Bird, you're hiding things. You know you don't have to do that, right? If you tell me about it, I can make it better."

Asaya looked down, remaining quiet.

What could be so disquieting for her? "You know, I have bad dreams too. Often in fact. It helps the fear go away when I talk about them."

Her little legs kicked up and down on the bench, as if trying to set her terrifying story in motion, or perhaps run from it. "The dream I had of you and Koji and Ira. You...were attacked by a dog in the middle of a road in the middle of a huge field like in the book, and it was all black with huge white teeth. Then it ran at you, and it wouldn't stop biting, and you and Koji and Ira took turns hitting it. It was really scary."

"Was this the dream you had a couple months ago?"

Asaya nodded.

Leaning, Aiya gripped her shoulders and looked her in the eyes. Asaya was growing into herself at an incredibly fast rate, her round face becoming more defined, with dark hairs running past her shoulders. She was still an innocent child, but the graveness in her eyes revealed anything but. "You never have to be scared, because neither me nor Kisane will leave your side. Not brother Ira or brother Koji either. Nothing bad will ever happen to us. We're stronger than you think."

Asaya grinned, comforted by Aiya's words. "Drink your tea," Aiya commanded. They weren't siblings, but Asaya looked up to her like an older sister, and Aiya cared for her like the younger sister she wished she had.

Asaya grabbed the tea steaming next to her, wincing in pain and nearly spilling the orange liquid onto herself. Aiya started.

"Asaya needs cooler tea, Kisane! It's too hot."

Kisane's came into view, face turned sideways. "Right away, my lady."

Aiya surveyed her for a second. Kisane seemed to have changed these past months. Melancholic and, upon inspection, ever so reserved. She was always an open book of delight, so it was strange now that somber notes were etched into her voice. Thinking on it, Aiya realized a pattern in Kisane's behavior, where for a time she would become, in her own way, colder and distant, reluctant to share the complex inner workings of her own mind, sooner or later to return to her natural disposition, like a family of passing clouds taking turns to blot out the sun. "Kisane, wait. Is everything alright?"

"Oh yes. Of course. I was just taken aback seeing you two like this." She smiled at her child next to Aiya, who wiggled her burning fingers against her teacup, careful not to let any one linger too long on the hot ceramic. "It reminded me of when my mother used to read me stories of the old nations. We didn't have any books, but we'd sit under the stars some nights and she'd recite them to me. My family...they didn't tolerate each other as well as this one." Her voice cracked on the last couple of words. She gathered the cup from Asaya's hands.

Aiya stood from her seat on the bench and took the cup, setting it on the ground. "Go play, Little Bird. Go and find Kotaru."

Asaya removed herself quickly, running through the gardens and towards the house. Aiya took Kisane by the shoulders and sat the woman next to herself on the bench. Kisane was no stranger to Uaya and Arusuke's treatment of their Ginju children.

She too was more than aware of the potential bloodshed that could occur between Takasa children when an heir was to be named who would take their father's place. Kisane never offered many details of her own past, leaving Aiya to ponder how much rougher it had been than her own. A common woman could suffer as much abuse as her noble counterpart. Aiya's heart ached, and blood boiled, at even the thought of a ruthless hand being laid upon Kisane.

Kisane wiped her eyes. "I'm so sorry, Aiya. My emotions got the better of me. My mother is the only good memory I still have before I was a servant of the Takasa. She would tell me stories of the hunting and poetry contests between king Omori and king Noh of Ochomo, of the wisdom of King Ieyasu of Ogasawa, who taught freedom and communal balance, who honored his family above his own wishes. So many stories. Those were the moments that gave me hope. My family, we were poor rice farmers a little ways west of here. My uncle would curse us and punish us with wood planks and cowhide whips, and his mannerisms caught on with many of my siblings. I used to wish desperately for a family like in those stories."

A lump formed in Aiya's throat. How could she possibly respond? What did she know of being powerless before her clan, forced into abuse, when she was bound by nothing but honor and duty? Still, the two could relate at a shallower point, for they both were born cursed into their families, sorely wanting for affection and love.

"Kisane, you're as much blood to me as Koji and Irashida. Asaya too. You're both our kin, Takasa or not. It's just...I can't bring myself to feel the same about the rest." In that unspoken chasm, it was understood whom she did not speak of.

"It's only natural to feel resentment towards one's own clan. Even those you did not spend your youth with. Sometimes I am so full of it myself that I feel it will soon burst out of me like a river."

Aiya nodded. "I obey Shozhu, mother and father through it all. I use my powers to kill, even though it never sits right with me. I desire to be strong and honorable above all else, and so I honor my clan and the established order. Despite how I feel, I carry out my duties. Is that not strength?"

Despite the public's misconceptions of what she was and her relationship with her clan, Aiya was a tool to be used by them, and so she kept herself from growing blunt by practicing contentment with the fact. Was there any better way of gaining strength or honor?

Kisane shifted, drawing herself away from Aiya, though barely noticeable. She smiled through a nearly impercepti ble wall. "True family is always smaller than one believes. It's forgivable to be selfish at times. I won't speak more of the things my family inflicted on me, but I will tell you I took a chance. I ran away and risked my life to bring a dire matter to your father's attention before he had inherited the throne. Back then, I was filled from morning till dusk with anger. I promised myself I'd never live in poverty again. Because of my actions I was made a servant and offered anything I wanted. I could have asked for more. For riches, for my own estate under fealty to your father. But I didn't."

She paused. Aiya could suddenly see, as if a veil had been lifted, the many years Kisane had trudged through, marked in the slight creases in the corners of her eyes and lips, formed over a lifetime more than twice as long as her own. "Why didn't you?"

The smile returned to Kisane's face. "Because the only thing I wanted was a child, to give her the life I could never have for myself. Because everyone makes exceptions for those they love."

Later in the day, as the sun slunk halfway into the horizon, pulling its dying light with it, Aiya parted from her meditation to answer the knock at her room's screen door. She was freshly bathed, her hair still wet and matted at the back of her robe. The river was a comfort like no other, ensuring that for the Ginju, there was no such thing as wasted or idled time. Each second spent in alignment meant learning and understanding their deity and its implications within the physical world to a greater degree. It was more an intellectual than practical pursuit. There were limits to the amount of the river they could draw, and by now she and her brothers had grown accustomed to using it like second nature. So why did she still lose control when wielding it to her limit?

Ira stepped in, holding a book in one hand and a small blue flag attached to a stick in the other, for waving harmony and good fortune into the new year.

"Since tonight we'll be deciding where to host the next few gatherings," he said, "we can use this opportunity to see which clans are really loyal to us, and which ones might be planning on using lord Owa's death as a way to stir another wave of dissent."

Unlikely that there were any conspiring against her clan. None of the nobility would foolishly go against them so soon, would they? She hoped not. She was a Takasa, but she had made human connections too. "Empress' soul, it's been so long since we've played this game of cat and mouse," Aiya said, taking the flag. She wasn't ready to give up these past two months of quiet, where she'd been able to interact with rival clans in a more amiable, most of all *genuine* manner. "I guess the saying is true that real friends don't exist among the nobility."

"We should keep our guard up at all times," Ira said, "there's no telling when someone will backstab us. This should be a sober night."

Aiya laughed. Ira must have inherited his tendency to fret from their mother. "And who in their right mind would dare try something like that right now? It will be at least a dozen full moons before any clan works up the gall to risk the same fate as the Hebi."

"I'm just saying that it could be anyone. Besides, gatherings among the nobility are always the optimal time to make a big move."

"And I'm telling *you* that I can tell when you're saying something without actually saying it. I think you just have something against me and fine wine."

"I *do* have something against it. Lay off it, Aiya." Ira's expression tightened, his head turned away for a moment. "Maybe I have just been on edge lately, worrying too much."

"By the Empress, Ira, you spend far too much time cooped up with your own thoughts," Aiya took the flag, waving it in his face. "So help me pick out my dress instead?"

The common grounds were already bustling by the time Koji arrived. Festivities were set up around the entire city, and commoners were forbidden from the meeting grounds for the remainder of the night to keep plenty of space for the nobility. His clan entered the scene in carriages with curtains of spotless white. The nine of them were welcomed with bows, proceeded by great cheer, and shortly after they split themselves up. It was important for each to interact with as many of the nobility as possible, of all ages and of every class.

Koji watched Ari whisked away to the far side of the meeting grounds by a couple of her friends, where a group of ribbon dancers spun as they welcomed onlookers into their circle. He didn't get a chance to ascertain which clan they were from, but Ari was devious enough to handle that. Even the young had a part to play.

Shozhu scowled as Kitani's friends approached him with an air of caution and feigned coolness. "Kitani-shen, we thought we'd down our fifth drink before you arrived!"

"Then you'd only be a third into your fill for the night." Kitani had a smug voice but commanded enough respect for his age. He greeted each with an amiable grin before smoothly leading them away to mingle in the crowds. Koji made his way into the meeting tower.

The interior of the tower was more decorated this time of year, flags of light blue, deep blue and white strung around the ceiling. Men and women danced to the flute in extravagant attire, colorful and slim like the peacock. Gourds of wine sat on shiny red iriswood tables of steaming fowl, whale buns, fish, and clams, which were themselves surrounded by rings of rice cakes.

Koji slipped out his notebook, making a quick note of the room's atmosphere on the parchment. A party was no place for writing, but he could surely spare a few minutes to take this opportunity. "A banquet for lovers, a night for glistening passion...."

He needed every word to fit perfectly. The setting made for good romantic scenery but the liveliness shouldn't be forgotten. *How the hell do I convey this through imagery?* These things were a pain to capture.

Two men suddenly began shouting outside the doors, sounding rather drunk.

"By the Empress," Shozhu cursed. He promptly excused himself from the room, to Koji's raised brow. Why he'd taken that matter upon to handle himself, Koji knew not. Nevertheless, he was grateful. Celebrations like these could be considered the antithesis of his uncle and were more welcome without him.

Either way, he put away his book to carry out his present mission, thankfully with minimal killing and burning. Koji slipped into conversation with the Ganha family. They were polite as usual, their newborn daughter wrapped in her mother's arms. Koji had been a friend of their son Giba since their younger years, an aspiring artist who shared Koji's love for books. They gave nothing away.

"Remember that time we got wasted during that Wailstorm?" Giba asked with an embarrassing giggle, sunken well under the influence by the time Koji had arrived. "Hino was there, and she wanted to leave and go out dancing in the storm. You tried stopping her, but as soon as she opened the door she fell over and passed out after just three steps!" He let out a chortle. Koji smiled, amused by the memory, but moved the conversation along. He had more important things on his mind for tonight.

"Seen the Hoda clan yet?"

"Negative. Haven't been around them since they lost their hold on textile mills. The swine just got their turn of chaos if you ask me."

"And your family took how many of their shares?"

Giba smacked his lips into a satisfied smile. "Thirty-two in all."

"A good margin," Koji mused. "Should add about fifty thousand empirical notes to your clan."

"So you've done your research. Fifty-two thousand three hundred to be exact."

"I'd say that would be a surplus to what you made last year." Koji kept his friendly charm.

Giba looked down to sip his drink. "I'd say it's enough to not be too worn out by the tax increase, if that's what you are getting at."

Koji took a turn at his cup, then glanced around the ballroom. "I don't mean to be a bully, Giba. I admire you and your family a lot. My father doesn't mean to force too much on you either, but the Empress gets her cut, and we have to find it one way or another."

Giba placed a hand on his shoulder. "Koji, shenshen, you don't need to explain these things to me of all people. I understand, it's a dog eat dog world. I'd be your first informant if another clan was planning a revolt."

Leave it to Giba to tell it like it was. He was one of the few people Koji knew personally willing to speak so brazenly. It was in his careless nature.

"Of course, Hino would be out of the picture."

Koji followed Giba's sight to see Ohmai Hino walking across the room in an elegant purple dress, hair tied back into graceful knots. Her face lit up as Koji noticed her. She made her way over to them. Giba patted Koji on the back. "I'll leave you to it."

Hino stopped just short of Koji, her eyes glued to his. Amethyst ornaments graced her ears. She was stunningly beautiful, a perfect oval face cut from the finest amber.

She was a foot shorter than him, her wide eyes seductively inviting as they peered up at him.

"You look...gorgeous," Koji said.

She smiled wider and brushed a strand of hair from her face. "Thank you, I would say the same for you."

"That I look gorgeous?" Koji asked.

"Yes." Hino grinned mischievously. "I suppose 'handsome' would be more appropriate."

"Or striking," Koji added. "Heads turn wherever I go. There must be something about me."

"It's your confidence, of course, Koji. So...."

"So?"

"My poetry. What did you think?"

Koji fought the urge to slap his palm against his face. Hino's family were second-class nobility, scribes who bound and sold books. She herself was a romantic, a poet ever since he could remember, whose work was admired among a sizable subset of the nobility. Despite his business, he'd meant to read it sometime this month.

"I'm sorry, I never got around to it. You probably want to stab me now, but hear me out. How about you read it to me tomorrow at midnight, right outside our estate?"

Hino's eyes narrowed. "You and your impeccable memory. Did you run this by your mother first?"

Because of the status of the Ohmai, Lady Uaya did not approve of Koji's affection for Hino. In fact, it was because of her that he'd never even courted her, despite their years of companionship. They'd only shared a single kiss, three years ago, before he'd pulled himself away. He'd lied to her, told her he had not shared her feelings. In truth, he'd been scared to defy his parents. Hino was hurt, but on the inside, Koji felt humiliated. He would prove himself more a man now. With or without his mother's approval, his life was in his control.

Koji only smiled. "Didn't need to. As they say, nothing good happens after sunset."

The clans moved about like schools of fish in the water. Back and forth, seemingly with purpose, until they abruptly switched direction again. Aiya viewed none of them as threats. Still, she kept Ira's advice and stayed mostly clear of the wine, renowned and imported directly from Rain province.

She utilized her more solid relationships first, chatting with the most influential nobles. Her slim yet flexible blue dress went an inch past her knees, a solid ocean blue with tight sleeves slightly billowed at the wrist. Aiya noted it wouldn't be a night of drunk partying without at least a couple men hitting on her. She entertained Sibachi, genuinely interested in the son of the famous Shinsato Hirofumi, an authentic leatherworker, while politely declining Chiba, who shyly made his advances every twenty minutes.

There were certain aspects of Sibachi to truly admire, such as his thick arms and kind smile, his easy laughter around her and the honesty in his work. He was the least in character like most of those present, which she gleaned from his playful openness whenever she inquired into his life. There were certain ways, however, in which he was not so relatable, and Aiya wracked her brain for a way to articulate them, even to herself. Ginju did not marry out of duty to their clan, but lovers were no obstacle to that. Ideally, hers would be somehow isolated from her clan. She would not share them with her family, not even allow the possibility. Finding love, in her mind, had always been synonymous with starting anew, to become one with a new family. Something she didn't deserve, for how could she be a good woman to her man if she could not honor her own family as it was?

Otherwise, what man might be good for her when she was bound to be so much stronger, so much higher status than him? That fact would leave him feeling intimidated, or worse, emasculated. She would cause him shame, and he would despise her as much as her own father.

If only these people knew who she really was, who she and her siblings were, maybe they'd try to appeal to them, raise the three Ginju up as the new heads of the Takasa clan to rule over River. Would they do so out of love or fear? They had nothing to love about her, for she was the dog of her clan. There was everything to fear, and talks of peace wouldn't change that.

"And then I said," Chiba laughed nervously, "if you don't want to be mistaken for a doormat, get off the floor!"

Aiya turned her head in confusion before realizing he was referencing some joke he'd made during their last interaction. Ira showed up by her side as Chiba excused himself, hanging his head.

"Any potential disruptors?" she asked him.

"Looks like we might go into the new year with some relative peace."

Ira studied the glass in her hand. "That is water, right?"

"Nope," she lied, downing the make-believe sake in a single gulp. "That's the first glass I've cleared tonight." Aiya grinned.

"You're supposed to be on guard!"

"I'm doing that by appearing as if I'm not, obviously. You know, if they really wanted to kill us, the best way would be an underhanded tactic like an arrow, or poison."

Ira didn't hide the distrust on his face. Finally, he said, "Underhanded tactics would be the only way." He offered a smile. "To think, we're almost like the Kiru compared to them, and yet we can be disposed of by the same illnesses as the unblessed. The heavens surely mock us."

"Stop it, Ira." Aiya said it louder than she intended to and drew looks from a couple directions. In a more hushed tone: "Don't talk about yourself like that. You're going to be fine. The physicians told us you just need to rebalance your energies–"

"I understand that, Aiya. I do. I don't mean to be pessimistic, all I'm saying is that *I'm* the prime example for why we can never fully let our guard down."

"Listen, save it for later, okay? You can mope then. We're here to celebrate like everyone else."

Suddenly, a series of yells set off at an impressive volume from outside the tower, considering the noisy chatter and sway of the violin. Aiya assumed it to be some argument, which–at such magnitude–would probably end in an honor duel. Then came more shouts, multiplying.

"What is that?" said Ira.

Everyone in the room slowly came to a standstill, listening. For every moment the shouting dragged on, the obvious answer became dreadfully more clear. This was no sound of celebration or a fight, but of mass hysteria and violence. Soon the shouts were melding with screams, and with every second they went on, Aiya's heart beat harder against her chest.

"What the hell is going on out there?" someone asked.

A Jodai guard wearing a plain white theater mask approached the door.

Before he could get a hand on the frame, it flew open and a messenger came nearly tumbling inside, kneeling.

"My lords and ladies, I bear emergency news! Fighting between Jodai forces has erupted outside! We are under attack by both River and Agriculture soldiers!"

# Ploy

No reply came in the moments following. There was no longer music, nor laughter. Nothing but the exchanging of looks on shocked faces, and quiet dread.

Next came the reactions, confused and growing more hysterical by the moment. It was as if a song were playing up into a crescendo, and with every higher pitch Aiya felt the tension expanding, morphing, becoming more surreal. She gauged Ira's response, but he remained as speechless as her. She tried mouthing words but her mind seemed to have gone blank, stripped bare.

"Repeat yourself!" Lord Arusuke's voice boomed from the front of the room. He stepped from the large company that had been entertaining him, face hard and imposing. "I'm not sure we heard you correctly! What did you say?"

"My lord, River and Agriculture forces have begun attacking the city and have already made their way towards the Takasa estate. The River forces seem to be those of the former Hebi clan, the Suno clan, the Ganha clan, the Hine clan, and an assortment of others. Takasa and Hoda forces are currently engaged with them and Agriculture troops, but they are not far from where we currently stand."

Arusuke said nothing for a minute. It seemed a minute stretched forever. "Impossible. That makes no sense."

The messenger simply looked him in the eyes. It was a look that said everything.

The guard at the door stepped up to the kneeling messenger so that he stood right above him, features hidden behind the mask. "I'd say it makes perfect sense." Before the messenger could react, the guard snatched the sword from his hilt and sliced the man's neck.

Aiya inhaled sharply. The man fell over, his head half severed from his neck. They could hear him gargling, choking on his own blood.

The crowd took that as permission to run from the guard, and all other Jodai in the room. Speech remained suspended from some, while others stood back, clutching both friend and kin protectively and making threats. The guard removed his mask, revealing an all too familiar face.

"Sano!" Arusuke shouted. His expression went cold, almost distant. "What's the meaning behind this? Explain yourself!"

Sano took a step towards the High Lord. Arusuke's usual strong presence seemed somehow to have diminished. "This entire night was a ploy, my lord. Everything was a ploy. Over the past few months, we have conspired against you, myself and over a dozen other clans. Your own soldiers. Since the end of the summer harvest, in fact. It was bound to happen eventually, you just couldn't see it. Right now, we have five thousand troops seizing the city. I'm assuming around a thousand soldiers oppose us right now, including six hundred of your own Jodai. Most of your troops remain loyal. They are good men, and they will die here, tonight. You will die too, I'm afraid. We've judged you unfit to lead. The rest of the nobility and their troops will be spared as soon as they pledge allegiance to the new River lord, to Lord Hebi Owa."

*Owa?* Aiya thought. *What does he mean by that?*

Arusuke was almost at a loss for words, and it dawned on Aiya that this was the first time she had ever seen him this way. He stepped forward, enraged, fists to his sides. "Lord Owa is dead! His entire family is dead! Where's your honor, swine?"

"Right where it's always been," Sano answered. "Your authority, unfortunately for you, has been vanquished forever."

The room's Jodai began making their way towards her father and mother, who clung skittishly to his side with an arm groping his bicep. Lady Uaya twisted the High Lord back, possessed by terror. Arusuke resisted, standing his ground, but even in his rage, the crowd could see loss in his eyes. Loss and devastation.

"Find the children!" Sano shouted to the other Jodai. "Everyone must witness this!"

Ari and Yuuki screamed, while those around them shuffled about, unsure what to do. Sano turned to Aiya's direction, and suddenly jerked towards her, pushing past the panicking crowd. Aiya was frozen in place, ready to kill him at the first sign that he meant to take her life. He reached her and tried grabbing her arm. Aiya stepped back and slapped his hand away, but Ira stopped her.

"Go with it!" he hissed.

Aiya looked towards him, repulsed and perplexed, but let the man take her arm anyway. She and Ira, along with Koji, were roughly escorted to the front of the room with the rest of their clan. Kitani kicked and cursed the Jodai, earning him a hard smack to the back of the head that sent him crashing into the rest of the family members. Uaya rushed to catch him. She shot Aiya an expectant look.

Up front, her clan suddenly stood in a different light. Years of power and prestige stripped away. Crying, shaking, cornered, they were not the powerful Takasa family anymore; merely a group of scared, vulnerable, and despicable Erru.

Sano stepped behind Arusuke and addressed the crowd. "These nobles have been detrimental to River society since the day they came into power. For forty long years we have been under their heel, as they made us writhe, wretched below their feet. They oppressed us, and now they will receive their turn of chaos."

Aiya knew what was coming. She saw the jerk of Sano's arm, the flick of his wrist. She heard the conviction, the *passion* behind Sano's words, words that had surely echoed in his mind for many years prior to this moment. Hesitating, she moved to stop him, but it was too late. Sano's blade had already plunged deep into her father's chest.

It was just one of many deaths she'd witnessed in her life. A death which, in reality, was no different than the others. Then why did this hit so hard, like a blast of violent wind straight into her gut? Her mind exploded into shock, the savage sight yanking, sucking her in to behold every gruesome detail of her father writhing at his former retainer's feet. He was clawing at the sword inside of him, attempting to curse, then he wheezed until he no longer drew breath. Her father of eighteen years was gone.

Children and adults alike, everywhere, screamed. Kitani broke loose of his captor's grip, ran, and fell on his father. He hugged him and cried, before being violently torn away again. Uaya covered her mouth, and could do nothing but utter high pitched noises as Sano grabbed Arusuke's hair and pulled up his head.

"Why didn't you stop them?" Uaya accused, full of horror. Aiya turned and saw her mother's eyes nailed on her.

"Take the rest of them to the Kawanura dungeons where they will await judgment." Sano began sawing as gasps and stunned curses lit the room. Aiya wanted to puke, feeling her stomach doing somersaults. Ari did.

Jodai flanked the seven of them on all sides. Sano handed away his prize and Aiya watched Lord Arusuke's head being strung up right outside the building. Past the doors and past the men decorating the tower with Takasa blood, she saw her family being led outside and then underground, spending anywhere from days to weeks locked away in the dank dungeons. She saw Owa, leering Owa, coming finally to release them from their torment, bringing their death on stage before all the nobility. Still, Aiya remained focused on what was in front of her as they were led away. The traitors had taken her father's head, and that marked the end of an era. The end of the Takasa rule.

The doors swung open, and the soldiers forced the seven out into a single file line. A Jodai kicked at Kitani's feet to keep him in place. The men pushed them forward, making them trudge along to the sounds of battle in the background. Aiya's heart pounded uncomfortably, her soft dress allowing her to move briskly. She wanted to look back, to watch as they got further from the building, but forced her attention on Ira in front of her. Kitani, Yuuki and Ari sobbed uncontrollably, ignored by their captors. The street they walked down was deserted. In the distance, she could see a few places where fires had started.

Uaya continued repeating her accusations against her Ginju children. Koji was struck dead silent, though Ira betrayed nothing.

*We just let our father die*, Aiya thought.

"Shackle them," a Jodai man said. "We don't need to take any chances."

A couple hundred feet away, they turned around a corner where they could no longer see the common grounds except for the protruding top of its tower. Their trek was sending Yuuki into convulsing shivers, and Ari was too distressed to comfort her, Uaya too distracted by her own mumbling. The guards gathered a small bunch of iron chains.

"It's okay, Yuuki. It's okay. We'll-we are going to be alright." Aiya did her best not to stumble over her words, turning to face her youngest sister of twelve years. *They won't hurt Yuuki, most of all Yuuki. I won't allow it.* She turned back to her brother, only a year younger than she. She trusted him with all her being, yet now she could hardly recognize whatever strange intentions lied inside him. *What the hell is going through your mind, Ira?*

"Stay in line!" one of the guards to her left shouted, wrenching her back.

Aiya glared at him, feeling close to murder. She looked ahead of her at Ira, who turned to meet her eyes. This time he didn't stop her. "Now!" he shouted.

The guards tensed, hands going to their hilts. That one moment of hesitation from them was all she had needed. Calmly, all her senses sunk into the river. She had access. The immense aura was there, within her, which she could grab hold of anytime, flowing and ebbing above her tuned soul.

She backhanded the guard next to her, her knuckles crashing against his skull. He spun backwards and landed on his back, silent. The others stopped to look at their fallen friend, while the other two Ginju took their turn. Koji grabbed one and dealt a deadly blow to the head, then threw him into another guard. Ira cracked two spines before stealing a sword and slicing down the rest of the Jodai approaching him.

The men wisened up quickly to the danger they faced and began to retreat. Aiya leapt across Kitani, who stood in awe, delivering a wood sandal to the chest that shattered the man's rib cage. He flew backwards ten feet, blood sputtering from his mouth. Her dress sounded as if it tore from the sudden extreme movement. Ripped a few inches up her thigh, she cursed, then made quick work of the last two guards with no hesitation. Before long, twelve bodies lay sprawled on the stone ground.

"Ira, can you explain *why* we waited so long to do that?" Aiya shouted, almost hysterical.

Ira didn't respond. Instead, he turned to their younger siblings and mother. "The streets look mostly deserted. It seems as if they want it that way. Come morning,  everything will have changed overnight. Seek shelter in one of the commoner homes, we're going back to the estate to save Shozhu." He began walking away, leaving them speechless at his brevity.

"Ira!" Aiya shouted again, but he continued walking past her towards the direction of the Takasa estate. She stepped forward, prepared to shake the answers out of him.

"MONSTERS!"

The violent cry from their mother stopped Ira cold in his path. She'd finally broken from her spell of shock. "You let them kill *him*. Your own father, my husband! Your lord! You've let them disgrace us and steal our province!" There was such venom in her voice that Aiya was taken aback. Her mother, a woman of composure, had never displayed such intense emotion. Even when she'd lost that composure on them in the past, it was invariably handled with a measure of restraint.

Koji stepped forward. "Mother, wh-"

"Heavens damn it, shut the hell up! *Shut up!* You're not my child, swine! I'm not your mother, you little son of a bitch! NEVER call me that again!"

As if Aiya had been stung in the abdomen, her stomach clenched. Together, they had committed the worst betrayal. She wanted to back down and apologize, barely able to stand or believe what she'd done. The other part of her kept her standing, vindictively content with her mother's suffering.

Ira was now between them, Uaya having removed her dagger from her bosom with a snarl that sealed away any remaining sliver of sanity within her frame. His voice was stern. "Listen, Uaya. Your time is limited, and you'll likely be found sooner than later. So if I were you, I'd take the children and try to escape the province while you still can. Your reign is over."

With that, he took off towards the estate. Aiya and Koji followed, not giving their mother another second. Her blue dress was less than optimal for it, but offered enough flexibility that it wasn't an issue. The tear in it helped. She kicked off her sandals, running barefoot. In the distance, Aiya heard thunder and noticed that the night was starless. It might rain soon.

"Ira," Koji shouted. He kept pace with Aiya directly behind his brother. "I'm going to ask you this once. Under heaven's witness, what in the hell is going on, and why did we allow father to die?"

Ira took his time answering. Finally, he said, "We're free now. We're no longer bound to the hell of living double lives, disgraced by our own family. Thanks to our deity, we can start over, with a new family. We won't be killed or outcast like the rest of them."

An irritating pang of guilt formed in Aiya's stomach. "So why are we saving Shozhu then?" Though he had not treated them much better than the rest of their kin, they owed it to him that they knew their deities in the first place. On that alone, his life should be spared. "And how do we know he's even at the estate?"

"It's not just Shozhu," Ira replied. "Kisane and Asaya too. We don't know what could happen with them. We need to hurry."

At the mention of Asaya and Kisane, Aiya perked up. Her heart resumed its crazed rhythm and she almost threw up at the thought of finding them sprawled on the ground like Arusuke, lost heads trailing blood or impaled through the chest. They were almost there, glimpsing the mass of both River and Agriculture troops lined outside the garden premises. Surprisingly, most kept about ten feet from the garden, and the household had not been set ablaze. River Jodai, however, were all around, apparently the dogs of Lord Hebi Owa. It seemed only one family would now be permitted to enter the former Takasa grounds.

"How is Owa still alive?" Koji asked. "Don't ignore me, Ira! Aiya and I saw him kill himself, right in front of us! We burned his estate to the ground!"

"Follow me," Ira said, struggling to keep pace. All this running was surely taking a toll on his sick body. "We'll sneak in through the back."

Contrary to their expectations, they didn't find guards swarming there. The Hebi lord was evidently confident that his plans would not be interrupted. If he was alive, was it possible he had some magic to counter even that of Ginju? Aiya struggled to conceive it.

The training grounds were in front of them, vacant and still as if nothing had changed. To the side stood only two Jodai at the top of the back porch steps. They sported green armor the shade of forest-jade, erect and alert. Agriculture Jodai.

Koji raised his sword stolen earlier from the prison guards. "Now or never." He stood up quickly, rustling the bushes.

"Hold on," said one of the guards, "I heard some scuffling, what was that?" The other guard shuffled about before drawing his sword. Aiya and Ira got to their feet.

"I heard—"

What he heard, he didn't get a chance to say. Koji's black form darted above him. The guard jumped and followed it with his torch. Koji landed behind him before the man stole a good look.

The guard spun, catching him. "What the? S-sound t—!" the other man yelped, backing up, eyes wide.

They didn't get a chance for that either. Koji drew his sword across his neck and the man slumped to the ground. The other tried defending himself, to no avail. Koji rounded on him and brought down his hilt, slamming the butt of his weapon into the side of his skull.

Aiya and Ira were right behind him, grabbing the weapons from the fallen men. "Think that undead bastard Owa is really on the other side? Would be nauseatingly poetic," Koji said.

"Only one way to find out," Ira huffed.

"How are you feeling?" Aiya's unsettled eyes lingered on Ira.

"I'm managing, but now isn't the time to get soft. We're too far down this road now. Let's finish."

They burst inside.

Oil lamps beamed in the background behind the nearest walls. The air, for one reason or another, felt a little more oppressive. Light flooded out. The main room of the first floor was a split chamber, a large entrance room divided into half, with the second room behind another sliding door.

Jodai stood, forest-jade armor clinking among the beautiful decorations of the room. It was like something out of a stage play, except Aiya and her siblings were unwitting participants in it.

She rushed forth, the guards growling in confusion. There were seven of them, more heavily armored than the last, but they went down just as easy. One standing a foot above the others held a mace, its ball half the size of his head. He raised it, then brought it down on Koji with skull crushing force. His attack never landed. As the weapon came down in an arc, Koji sprung off the floor and kicked it, smashing the ball backwards into the Jodai's forehead. He thudded on the floor, safe to say for good.

Five swords made for the three of them, the sixth guard running to gather reinforcements. He'd been quick to choose self-preservation, and Aiya couldn't blame him for it. The others had chosen certain death.

"W-what the hell are you?" a guard asked, mouth trembling as he crossed blades with Aiya. They pressed their swords against one another, pushing to test the might of the other. Aiya did not test, only allowed him life a little longer.

"What did you do with the servants, swine?" she demanded. "Answer!"

"Damn you," he said through gritted teeth. He almost flinched as Aiya brought a hand up, grabbing her opponent's blade. He watched in horror as she flung it to the side, pulled back her sword hand, and buried her own weapon where his neck met his shoulder. He grunted, blood cascading from the wound. Just like all the men before she had killed, childlike and helpless.

By the time she looked up from his lifeless gaze, the rest of the guards were finished, and Koji had already caught up with the last. His prey hadn't even made it to the door, slouched as he clutched at his stomach on the floor where he'd been stabbed.

"I don't think they've killed any of the servants," Ira said, face mere inches from the screen, "but I think someone is behind that door, waiting for us. They've just used the others for bait."

Aiya glowered. Were they aware of who they were baiting? "You're saying they're intentionally inviting three enraged Ginju to a sparring match?"

Ira pressed his ear against the door and listened...nothing. Aiya hoped to the heavens he was right about the servants being used as hostages. She was tempted to tell them to split up to find Asaya and Kisane, but something in her told her this was where she needed to be, that even before they went through this door, they were unsafe.

A tight steel grip seized Aiya's arm above her elbow. She faced Koji, his face hard. "You took that injury from mere soldiers. Behind those screens is something worse."

"What's he on about?" questioned Ira, ear still pressed against the rice paper. "What injury?"

Aiya yanked herself from him. Though barely perceptible, he recoiled at her aggression. "You're really trying to stop me from this? Asaya needs us."

Ira stepped back, and, taking a breath, swung the sliding doors open.

The room was pitch dark, sheets having been placed over the walls and windows to block any moonlight. The faint glow of the lamps in the first chamber weakly illuminated the room. At the back was a dim figure sitting in silence. He looked straight at them, a man with a beard matching Master Shozhu in volume but not length, gray hair tied into a bun. Whoever he was, he clearly was not Owa.

Aiya raised her sword, the faint silhouettes of her brothers beside her. "Who the hell do you think you are," she snarled, "sitting in our damn house?"

The man said nothing. Aiya stepped a few feet forward, ready to repeat herself when she heard shuffling to her side. Before her eyes adjusted to the dark, something with the force of a thousand tons slammed into the side of her face. She saw a flash of white as she flew across the floor, almost into the other wall.

"Wa-what the?" she sat up, spitting. She tasted blood in her mouth. Her brothers rushed forward, Ira tackling the body that stood where she'd been seconds ago. As they struggled to the floor, braziers flared to the sides, four in each corner, illuminating the room completely. Aiya saw they had more company than expected.

Besides the boy Ira wrestled with, another young man stood on the far wall from Aiya, blade at the ready. She turned to see a female form behind her, two short swords drawn. Koji jumped to his sister's aid. "Watch out!" he screamed.

The female swung down her swords. Aiya rolled out the way, drawing her blade and forcing it into the woman's chest. She tried dodging, but Aiya proved too fast, and the woman was already too dedicated to her attack. Aiya's blade punctured with enough force to have pierced through her back, yet only sunk a third of the way. The girl grunted and crumpled as Aiya pulled her blade free. Koji kept his sword trained on the assailant as Aiya turned on her feet to face the second opposing male figure.

He was dressed in similar black clothing they had worn the night they'd brought destruction on the Hebi estate. He couldn't be any older than herself. His features were hidden, but his eyes, with their dark intensity, furled in the rage of youth. An Agriculture man, here to spill innocent blood, with the audacity to look at her as if his anger were righteous. Aiya's chest thumped with fury.

The sitting man chuckled, bringing her attention down on him, then back at the man before her, careful not to lose him.

"Seems you've been expecting us, old man," Ira said roughly. He'd gotten out of his scuffle and stood facing his opponent.

The old man showed teeth. "Surely you didn't think I'd let you interfere without consequence."

"And you are?" Koji demanded.

His smile remained for a long minute. Finally, he answered. "Lord Tabeni Tsugo, High Lord of the Tabeni family, ruling clan of Agriculture province. I, and most others, have come to an understanding that Hebi Owa is the rightful ruler of River, and you Ginju are the only ones standing in the way. Did you think we'd allow that?"

"Of course not." Aiya grinned bitterly, wiped sweat from her face, and lunged.

Her opponent didn't miss a beat. He engaged her attack midway, the point of his sword aimed straight for her left eye. Aiya's blade, face down, made for his leg.

Their steel rang, and the force of the collision shook Aiya's bones. She grunted. What was this strength, this speed that was enough to follow even her movements?

Eyes locked, she saw deep in his expression a look of defiance, somewhere in the green of his irises, so intense it sent chills down her spine. Whatever his past, he was ready to protect and kill for his lord. Struggling, Aiya realized she'd never faced an opponent with such ability who wasn't one of her siblings. It became abruptly clear to her who she was crossing swords with, why that smiling man named Tabeni Tsugo oozed confidence in the face of death. There had not been much resistance to their entrance because Owa had been expecting them with the perfect counter. Freaks of his own.

*We finally meet face to face*, Aiya thought, *Ginju of River and Agriculture. Let's see whose deity is more worthy tonight.*

She threw her left elbow at the man's face with all her strength. He could follow her movements, but she was faster by far, and he barely managed to catch it with one hand. The force of it set them both off balance. Aiya disengaged her blade from his and went to cut him across the chest. He fell to the side, spun, and pounced back with a roundhouse kick that would have bruised and bloodied her jaw. She fell to the side of his leg and grabbed it to throw him off balance. He toppled, and she proceeded to gut him as the room changed, darkening, before pulling her blade free with surprising weakness.

Stunned by how easily he'd fallen, she turned to the others, recalling her torn bicep as dark tethers in her vision marked the coming of the drowned man. Each breath was shallow, each thought magnified in fear. Her skin grew cold.

*No! My brothers need me! Kisane. Asaya needs me!*

She became aware of the river, aware of it coursing through her veins. She ceased drawing it, trusting her years of training and experience, letting angry determination fill its place. The darkness left her, replaced with the clash of swords, fire, and blood.

Ira and Koji's opponents were keeping up better than Aiya's own, though they still struggled against the river's speed. Blood stains formed all over, drawn from the hideous wounds the Agriculture Ginju received.

Aiya held her breath. Koji was engaged in a sort of arm wrestling match against the same female whose chest Aiya had gored. *What?*

"D-damn you! Why won't you die?" Koji managed through gritted teeth.

Someone was behind her. By the time she saw him, it was too late. Her opponent's crushing grip got the back of her neck, and she felt the tip of his sword poking into the small of her back. She let out a small cry, grateful when he didn't go further. "H-how are y—"

"Any last words, River bitch?" he growled, not sounding like he intended to let her finish if she did.

Aiya's mouth turned dry. She strained her head to get a look at the spot she'd sliced just moments before. His grip wouldn't allow it. "You don't get to look at your killer before you join the storms. Your last breaths will be spent watching your fellow River scum succumb to your same fate."

Dropping her blade, she brought her hands up and grabbed his wrist from behind her, flipping over him, throwing him off balance. Before he could react, she landed a fist in his cheek, knocking him two arm lengths back. She ran, retrieving her sword and lunging for him. "Join the fucking storms!"

He scrambled to his feet, inadequate against her speed. Her alignment wavered, splitting her vision and shaping a horrible sensation that her mind, body and soul were separating, each stripped from her control as she made for her prey.

*I am in control!* She grasped for the river, reached for its raging currents, losing herself as it flooded her soul. *I am in control!*

She lacerated him in two criss crossing strikes from chest to ribs. Stringy droplets of blood flew from him with each swipe, and she finished by cuffing his throat with her free hand as she fell to her knees. He tumbled across the floor, almost into Ira, who had cut his opponent across the arm in what would have resulted in the loss of a limb in a normal match. The opposing Ginju took it and went for Ira's neck.

If it wasn't for his height, Ira would have suffered a hole through the apple in his neck. He leaned back, kicking the Agriculture Ginju back into the paper wall. He ripped halfway through it, slowing himself by grinding his feet into the floor.

The night devoured Aiya whole, light by the braziers swallowed like fireflies. She held herself up on her hands and knees, pushing to stand, but to no avail. Her frame shook uncontrollably, swaying side to side as if submerged in the blackest waters, so dark her senses became distant, drifting away. Terror lodged in her throat as the hands of a dead man grabbed her from behind, clammy skin warping around her elbows. That terror expanded to the point of bursting. Unable to see her enemy, Aiya twisted, jerked, opened her mouth, and screamed.

The river evaporated from her mind as she collapsed. Every part of her twitched numbly with the most profound sense of dissociation. For a moment, she'd lost all control over her own body, mind and spirit, filled with pure *cold*. She wasn't sure a greater horror existed under or above the heavens. *Need to get to your feet!* She let the feeling pass, summoning the strength to stand.

Aiya flinched with awed horror as her own opponent slowly rose to his feet, tears along his clothes. Ira pounced in front of her and grabbed him, ramming his sword through the young man's chest. They both fell to the floor and Ira pinned him down, aiming to stab him again.

The Agriculture Ginju winced from the pain but didn't make a sound as he shoved Ira away with all his force.

Ira's foe came bounding after him, sword trained for the kill. Aiya leapt in his way and slammed a fist into his nose. He took it with ease, Aiya realizing her strength had left her. She stood weakened, vulnerable, exposed. She'd failed, and would be killed in her own household. "What are you?"

"Same as you, but stronger," the Ginju replied. His voice was less full, less commanding, but contained equal menace.

Her own opponent, eyes still on Aiya, stood and removed his shirt. Bare skin was now visible, revealing stab wounds inflicted by Ira and the horrifying lacerations she had given him across his torso. Somehow, the wounds were stitching themselves back together, blood no longer seeping out of them.

"Impossible..." Aiya said absently. Was it the power of their deity? That was the obvious explanation. Still, how could such a thing exist?

"It's been an interesting night, hasn't it?" the Agriculture lord said, clearing his throat. He'd nearly been forgotten. "Agriculture is not just about growth, but rebirth. Now, I should ask you all to refrain from killing each other."

Aiya squinted at him, sitting calmly where he was, not afraid in the least of the beings fighting before him. Looking back at the young man she'd lacerated, she was astonished by how well he fought, how he'd even found the chance to kill her. Why hadn't he?

The river surged within her again, along with an overwhelming urge to finish him.

"Your deity is impressive," Koji said through a smile, "and I'll admit, we were caught off guard. However, it's nothing compared to the power of the river."

He lurched forth, swinging his sword in one powerful motion. His target, alarmed, allowed herself to be cut down the torso as his blade split skin. She grabbed Koji's hands, held them down, and jabbed a fist into his nose. "Back off, insolent bastard!" she screamed.

Koji flew back, nearly losing balance, but quickly caught himself. "Who's the bastard here?" he asked, raising his sword again and preparing to charge, wobbling.

"Enough!" called Ira, murderously. "We're no longer fighting, Koji!"

Aiya's opponent spoke up. "Stand down, we're not going to harm you."

Koji refused to drop his stance. "Yet you still stand here, desecrating our house like swine fresh out of mud." Aiya tensed. She'd never seen him in such a state. His nose indeed gave reason for righteous anger, blood trickling from it, his voice coming out nasally.

"I anticipated you coming tonight," said Tsugo, speaking quickly in an attempt to divert their attention back to him. "I had to see your power for myself, so forgive me for trespassing. And the violence."

"You should have brought more guards," Aiya said through bloody lips. "And Ginju. You're no safer now than if you were all alone."

Tsugo scratched his beard as shadows created by the burning braziers danced across his body. "I admire your tenacity. That will be useful for you in the near future. But now that our business here is done, we must be quick to take it elsewhere."

Koji scowled. "Elsewhere? We're here to kill you. What in your right mind makes you believe you'll be leaving here with your head still attached?"

"He understands we'd not let you do such a thing," Aiya's rival spat. "And he understands that, from our fight just now, the Ginju of River are inferior."

"Relax now, Totane. River Ginju, I sincerely ask for your forgiveness for the events of tonight, but there was no other choice. Due to the astuteness of your brother, Irashida, who would give his life for you, you are free from the shackles of the Takasa clan. Lord Owa will reign, and he will of course want you removed from play, the power of the Ginju transferred to his own offspring. Instead, we will retreat now into Agriculture province, for the purpose of preventing a night like this from ever occurring again."

# Trust

A long silence followed, so deep and true that Aiya forgot they were all in the middle of a dire battle to the death. "Agriculture province?" she asked, perplexed. "You've got a real smug sense of humor."

"I say he's bluffing to stall time," Koji said, returning his gaze to the opponent before him. The long cut down the front of her body had already begun healing, though visibly much slower than the other injuries she'd received. "We should finish what we started and not get distracted by this old man's rambling."

"The only outcome of that would be the three of you unfortunately joining the storm," said the young woman, whisking her swords out to her side, though she grimaced in pain.

Aiya held her own weapon up and pointed it to the one called Totane. Aware of his abilities now, she was sure she could take him down with less effort. She tried to summon strength back into her muscles, still slightly numb.

"I sincerely ask that you hold." Tsugo's voice was firm. "What I speak of is a serious matter. We *must* leave now. I am impressed with your abilities tonight and it would be a shame to put them to waste."

"He's gone crazy with fear," Koji said. "Don't worry old man, we haven't come—"

The female Ginju stepped forward. "Talk to our father with anything less than utmost respect again, and it'll be your last words. Mind you, I'm not too keen on stopping this fight either. We don't yet trust you."

"The feeling's mutual," Aiya countered, gaze steady on Totane.

"For the Empress' sake, put your weapons down!"

Ira's command left Aiya startled. He tossed his own weapon away. It clattered on the floor, begetting silence.

Koji looked back and forth between him and Tsugo. "What did you say, Ira? And how does this man know your name?"

The fact dawned on Aiya, having somehow evaded her. Despite herself, she found herself unable to take her eyes away from her brother.

"That goes for you first, Risako," said Tsugo. "This discussion can't happen with our blades pointed at each other's throats."

"Then it can't happen at all." Koji took three steps towards Risako, his blade aimed directly for her.

Risako scowled, staring at Koji, before sheathing her double blades in disgust. Koji did not mirror her concession.

"Please, River Ginju, relax. I only had my offspring here to stop you from taking my own life, and as reassurance that you'll sit and listen to what I have to tell you."

Aiya thought. It was possible that tonight marked the first time during the Shikkin era that Ginju had fought amongst each other. Possibly, for the first time in the history of the empire. The man called Tsugo likely wouldn't risk his most important assets for no purpose at all. Even outside the advantage of his Ginju, with his current manpower, he *could* overcome the three of them, if not without heavy losses. Even three Ginju couldn't defeat three thousand men. Aiya considered him for a long moment. "How does sitting down and making fools of ourselves with you change our current situation?"

"You'll live a little longer, for one," he replied. "Put away your arms and I'll explain everything. It's fruitless to try when you're on guard like that."

She looked to Koji, then to Ira. Hesitating, the two threw down their swords. Aiya grew heavier, almost as if her feet had sunk into the ground, and she refused to take her eyes off of any one of them.

"I assure you we mean no further harm. My children understand what pressing matters we must discuss, for it concerns them as much as it does you."

"Whatever you say, old man," Koji replied, "just explain to us what you want before we change our minds." The boy next to Ira shot Koji a look of hatred that might have evolved into a murderous rage had Tsugo's words not rung true.

Tsugo looked relieved. "I'll be as brief as possible. I assume you are more than familiar with the tale of the River Prince."

"Prince Tsae? Of course," Aiya said. "Son of King Omori, and the last king of Nirogawa, who drowned three thousand imperial troops in the Yunan river before surrendering to the Empress."

"Then you know he upheld the righteous virtue of charity, and you know of his practice of nurturing community. He was a man of courage in times of great honor and even greater bonds between the Erru. His father knew Agriculture as Ogasawa, before it was conquered by the empire, and shared with his son the sagacity of King Ieyasu, who imparted his wisdom to Omori in his own pastures. Two kings, speaking freely of their own accord, beholden to none but the kingdoms which they loved."

Aiya considered him with hesitance. "What's your point?"

"It is a shame you don't already recognize it. You've lost your ways as much as us all. Your eyes are veiled. The River Prince may have given up his kingdom, but not his spirit. Even today, his remorse has not been forgotten."

Aiya recalled the lamentation:

*Yet once more, would I see our freedom be*
*One year more, I trust would have saved our plight*
*One day more, her blood spared another night*
*One night more, our right to mourn freedom's flight*

Tsugo continued. "What he and all his kingdom lost on the day of his surrender is a shared death with all the kingdoms and tribes of southern Egaisha. We lost our identity, our individual honor. Gone are the days when a sister's hand was not forced upon her brother to take the throne, gone are the days when war was only a thing of necessity, to be waged with the northern peoples. All are forced to serve one clan, under threat of your kind, and the High Clans are in turn forced to serve the Empress. The storms are an eternal reminder of that.

"Like River, Agriculture province values its independence. We long for the old days of old, and we have grown exhausted from the constant fighting for expansion, losing trained soldiers to that cause. Taxation, unending involvement in imperial statecraft. Every single Agriculture citizen desires to exist as a people of our own, independent from the empire. For that, we need to plan, to take action, and Lord Irashida here is the one that has brought that into fruition."

Aiya's head snapped towards Irashida with a look of bewilderment. He returned Aiya's gaze dead in her eyes. "I'm sorry for not telling you. It's shocking, I know, but we all do what we must for what must be done. No more questions for now, let's leave while Owa is still occupied. I promise I'll answer everything."

"Is this a heavens forsaken joke?" Koji asked, shaking his head with a thousand other questions and demands.

"By the grace of heaven and the Empress' sovereign soul, we will explain everything once we are in a position to do so." Ira began walking back the way they came, "but right now we must go. Through the back door and into a discreet carriage?"

The last question was for Tsugo.

"Quietly, and retrieve your weapons too. For insurance purposes."

# Freedom

The carriage was outside the gardens to the left. Aiya found that the man spoke in his own uniquely decorous manner, even for a nobleman, as Tsugo explained the 'official' plan: he was to exit through the front door and reveal their dead bodies to Owa. Instead, they had distractions set in place. They'd leave without him nor any of his men taking notice. Aiya wanted to object. She wanted to reveal herself to Owa, to skewer the life from him as he did her father. Though she was repulsed by his actions, his sudden gruesome death tugged at her chest. Was this the beginning of grief? Her thoughts and emotions spiraled, as if her mind had lost a portion of its ability to articulate itself to her body. Her only clarity was anger, and a powerful curiosity to see Owa in the flesh, standing alive in front of her.

There were no soldiers in sight. Through the gardens, their surroundings appeared unfamiliar, almost otherworldly, even with the routine skywater that lightly fell. Ira stopped to whisper in her ear that Kisane and the rest of the servants would be taken care of. Aiya stopped herself from audibly expressing her doubts.

They all slipped into the carriage without a word, and no sooner did it take off. Curtains covered their view of the outside, giving the somewhat spacious box a confined feel. They were not stopped once on the way out of the estate. Apparently, whatever distractions had been set in place had proven effective.

The first five minutes or so passed by in uncomfortable silence, until the driver confirmed they were outside Owa's radius.

"Now that we're in the clear," Tsugo said, "allow me to explain."

Aiya took one look at Ira. *Trust me*, his face said. She would at least listen.

"You must understand this was all a front. One with tangible consequences, but a front nonetheless. Lord Owa is to be put in Arusuke's place for something bigger. Let us go back to when this all started. Three months ago, we joined your father and Lord Shozhu in a meeting. We understood that civil conflict in River was escalating, and being a supporter of the Takasa bloodline, historically speaking, we came to offer assistance. The meeting did not end as planned, so Shozhu approached a vassal of mine away from everyone else. He revealed he wanted his brother, your father, gone from his position as High Lord. Shozhu understood he could not so easily take up the mantle himself, thus he promised we would be reimbursed tenfold through our newfound grace with Lord Owa if we helped him. So, they made a deal, my vassal promising to bring this information to me. I wasn't expecting Irashida to have eavesdropped on their conversation all along. Your brother later approached me with what he had seen, threatening me. A thoroughly frightening experience. When I told him my true intentions-which were hidden from Shozhu-he offered himself along with the two of you. In retrospect, I couldn't have had better luck.

"Irashida revealed to us the details of River politics your father wouldn't delve into. He informed us that Hebi Owa was the second best fit to rule and would eventually take his chances at it. We found a lookalike in Agriculture province, someone close enough in appearance to Owa to be mistaken for him in the dim of the night. Then we went to Owa himself about it. The real lord and the fake were switched out the night you went to kill him. A few nights after his death, Owa went quietly to the nobles all across River province, revealing his body that could not be slain and promising to end Arusuke's rule. Needless to say, much of the nobility were quite easily swayed to join his cause. You'll forgive me that I needed to see how River's Ginju fared against my own. Your brother could not tell you any of this for that reason."

"So you knew father's death would happen. You were only waiting for it," Aiya watched Ira, who did not seem the same boy. It was beginning to make sense.

"Sorry I couldn't tell you," Ira replied, "Not sorry about father."

"None of us are," said Koji. "Things could have ended a lot bloodier though."

"What about Asaya and Kisane?" Aiya asked, heart suddenly racing. Ira's reassurance had done little to stifle the fear within her. She couldn't imagine Owa showing mercy to any associated with the Takasa family after what they'd done to him.

"The servants will be accordingly fine," Tsugo answered calmly. "For the record, Owa's children escaped the fire through a trapdoor hidden in the floorboards the second you left, so the grudge Owa holds is at least somewhat mitigated by that fact. As Lord Koji expressed, things could have ended far worse, but we took all necessary risks and precautions. I ordered Owa not to kill any servants, unless he wants to be seen publicly just as ruthless as the late Arusuke. As for Shozhu, ironically, he will also be put on trial for treason.

"It's a lot to ask, but put tonight's developments behind you. From here on we must have a very narrow focus. You three are to help with the most important task of Agriculture in decades, perhaps in all our history. We need your help in saving Lord Sen, heir of Forgery."

"Lord Sen?" Koji asked. "The lordling father rejected two months ago?"

"Correct. He has been involved in a desperate battle of inheritance for his province for six months now. Having killed all her other siblings, her sister wages war with him as her last obstacle. Sen has put up quite the fight. If we aid them, we will position ourselves for an arms deal that will pay us handsomely. Their victory is near certain with our help, considering he's kept up this long."

"So you're recruiting us for your own political gain," Aiya mused. "Charming."

"I'm afraid not. The three of you are actually being recruited for a much grander cause. This is the beginning of a revolution, a war to take down the empire from the inside."

In what felt like minutes later, the words still didn't register. "Do what?"

"A revolution, to take down the empire," the one named Risako repeated, slowly this time.

Aiya started. "Take down the empire? As in take down the Empress? Am I hearing you right?"

"You are," Tsugo said.

"She's immortal," said Koji. "All powerful. She might as well be one of the Shinti compared to us. The last ones that tried going against her caused the Wailstorms, according to legend."

"The roots of Agriculture go much deeper than you may think. In days of old, wealth was more diffused, and the common Erru once prospered near as much as the second-class nobility. No longer. For far too long, The Empress has unjustly conquered and ruled over the Erru people. For two centuries, she has broken the honor of the Erru, stolen from us, divided us. But we are not hers to command. This deviation has been a long time coming, and thanks to Irashida, the path has opened."

Aiya observed her brother. The perpetually bedridden Ira had somehow outmaneuvered them all, secretly upturning the lives of their entire clan–no, their entire *province*–under every one of their noses. He no longer appeared as her meek and feeble brother, but as a true peer, resourceful and intelligent. A younger version of their father. She supposed he'd always been. "How did you know you could trust them?"

Ira took a long look at her. "It was better than us suffering in our estate for the rest of our lives, better than possibly watching our siblings kill each other when they got older. Being humiliated and unwelcome in our own house. All that time I was sick, I felt like a burden. I grew as skilled as you and Koji, but once I turned twelve, I couldn't maneuver through the nobility with you. I couldn't uphold the Takasa name, even if it was wrong to do so. I felt this was the only way to help. To secure another life for the two of you. I know we are sustained better than most. We have servants and get our fill. We are protected and feared on the outside, but in our own home our clan rejected us. I couldn't bear watching you two be disgraced. So I took a chance. I had faith."

Aiya considered him for a long moment, unsure of what to say. There was a warmth blossoming within her, a tenderness that spread through her insides. He'd done what he believed was right.

"You're no burden, Ira," Koji said, looking as if he were about to stand up but thought better of it. "And don't let us ever hear you say those words again! We'd walk to the end of the continent for you. More importantly, don't ever lead us on like this again, or I'll make you bedridden myself."

Ira looked away.

"Be that as it may," Tsugo continued, "Through him we were able to secure you three, now having six Ginju in total. We'll need as much strength as we can gather, and Forgery is our next destination."

"So we are your captives then?" Aiya asked.

"You are free to do as you please, my lady, but rest assured we will show you why you will come to support our cause and trust us."

"Except you'll have to kill us now that we know of your secret plans."

Tsugo laughed, and Aiya eased reluctantly. "The days where Ginju paid their loyalty towards the Empress are long over! You've no reason to be concerned with our machinations past this point, and so we've no reason to take your lives. This is one issue of many with empirical expansion. As more provinces are established further from the Imperial Seat, their peoples feel more isolated from it. The ordination of your clan was meant to strike fear in the hearts of nobility and common alike, but they forget the Sovereign's favor bestowed upon you, and only see an unsavory High Clan, and only fear endless subservience. They wage war, the unlucky suffer from seldom unmet quotas, and the rest suffer from their depleting wealth. The war with Tarshan is unceasingly stalled. Such is the state of all southern provinces, save Agriculture of course. The north is not without its problems either. These cracks in the empire present an optimal time to strike, as the concerns of the Empress become too widespread. You've no idea what the Empress even looks like. Have you ever been to the capital city?"

They shook their heads, though it was rhetorical. Sanaba, the Jewel of the Empire, as it was called. According to hearsay, it was unlike any city on any continent. Entry by Erru outside the city was forbidden.

"Once as infants," Aiya added, "when we received our blessings."

"There rests my case. Besides, I believe you will not betray your brother's wishes. I only ask that you simply come along for the ride, let us show you our province for you to make up your mind there. You are free to come back and clean up this mess anytime you please, and to forever miss out on the opportunity of true honor and freedom."

# Divergence

Aiya's slumber would last the entire way into the next province over. The distance from Kawanura to Agriculture was mere hours by carriage, and so by the time she awoke, they were already within its borders. She was surprised to find just herself inside. Her head pounded lightly with fragments of strange dreams from the previous night: she'd been running from many things. From her family in the forms of monstrous spirits, from devilish nobility, with crazed eyes and righteous anger, come to exact vengeance on her for all she'd committed against them, and she'd been fleeing to many places, bounding across mountains and landscapes and unending cities of oddly geometrical shapes. A night without liquor always resulted in strange dreams, with a side of general fatigue the next day. *I should start taking Ira's advice seriously. No more drinking.*

Outside was the familiar noise of droning chatter. Nervously, she sat up and pulled the curtains back from the carriage.

Sunlight flooded inside and Aiya squinted her eyes. When they adjusted, she saw commotion around her. Bodies, buildings and food stands. It was First Day morning. She realized that she was in some Agriculture city. Risako, the female Ginju, came to stand below her outside the carriage. Her long hair was pulled behind her, giving full effect to the impatience on her face.

"Finally up."

Aiya searched for any sign of her siblings. "How long have I been asleep?"

"Six hours. Your siblings woke up an hour before you. We took them to a bathing house nearby. Don't worry, we all needed one."

She opened the door and extended her hand to help her out of the carriage. Ignoring it, Aiya hopped out. She knew the terrain beneath her was only dirt, but still she felt as if she were stepping onto strange land. "I assume we've got the best beds to sleep in too?"

Risako smirked. "Don't get too comfortable, we won't be here long in Shujukin, and Agriculture isn't big on indulging in self-pleasures either."

Aiya was led to a bathhouse building, feeling awkward in her torn dress with blood splotches splattered over her left side and across her collar. She noticed one of the billowed sleeves was ripped at the cuff that went all the way to her elbow. She tried, to no avail, shaking off her overwhelming self-consciousness as they strode in. Though none paid her attention, she could not help but feel like a glaring oddity. Once they entered the steamy bathroom, she turned back to Risako. "My robes?"

"We put some new clothes over on the bench right there. Meet me outside when you're finished. Take as long as you need, but know that we leave for Forgery tomorrow morning."

The steam bath hit Aiya like a slow descent into nothingness. She ignored the other bathers, most of whom bathed out in the open, trying to relax against the warm stone wall of the pool. As that nothingness reformed and regrouped, all her thoughts and worries from before she had been taken away from this world by sleep had come flooding back. The horrors of the night before, what would become of their future. Had they really been having a conversation about destroying the empire from the inside? It was crazy, and had she not been so disoriented, she would have called them out for their insanity as well.

There was still a great deal of disorientation within her now, condensed into the void she felt for her father's death. While she bathed decadently in an outside province, his head rotted publicly in the city he once controlled, that she once called home. Would she or her siblings ever be allowed to return? What would become of their mother, Kitani, Ari? What would happen to Yuuki, at only twelve years of age? They would be at the mercy of Owa, and though Aiya had never felt much for them, she could not deny the confusing, intense guilt threatening to bubble to her surface.

As inconceivable as it was, the more she thought of it, the softer she grew towards Tsugo's speech concerning the empire, a rightful power that most River Erru saw as heaven's will. Even she had always seen it that way, but then again, she'd at many times felt the same about her own clan. Wasn't the natural order of things right?

If it were, she and her brothers deserved to be dead, and her province deserved to suffer in fear under the Empress. This 'Republic' compelled her, and if her brothers were here with her, she'd embrace it and begin their new lives, carrying out the rest of Ira's aspirations herself.

*And our duty to the Takasa, all that we worked for all those years, gone. Just like that.* Was this anger she felt at her sudden freedom from her clan? Indeed, all her dedication to her clan name had essentially mounted to nothing. It was right to be that way, but somehow unjust.

She got out to dry herself, then put on the clothes that had been left for her. It was a distinct pair of green robes, shiny silk, with criss-crossing line patterns stitched on the outside. Agriculture robes. It didn't feel right to put them on, but she figured she didn't have a choice. Reluctantly, she slipped into them and made her way back to the outside world.

As soon as she stepped out, a man stopped her. He was balding on top with a black ponytail at the back of his head. Four men traveled behind him. The man walked upright, with his head slightly upturned, and though he was her height, his eyes almost pointed downwards at her. "I believe you did not pay your due respects to the Tabeni family when you went into that establishment, miss."

Aiya looked at him, questioning. "What are you talking about?"

"You heard me, or are you deaf? You didn't pay your respects! So now you will have to pay another way, I'm afraid."

His hand went to his sword. The men behind him looked serious.

Aiya hesitated. Had they been in River, she would have immediately cut the man down for so brazenly threatening her like this. But she was a guest in a foreign land now, and she wasn't exactly sure what rules she had broken. Heat rose in her face as she looked around for possible clues from pedestrians, but she was only met with stares.

"That's enough, Tobirune," said a voice to the side. She looked over to see Totane approaching from within the crowd. Intense relief flooded through her as her muscles relaxed.

"Totane! What's the meaning of this?" Aiya asked. It was strange addressing him by his name, having been so eager to slay each other the night before.

"Apologies, Aiya. This is one of my uncles. Tobirune loves to mess with people. He won't be doing it again."

"Had to welcome you the right way," Tobirune said, winking. "And wisen you up, considering what I've heard of your lack of worldliness. Always remember to keep your head up and eyes open, and more importantly, to be knowledgeable of local customs." He nodded to her.

Aiya turned to Totane, annoyed. "Where is everyone?"

"Going through the same thing you are," he replied. "We're showing them what makes Agriculture different. Follow me."

Tobirune bowed as she and Totane left. She was more glad for his timely arrival than she wanted to admit, though she still eyed him suspiciously.

Totane led her down the streets which in some aspects were remarkably similar to that of Kawanura's. He explained that this was the capital city of Agriculture. It had wide streets, and she glimpsed the thousand lives walking down its paths. But she noticed different things too. The architecture was more simple, there were less elegant and grand buildings. There were more white painted buildings, and the attire worn by its citizens was a little less varied. The streets felt less crowded, likely because the way pedestrians moved through them was in some way more organized. They passed by food stands smelling of yama noodles and baked goods. They had yet to cross a fish stand.

"You won't find as many street performers here," Totane told her as they turned onto another street. The buildings here were tight and there were less people populating the area. At the end she could see the road led to a building which bordered the edge of this part of the city, its top story peeking over the city walls. "Our populace is always occupied with more important things. Our economy revolves around upwards mobility for all, for the one sole purpose of eventual independence. You are only as strong as your weakest link."

The phrase had gnawed at Aiya more times than she could count. "So I've heard." Just the night before, he had looked into her eyes as if he were ready to dice her two times over with his blade. Now, he extended casual warmth with a friendly demeanor that seemed an almost entirely different set of clothing on him. Who was he really?

"What do you think of nobility sacrificing a portion of their wealth for the common good?"

"How does that help with rebellion?" Aiya eyed him curiously. Even saying the word *rebellion* sounded strange coming from her mouth.

"For the reasons I just discussed. The weakest link breaks the entire chain. The empire is flimsily held together by the nobility closest to the Empress. They represent the neck. The Jodai armies that the Empress sends out for conquest, and the ones she takes from us, as well as the taxes placed onto us, those are its arms. The Empress, of course, is the head, and also the legs, which her empire stands on. It's long been said that eventually the empire is doomed to fail. Here we are."

She wanted to ask, 'who says that?', but they reached the outside of the building, and Totane moved to open the door. They walked through into a sparse room that smelled of cherry bush incense. Torches in the corners warmed the room, and a single man sat criss cross by a shrine, praying.

"This is a shrine house," Totane said in barely a whisper. He quietly made his way to the spiraling staircase that led up to the top of the building. Aiya could feel the reverence here. There were no shrine houses of this size in River, but most people she knew preferred them to be in the woods or on the edge of the sea, submerged in nature.

They climbed in silence until they reached the top. She was not expecting to see Ira standing along the wall, watching something outside, while Koji scribbled into his open pocket book. He shut it upon seeing her.

"Koji! Ira!" She nearly sprinted over to them. They turned and embraced her in a hug. "How long have you been up here?"

"Just a few minutes. We got done eating not too long ago," answered Ira. "It turns out that yama noodles taste amazing wherever you go."

At the mention of food, Aiya's stomach stirred. "What were you looking at?" She went over to the fence, past Risako and the other Ginju boy from last night. He introduced himself as Johori. He was the same height as Risako with a similar structure, fresh-faced with a slim and sharp nose, though he kept his hair cropped above his ears like Totane.

"You landed that first punch on me last night," she told him. "You're the only one I haven't yet forgiven."

He dropped his eyes, looking as if he was about to respond. When he didn't, Aiya decided she'd made him feel bad enough and turned away. At least this one had some empathy.

Looking out in the open, she nearly gasped in awe. The shrine building oversaw a massive stretch of rocky plains. In front of them were thousands of troops lined up and ready to march, a reflective sea of shiny green armor. Behind them, closer to the building were men sparring and training.

"That's the army we'll be taking with us shortly," Totane said, stepping up to her, "and below us are the sparring grounds. Commoners and nobles alike spar everyday."

"Both common and noble?" Koji asked.

"From the way you talk, it sounds like the distinction doesn't exist here," Aiya noted.

"It definitely does," Risako explained. "Commoners know their place, we just can't afford to waste such potential manpower, not with goals like ours."

"Our goal is to have fifty percent of the population prepared for combat at any time," Totane said. He gestured around the room. "Here lies the origin of Agriculture."

Aiya hadn't noticed all the crusty paintings on the wall before. They were massive, detailed, and looked ancient.

"These were painted here when this building was first erected, fifty years ago. They tell the story of the fall and rise of Agriculture. Let's start from the beginning." He pointed to the first painting, an image of a kingdom in prosperity. People of all sizes and attire stood around a large palace of gold. They were surrounded by crops of the deepest green, rain descending on them from gray clouds.

"This was the beginning, before we were known as Agriculture. Back when we called ourselves Ogasawa, the kingdom of prosperity. Our people traded with nearby nations, even your kingdom, Nirogawa, and even with the empire. We were wary of the empire, because we knew they would come to conquer us one day. And so they did."

He moved onto the next painting. It was the opposite, one of destruction. "The Empress offered to allow us to join the empire willingly, otherwise we'd join by force."

The same palace was shown crumbling, broken, and smeared with red. Those surrounding it cried out to the sky. Totane spoke with resentment. "Like any worthy Erru, we chose the path of war. Neither path meant peace, for the Empress forced High Clans upon her provinces, followed by forced quotas. She brought an army like we had never seen, over forty thousand troops. Soldiers from Rain province and the capital city. Soldiers from all the other provinces too. We fought anyway. Luckily, her efforts were split between us and what is now Stone province, so we were able to put up a better fight in the beginning than first expected."

The next painting showed an important-looking man being cut down by some large monster. His blood spilled everywhere on the floor and splashed onto both figures. "Our king was killed by none other than our own kind. Ginju, like us, sent from the Empress herself to stop the 'rebellion', as they called it."

The next art piece was different. Two groups of people staring each other down.  On both sides were two bearded men, with shorter men and women behind them, and children at the back. The background depicted buildings up in flames.

"After his death, the political environment was thrown into disarray. The economy of course suffered after that, and so did our people. The realization that we had lost began to slowly  weigh ever more upon our stubborn backs. Still, we fought the Empress, and each other, faction after faction vying for control where the king once sat. In the one-hundredth second year of Empirical Reign, Agriculture's two most powerful and influential clans came together, with a revelation that would change the course of our future. The first realized the power vacuum they all fought so desperately for could easily be won through the aid of the empire, which would be obtained through surrender. The second recognized the same, but also refused to give up on independence.

"This was the Tabeni clan, our own blood." He gestured to his siblings. "We recognized the only way to truly defeat the empire was from the inside. Thus we and the Kensei clan agreed to come together under one banner and rule within the empire. We surrendered and the casualties stopped for the short period of peace that followed, though unbeknownst to many, this was only the beginning."

Aiya thought the story seemed a little far-fetched. She doubted two families of nobles had managed to work together for over a century for the purpose of taking down the power that upheld them in their place. She stepped forward and followed his gestures, which now pointed out the second to last painting.

This one showed seven tall male figures. The tallest was in the middle, one of the bearded men from the previous painting. On the ground beneath them, they gazed at a litter of dead bodies, a pool of blood leaking onto the floor.

"The story doesn't end how you think it would." Totane stared up at the last painting, a grand castle burning, with men and women of various colored robes standing around it with their fists held high. Finally, he turned to them. "We betrayed the Kensei, slaughtering their entire clan and then covering it up to make it seem like an accident to the public. It was shortly after this we were able to take the first step toward our ultimate goal, and so we formed the Republic."

Republic. Where had she heard that word before?

"That's the word for the Tarshan governing system, isn't it?" asked Koji. "Since they don't have an empress overseas."

"Exactly. It's a form of government in which sovereignty rests with the people, in which the highest power is representative of said people. The Empress cannot represent all Erru people. They are best represented by the nobles of each province. We saw this way back then, and so we killed our 'allies' who certainly were not willing to turn their backs on the empire. Then we recruited seven other noble clans. To this day they help coordinate the underground rebellion, just below the Tabeni in rank. Every person in Agriculture is aware of this story, men, women and children. What we fight for is freedom, something we cannot, *will not,* live without.

"Our purpose for the last hundred years has been to eventually bring about the empire's downfall. We conspire to unite the peripheral provinces, eventually to attack the center of Egaisha. Recruiting every province on our side is likely out of reach. They and the Empress have been in bed together for far too long. Regardless, we will gain independence for each province, each becoming its own nation. You're lucky. You and Forgery get to be first in line."

Aiya eyed him skeptically, watching the blaze in his eyes as he spoke. This was life and death, an entire province willing to give up everything for independence. Most nobles she knew couldn't see past their own small sphere of influence. She wasn't sure how plausible his plan actually was, but it was beginning to dawn on her that she had been forced down a narrow path that would lead them to destruction. No, she hadn't been forced. She'd allowed their father to die, *chosen* for him to be killed when she could have stopped it. Now there was no going back, because the path behind her was completely burned.

She felt it verged on madness, but something about the conviction in Totane's voice opened a sort of window into understanding, to see that the Empress could, in fact, be overthrown, in some absurd dream. Perhaps, this was her chance, a chance for them all, to fight for a righteous cause, a cause echoed by the bravery in the stories of King Tsae. Perhaps, they should put aside their petty squabbling and fight beside each other for what their lives revolved around. "It's insane. How do you plan on bringing this about? Where do *we* come in?"

Totane took a step towards her. "Everything starts with you. Ira informed us that your father Arusuke would be too difficult to convert with his pride. He accepted no position lesser than a leader, apparently. Taking him out killed two birds with a single stone. Lord Owa will be much more likely to cooperate, eventually, and we will also have the cooperation of River's Ginju, should you choose to comply. Similar measures were taken way back then at our foundation. After slaughtering the Kensei, we recruited seven trusted clans to lead the beginnings of our revolution.

"Over the years we have been bolstering our forces, then we began securing ties with Sen once his own kin began hunting him in their reach for power. Now with the High Lord of River slain, the needed tension to kickstart this rebellion is set. An age of liberation and autonomy is approaching. Whether you want to be dead or alive to experience it, that lies in your own hands."

He took not a single glance away from her as he spoke. The passion in his face resonated with her, as if she was finally understood, *heard*. It was the same passion that drove her to protect her brothers, her family. Aiya kept her feet firm as every part of her was swept up, swayed by his words, and in the silence of the room, it was only the two of them. Something like a barrier inside her broke open.

"If that's what it takes for freedom, my siblings and I are all for it."

Totane's gaze remained, searching her for truth. When he saw her resolve was steel, he walked up until they were a foot apart. Close enough to smell his breath.

"There's only one way forward here. If you would have said no, I would have told you that you could stay here in the safety of our borders, free to take action only when the Empress came riding for you while you cower behind our burning fortresses. That is, if it comes to that, which we don't intend. Regardless, we leave tomorrow morning with that army posted out there. Once you're marching with us, it's march on or die until the very end."

"In River, we hold certain principles. We don't go back on our word. Even if all our suffering in River was for naught."

"It wasn't for naught," Risako chimed. "Were it not for your circumstances, you wouldn't be here. This may prove the greatest opportunity in a thousand lifetimes."

Her words did little to affect the bittersweetness of it all, but Aiya stifled the emotions within her. If she had indeed wasted her eighteen years under an evil man, she would spend the next eighteen amending that. "Put it that way and you're probably right." Totane sighed. "It's settled then. I'm glad you made the right choice." He turned to the others. "I suppose dinner is in store now?"

"I've a question though," Koji said. "We haven't been introduced to Lord Tsugo's wife or your other siblings yet. I feel like at this point we've been welcomed into the family."

"Mother is attending the gardens," Johori answered. "As for offspring, we're all he has."

"Only three?" Aiya asked. Most clans birthed at least five or six, and if not, they made up for it with illegitimate children, shameful as it was.

Johori moved to answer when suddenly Ira erupted into a fit of hacking coughs. They all turned to see Ira had fallen to his knees, shaking. He wriggled on the floor, hands moving about random and wild. His eyes had gone wide, his mouth drooping.

"Ira!" Aiya ran to him, heart thumping with sudden terror. Koji rushed to his other side.

They grabbed his body, tried to stop him from moving. "Ira, what's wrong? Calm down!"

It was no use. They patted his face, unable to elicit a response. Without warning, Ira entered into a massive fit of spasms, flailing his arms and forcing his two siblings to back away. His body continued this, refusing to be pinned down, until he went limp. When it was finally over, Aiya gaped in horror at the small trickle of blood that ran from his mouth.

# Conviction

Ira lay in bed as dim morning light seeped into the castle room. His chest heaved up and down as Aiya ran her fingers through his hair, grateful for the only indication that he was not dead. Koji sat on his other side watching, waiting for him to wake at any moment.

They both knew he wouldn't.

This had happened once before. Earlier in life, when they were Kitani's age, meditating out in a random field not far from some noble estate. They were down in the southeast of River province, on their way to visit Stone province and stopped next to a town called Kobachi. One second, they were all in a peaceful trance, and the next, they had thought Ira was dying. He had come close, according to the physicians.

They heard the door slide open behind them. Neither bothered turning to look.

Tsugo appeared by the front of the bed. A moment of silence passed. "He's still breathing, that's good."

Aiya was unable to tear her eyes away from Ira's face. She should've known this would happen after pushing himself for so long. They'd come all this way, and she'd barely given a thought to his health. She had been too concerned with what lay in front of them, and now she didn't know how to go on with him here, bedridden.

Tsugo spoke again. "I am deeply sorry about your brother. I recall him informing us of his health issues, and I wish I had taken it more into consideration. That being said, I wish you could have more time to be at his side. It's the crack of dawn, and we depart soon...you've been at his side all night. I pray you've not been beating yourself up over this. It's not your fault. Can you go on?"

Aiya watched memories of herself, Ira, and Koji bonding over the years. Ira at Koji's side, coming to her defense as Shozhu berated her for refusing her meditation at age eight, traumatized by nightmares of the drowned man. Ira teasing her for it at age ten. Ira engaged in an arm wrestling match with Koji, proving to Kisane who was stronger. Ira showing off to Asaya, leaping from tree to tree, snapping a thick branch before crashing hard and cracking the stone below, laughing. The memories played incessantly in her head.

Koji looked up. "Yes, we'll still be going. It was Ira who set this all up in the first place, wasn't it? We'd be damned if we abandoned you after coming this far."

Tsugo nodded. "Meet me at the front gates in ten minutes." He took his leave, closing the door behind him.

"So what happens now?" Aiya asked, moving her head up for the first time.

Koji kept his eyes steady with hers. "We march, as Totane said. As Ira would want. We fight. Then we come back for Ira and fight even harder. This is just the beginning. We can't give up yet."

In all the times she'd faced despair, she was indescribably grateful that Koji was at her side. He was a rock she could lean on when all hope had escaped her, guiding her out of the past, whereas Ira had always led her optimistically into the future.

Aiya nodded, then leaned forward to kiss Ira's forehead. It was warm. She stood. This was the last memory she would have of them together before riding into Forgery. She'd remember him as a fighter too, strong and unconquerable. When they got back, he'd be back on his feet again, ready for the next phase of this revolution. "Let's march then," she said.

Tsugo wasn't at the garden gates, but Tobirune was. He greeted them much less enthusiastically than his first encounter with Aiya led her to expect, then led them down the same path Totane had the previous day. They passed the tower and exited through the city gates into the field where the Jodai were gathered. Ten thousand troops lined up outside in ten rigid lines. The sight was as amazing as it was the first time she had seen it. Jodai soldiers stretched out as far as the eye could see. There were carriages for carrying food, tents, supplies and of course those along for the ride: musicians, medics, prostitutes, and noble men and women of beneficial trades.

"You'll be marching at the front," Tobirune said. "I'll walk you down and explain the different battle formations and tactics so you'll have at least some understanding before you set off for the battlefield, where you'll see it with your own eyes. Have you ever been in a large scale battle before?"

"No," Koji answered, "but we studied them extensively over the years, along with economics and logistics."

"Of course, stupid me. I would expect no less out of the upbringing of a Ginju. I've seen war though, been in it too. I've no doubt in the sturdiness of your character, but believe me, it's not something you can study or prepare yourself for. It's not something I'm willing to experience again just yet."

"You're not coming?" Aiya asked, striding just behind him. They could smell the musk on the soldiers now, walking in between the long rows. None that Aiya could see broke their statue-like position, waiting for the marching to begin.

Tobirune laughed. "Heavens, no! If you saw how large my plate was for domestic tasks, you'd walk quicker. Working from behind the scenes is what I do best. If I were as strong as you though, I probably wouldn't be so wary of charging into battle."

Tsugo finally made his appearance at the front of the lines, gathered with the Agriculture Ginju and important looking men. Likely generals and other leading commanders. Tobirune ushered them beside the Ginju, and the sight of the men from the front was just as breathtaking. No one spoke, and all eyes went to Tsugo.

Tsugo stepped forward, his feet scuffing the ground. The attention paid to him gave the High Lord an unmatched air of dignity. He was peerless. His head moved one way then the other, then he repeated the sweeping gaze. With one deep breath, he bellowed, "WE MARCH!"

The soldiers roared on cue, so suddenly and loud it was like thunder. Aiya's hands nearly flew to her ears. None of those beside Tsugo joined in with the yelling. It went on for minutes, a last attempt to mentally brace themselves for what was coming. Once they were done, Tsugo turned and the others followed, hopping into their carriages. With a single shout, the Tabeni High Lord had inspired ten thousand men. The same could never be attributed to any of the Takasa.

*This is it.* It dawned on Aiya that this was actually happening, that they were really on their way to join a civil war, likely the first of many, any of which could be their last. She was here, climbing into the carriage with Koji, in another province, about to take sides in a battle they had no business in. Their father was dead, the rest of their immediate family might as well be, and Ira...

Ira had really led them into this impossible plan to fight against the Empress herself, and against an empire centuries old. But if this was what he wanted, she would go with it.

"For Ira," she whispered, and no one turned whether they had heard her or not.

The march was to last two days. After the first they would be in Forgery, but it would take another to reach their final destination. In the meantime, Tsugo explained the plan in detail.

"First, we'll be assisting Lady Ueko, Sen's mother, while looking for an opening to turn on the 'official' Forgery army. They'll have fought seven days by the time we arrive," he explained with shallow breaths. His eyes were watery and low from clear exhaustion.

"Official army?" Aiya asked. "I thought we considered Sen the true inheritor, that's why we're aiding him right?"

"We are aiding him in an indirect way. Or rather, a round-about way. There are two reasons we cannot outright attack. One, we must prepare for the young lord's ascension to the throne. If his future subjects are to be partners in our rebellion, we'll need them in good standing with us first. That means not winning his battle for him. On the battlefront, I'll be making an additional proposal with his mother beyond our weapons trade agreement."

"Additional proposal?" Totane's eyebrows furrowed briefly at the statement.

"One I cannot disclose just yet, I'm afraid. It must be a surprise to everyone when they hear it. Convincing the mother to solidify this deal in the midst of other high families who will surely be present is a top priority. That way, once we reveal we were with Sen all along, it will be harder to protest any pacts we make with Sen that his mother, and her subordinates by association, have already agreed to."

"So you've been forming a double pincer," Koji remarked. "Maneuvering behind both parties. It's cunning."

"Always stay one step ahead of your opponent," Risako said, leaning back in her seat. "Rule number one of war and rebellion." She was striking, attractive in a conventional way. *She's generally well-informed. And not afraid to speak in her father's presence. He must put a lot of trust in her.*

"So it's his mother leading the opposing army?" Aiya asked.

"There are rumors that behind the scenes she's manipulated her gullible daughter to gain power. Her daughter would be High Lady by the end of her schemes, but Lady Ueko would be in actual control from the background, making her daughter more of a figurehead. She will use whatever means to control her family, courtesy of her husband's death. Which leads into the second reason that we cannot outright come out on Sen's side, which you no doubt are aware of but perhaps forgot to consider. In Errunese tradition, a province only follows a strong inheritor. This is especially true in Forgery.

"Outside help is permitted, but if it appears that he would have stood little chance without it, he will lose respect regardless of the outcome. Additionally, he must kill his siblings himself to inherit the throne, or that would undoubtedly introduce new reasons rival clans could try to seize the throne."

Johori sighed. "In other words, leave it to our Errunese pride to make things as difficult as possible. History teaches that men and nations only behave wisely at the exhaustion of every alternative." He had soft features like Ira, though he paused in between his sentences, possessing a less forward demeanor. Aiya took a liking to it, having encountered enough Errunese pride for a lifetime.

To sit in the presence of Ginju outside of River province felt humbling on some level, and on another, amusingly mythical.

She had to stop herself from shaking her head in confusion. "So how the hell are we supposed to bring Sen out of this alive if we're attacking the very army defending him first?"

"So far, he's held the advantage, having gathered more nobles to his aid than his mother anticipated, dragging this battle of inheritance out for six months. We clearly have a very intelligent lordling and warlord on our side. If worse comes to worse, we will turn on our supposed allies the minute things look over for Sen. The main objective is for him to kill his final remaining sibling. Also, Ginju are rarely involved in open battles, but in case Lady Ueko gets fed up and sets one of her hounds on Sen, we've got five of our own to stop her."

Five, now that Ira was sidelined. Still, the number seemed reasonable.

The rest of the day was spent idly contemplating this conversation. Aiya realized that their rescue plan was a lot less concrete than she previously imagined. The fact left her anxious, and she, more than a few times, longed for somewhere to pace so she could rummage through her thoughts. Koji offered no encouragement, preoccupied with himself, which did little to calm her.

She'd lied to Asaya. Despite her claims that nothing could ever hurt them, the opposite proved true. They'd fought

Ginju like themselves, and as much as she resisted admitting the fact, they'd been evenly matched. No, her brothers had proven themselves equals. She'd been shown to be inferior twice during their match. Further, if anyone could threaten them, it was the Empress herself.

Fortunately, the monotonous journey passed by quicker than expected. As the sun dipped below the horizon, they began to set up camp. Temperatures began to dip uncomfortably. This was northern Agriculture, further up the continent than Aiya had been in a while. In two days, they'd be at the battlefield, at the Hijimata hills.

Camp was set up with lightning speed, and this was the first wonder of war Aiya experienced: How quick and efficient a large group of men could be. Soldiers were straightening tents while those in higher ranks handed out rations. Some went out to forage for food in the plains to try to catch whatever rodents they could find.

The musicians had finally got into their instruments and were working up a tune as soldiers laughed and danced and cheered. She figured having the knowledge that some of them would not make it out of this alive would be more sobering, but on the other hand, their odds sounded rather high. Many of these men were undoubtedly prepared to die for their province, for this Republic they so foolishly believed in. But was it really foolish to fight for a cause one so strongly believed in, a cause for the greater good? Tsugo's sentiment struck a chord with Aiya, the revival of the many kingdoms from the days of old. It was true that many in River looked back on their history with wistful reverence and fondness. Secretly, the River Erru never lost hold of their

Aiya remembered Tsugo had mentioned that Johori and Risako were twins. They certainly looked the part, though their personalities were distinctly different in some ways. So far, Johori had kept shut, unless forced out of himself. While Risako was the same, she carried herself more openly, and expressly drew herself towards any matter of her concern. Two sides to the same coin never fit a pair more aptly. Intriguing. "How old are they?" she asked.

"They'll be four come Toma, my lady. All the coin in the world couldn't come between me and them, not that I have much anyway." Was he a commoner?

Aiya smiled. "What's your name, soldier?"

"Korui, your ladyship."

"You are an honorable man, Korui." She found the gesture touching. A blade was more honorable than a spear or glaive for foot soldiers. Polearms were to be won through rising through the ranks into the position of lieutenant or general.

Behind her now, she listened to the younger man's voice: "I can barely stomach this soup after earlier. Not with this texture."

"Hmm. You should be wary from now on. Horses blow snot whenever someone deceitful or troublesome approaches their rider. Take it from me," came the older man's reply.

"No. That's just old superstition."

She smirked halfheartedly, ignoring the confused emotions that hit her like vertigo since leaving River, and continued walking, unsure exactly where she was going. For some reason she wanted to see the troops, to be in the midst of those that would be fighting. She circled back around until she came to the noble quarters again from the opposite end. A bunch of tents were lined up in an orderly fashion. Turning the bend of one line of tents, she came across the sight of a man pushing a robed woman against a carriage wall.

"Where are you going?" the soldier asked, not releasing his hands from her collarbone. "There's no reason to leave yet!"

His words were slurred and he lacked the proper footing. The woman slapped his arm away with surprising force and pushed him back, making him stumble. "Listen, you entitled *prick*. I've been at work since we set up camp and I'm tired now. I'm finished until we get to the Hijimata hills. If you have an issue with that, there are others who can service you, like your Jodai friends for instance!"

The man growled. "That's a whole day of waiting. I need something to get my mind buzzed *now*. You expect me to wait till then?"

"Yes, now move aside."

She attempted to walk away but the man grabbed her again. They wrestled while she demanded he let go, the soldier demanding she calm down.

"I should have you hanging by your ballsack," Aiya said, stepping in close. If this were River province, he'd undoubtedly be worm food by now. Forcing oneself on prostitutes was a high crime. "But instead, you'll get off with a warning. Now begone."

The man stopped briefly to assess her. He grinned, eyes low. "Are you suggesting you'll use force if I don't?"

Aiya's blood began to boil. She imagined cutting him in two, here and now, his body soaking in a pool of his own blood. Killing might be a bad idea though, and she didn't want to be involved with an outcome that serious in a foreign army she was so recently accepted into.

More men began to wander over, seeing what the commotion was about. The man looked about and quickly released the woman, who gracefully managed to regain her balance. She turned and slapped him with all the strength she had. Rage set in on his face.

Aiya barked, "You defy your orders? You're not even a lieutenant!"

The man looked from her to the woman, bowed, then hurried off. Aiya approached the woman. "I'm sorry about that. Were you hurt?"

She returned a slightly disgusted look. "I'm fine, and don't assume I need help either. I've been in plenty of worse situations, so I know how to defend myself. You have to know in this profession."

The woman stalked off, leaving Aiya in a perplexed state, and an even weirder position. Aiya had not even the chance to correct herself. The woman's unexpected criticism was a light jab to her gut. Had she done something wrong? Something shameful? Should she pick up her pride or toss it to the side? The soldiers around her remained standing, so she shooed them away. "Carry on about your business!"

The men dispersed. Unsure whether she'd made the right move, Aiya continued making her way back to their campfire. She turned a corner and nearly smashed into Totane, who was briskly walking around the tents.

She skidded to a halt. "Oh shit, sorry-"

"You need to come with me." The expression on Totane's face was dead serious. "It's urgent. And dangerous."

# Hope

What was so urgent and dangerous turned out to be a game of Perish. Two soldiers, a youthful man with a beard and his partner whose hair trailed down to his shoulders, stood opposite from each other at a table. The game, popular in taverns across Egaisha, was simple. One drew from a deck of cards hoping it was lower than the card in their opponent's hand. If it was higher, they took a shot of fiery liquor. The first person to pass out lost. The young bearded Jodai was so drunk his eyes seemed almost shut and he looked constantly on the verge of toppling over. The other swayed in laughter. Totane watched them, amused.

Aiya was confused, to say the least. "This is what you called me for?"

"Of course, what did you expect?"

"I don't expect you to be surprised when I slap that stupid grin off your fucking face." She found his amusement contagious. "It's definitely urgent if you plan on saving that man from drinking himself to death, I guess, but there's no danger."

"There's danger for him. Did you know this game used to go by the name *Fires of Hope*, before we became part of the empire?"

"Interesting," Aiya replied. "Let's hope their hangovers won't impede them tomorrow."

She was tempted to take the vessel of liquor for herself, but thinking of Ira, thought better of it. She'd made drinking far too big a habit in her previous life, and that, along with the emotional stress it had brought on her, was gone. It was time she gave alcohol up for good.

The flaps to the tent opened as an armored man entered, lamellar plate clinking. She noticed immediately his right arm was missing. His helm, a winged dome, indicated that he was a commanding officer. His eyes passed over the game and the two of them watching. Aiya shifted uncomfortably.

He turned to the men quickly. "That's enough drinking for now. Most of your comrades are sleeping, I think it's time we do the same."

The men tried reasoning with him, giggling like children. The commander demanded they get out, and they stumbled away.

"My name is Lieutenant Gaku Hedi. Apologies for any inconvenience." He bowed, glancing up at Totane, then Aiya.

"It's. Fine. Thank you, lieutenant," she said.

"I see where my sister learned to be a killjoy from," said Totane. "What am I saying? You learned it from her."

"I'd engage in your banter, Lord Totane, but tonight we must remain diligent." The man nodded at Aiya and took his leave.

"I wasn't bantering," was Totane's reply.

She followed him awkwardly to close the tent behind him, then turned to Totane, who sighed heavily. "Look what you've done. You've got us into a quiet tent all to ourselves."

"I don't want the quiet any more than you do," she replied. "I've had far too much on my mind these past nights."

"Agreed." A moment of silence passed. "On a scale of five, how nervous are you?"

"About tomorrow?"

"About tomorrow's battle."

"I'll be ready for anything, don't worry."

"It wasn't a test, Aiya." He spoke to her as if confiding in a longtime friend. "I'm at a six in case you were curious."

The commotion outside had died down, and a restful atmosphere set in for the night. Totane's nose was actually rather large, but it complimented his imposing yet friendly face. His irises were not the green of the night they had fought, but instead a familiar black. She asked him, "Are you nervous about fighting Forgery Ginju?"

"Of course I am. We've no idea what we'll be up against. But more importantly, I'm nervous about the other things that could go wrong. I think about us failing, of Sen dying. Then I think of things continuing as they are. The Empress pressing on with her tyranny. And that makes me angry."

Aiya imagined Totane's speech from the day before being given to her own family, and any of the prestigious clans of River. Though most despised imperial rule, and especially the many imperial taxes, how many would be willing to do as the Taheni, to forsake their ordinance and fight the very hand that positioned them in their place of power? She ventured the answer was none.

"I won't belittle you when I ask you questions like that," he continued, "I understand you're just as much the warrior I am. I want to let you know that despite our passion, letting your concerns out there is still important. Courage isn't about never feeling fear. It's pushing past it to act on your values."

"Were you nervous when you had to fight us?"

Totane's smile returned. "I knew what the outcome would be in the end."

"And how is that?"

"Faith. Having faith in yourself is the most powerful trait you can possess."

"Because if you don't," she replied, "no one else will."

He nodded.

She walked and sat down at the table the men had been at, pondering for a moment. "What's it like? Your deity, I mean. Agriculture sounds like kind of a strange deity when you think about it."

"No stranger than the river I would imagine." He sat down with her, sliding up his sleeve to reveal a black shoulder tattoo. Three undulating streaks that became thinner the higher they traveled up his arm, converging and joining on the inside of a circle. "We received this at seven years. We had to dedicate our entire lives to our deity, so I understand sacrifice more than most."

Aiya showed her own tattoo on her wrist. "I feel that. This was pretty painful for a seven-year-old too. But how is it when you meditate? When you become one with agriculture, or whatever, what does that look like?"

He paused. "I suppose with the river it would be equally as hard to describe, but it's something you have to experience. It took me ten years to feel like I could fully understand agriculture as a deity. Hell, even now, I discover new things every day. What we as a civilization run on is growth, and for that we require sustenance. We require gradual change. Most importantly we require community. Agriculture embodies all of that. It is a method of survival, but it is more than that. Words can't really do it justice."

There was a certain deep knowledge of his subject that Aiya empathized with completely. *Agriculture*, she thought, *sounds as beautiful as the river.* Truthfully, however, nothing could ever compare.

Totane stood. "It's about time we sleep. We'll make it to our destination before tomorrow's end, so we're going to need it."

"You're right, I was thinking the same."

Totane smiled. "Goodnight." He left the tent, leaving Aiya to contemplate how similar they might be after all.

The next morning, they were up before the sun had snuck halfway over the horizon. The night's chill had yet to depart them, but the sun was promising its warmth. Whatever hangovers the men had from the night before had to be dealt with as tents were packed up and belongings hastily gathered. Tsugo explained to them they'd be riding by horseback today so that they'd be ready to join headquarters upon arrival. *Better than sitting in a cramped carriage all day*, Aiya thought, groggily hoisting herself onto her mount's back.

She was proven wrong when the first of lower back pains showed up an hour into their journey, and a man who went by General Yko had to correct her and Koji's posture. He was a strong burly man, with little hair and a prominent mustache. She'd been so lost in thought that she'd been slouching, a distasteful posture communicating an odd lack of experience for nobles as high as themselves. Aiya pushed back her shame for the rest of the journey.

"We're here to honor Ira's wishes," she told Koji, who churned the last bits of his breakfast in his mouth which pacified his grumpy morning mood. "But also, something in me wants to make up for father's actions. What we did on his behalf. And, I think, for the lordling he neglected two months ago."

Koji squinted against the rising sun. "I don't know how much hope I have in our cause, but the more I think about it, the more I see it as right. It sure feels better than what we did for father, the bastard. I'm with you on saving Sen too. However, you and Ira come first in my eyes. Before Sen, before revolution, before anything."

The land became more and more arid as they marched and the day grew warmer. They were informed that they would be heading straight into battle and thus would not be passing through any cities, though they would certainly pass by a few.

Further conversation was sparse, and Aiya found herself off to the side at one point thinking about nothing in particular, trying to keep her creeping anxiety at bay.

"Your brother seems excited to take on our enemy."

Aiya turned to see Johori on his horse trotting beside her. He really did look a lot like Risako the more she got to know his face, though he appeared a bit more sheepish.

She gave him a confused look. "Did he say that?"

"He said he'll be glad to prove his dominance over any other Ginju the way he did us." Johori grinned as he said it, and Aiya realized that he was being hyperbolic. She forced a smile.

"I'd have to agree with him then."

"Well. Our involvement won't likely be needed though, you know. After all, it'd be a terrible decision to risk our most valuable assets so early on."

Aiya shrugged. "I figured we were the keys to victory. We'll have to intervene at some point."

Though he had initiated the conversation, she got the notion that he was slightly out of his element. Johori was introspective, reserved, never immediately letting out what was on his mind. Finally, he said, "It's our hope that we won't. There's no telling what could happen, and we're not exactly replaceable."

"Well, I think we all understand that. Why are you saying this, are you afraid?"

Johori laughed, though by its abruptness she questioned whether it was genuine. "Just letting you know not to get too cocky or eager to jump in. Even against Jodai, sufficient numbers and tactics can easily pose a threat."

"We'll just have to be prepared for whatever comes," Aiya replied. It may have been arrogant, but the Jodai were not on her mind as a threat. She found herself thinking again of another possible surprise encounter with Ginju.

She was surprised not to be overly nervous about such a scenario. After their encounter at the Takasa estate, she discovered even greater confidence in her own abilities. She was even more surprised to find eager anticipation for another such encounter. It was an opportunity, in fact, to gain more respect, to put her abilities to the test. A Ginju opponent was undoubtedly dangerous, for the deities held terrifying power. *But that makes my power terrifying too.*

Camp was set up that night just as quickly, albeit enjoyed more cautiously. The morning that followed on Seventh Day, they passed into Forgery province. Jodai patrolling the border in dark orange armor merely bowed in their direction, though they were screened by a small group of armed Forgery messengers in dark robes of maroon. The men left to inform their superiors.

All of Forgery would be  aware of their presence. They marched parallel to a city wall, spotting soldiers lined outside as their march brought them close. When they were nearly across from it, Aiya came to the conclusion that it was the local city lord saluting to them outside his gates next to his troops, judging by his front position. The sight filled Aiya with a confusing mix of warmth and honor and strange guilt. Little did they know their army was a hound disguised as a sheep.

According to Tsugo and his generals, Sen only controlled the northeast regions of Forgery. These were their victims.

The day progressed torturously slow, until late afternoon set in. Tsugo informed Aiya and Koji that they were getting close, their destination only a few hours away. Any doubts they possessed evaporated upon crossing their first dead bodies.

As the sun lowered itself, the entire mood of their army grew solemn, suddenly serious in the face of bodies littered across the ground. Every few hundred feet their nostrils were assaulted with the stench of decay right before they crossed scattered corpses, swarmed by buzzing flies. Some held onto expressions of horror even in death, illuminated by the setting red sun, others expressionless as if in a slumber, lying in a bed of their own blood. Some were missing heads. Soon enough, the first of the hills came into view. A massive brown-green lump like a boil upon earthly cracked flesh. In the distance they heard shouting, the banging of steel. The air was eerily still against the backdrop of marching.

Despite her confidence, Aiya's heart beat against her chest in dire protest. Koji gave a long look in her direction, one meant to snap her into focus. She took hold of herself, watching the soldiers do the same. Soon they were climbing the hill in which they knew a battle raged on the other side. The battle of Hijimata. The atmosphere was almost suffocating at this point, like a blood-soaked animal hide draped over their bodies, weighing them to the ground. They crested the hill and came face to face with the most horrific assault of the senses Aiya had ever experienced.

Sandwiched between the two gargantuan hills, thousands of soldiers collided in a wave of death. Gore and tragedy everywhere. Aiya couldn't tell who was who. The clang of armor and metal rang, so intense that she felt a pang of pity for the men about to be thrown inside of it. It was a sea of chaos and violence, terror and fury, where life was snuffed out from one second to the next like a row of candle flames.

Above it all was HQ, three large tents with the largest in the center at the crest of the hill. The soldiers from here viewed the plains in front of them with dutiful expressions, shouting out orders here and there to the surrounding guard. They wore the same burnt orange armor as those below, some with jagged horns ornamenting their helms. At the crest of the opposite hill were Sen's headquarters, resting in one large tent.

Tsugo shouted, "All troops, this is our time! Proceed, men of honor, men of faith! Men of courage, men of brawn, and men who bring death with haste!" The men roared, and did just that.

Aiya could do nothing but sit by on her horse as the thousands of feet stampeding beside her went down the hill into the tumult. It was like storm winds passing, and as dust blew into her face, she was forced to cover herself.

When it was over, Koji grabbed her arm and held it down. They locked eyes for a moment. He motioned forward, where Tsugo led the rest of them to Lady Ueko's headquarters. The battle raged on, sparking a new fury by its latest arrivals. The Agriculture men stampeding down the hill were an unstoppable force.

"How's Sen supposed to get out of this?" she shouted. The battle appeared at a deadlock before, but now the Forgery lord would be massively outmatched.

"Let's just follow Tsugo's footsteps," Koji answered.

At headquarters, there was a raised seat like a throne near the edge of the hill in front of the main tent. In it, a girl no older than Aiya sat with an angry expression. A woman in an orange robes tied by a golden fleece belt stood beside her, watching intently, a scourge of wrinkles consuming her face. The girl in the seat was seething about something, and every once in a while, the woman said something to her in response. Twenty or so Jodai guards surrounded them.

"You've arrived just in time," Lady Ueko said, not bothering to turn her head. Tsugo was merely feet away from her. He unmounted his horse and gave her a quick, courteous bow.

"You notified us that you were being pressed into a stalemate. My troops are ready to pincer Lord Sen's forces so that we will be at an even greater advantage come tomorrow."

"*Do not*," growled the girl on the seat beside them, attracting the gaze of everyone, "*ever* refer to that scum as *Lord Sen* again. He is no Lord!"

"Calm yourself, Hasa," Ueko said in a voice smooth as butter. "Lord Tsugo only meant to be polite. Your brother won't be too happy now."

Aiya shifted uncomfortably. The newly arrived troops attacked Sen's army from both ends, collapsing their formations. The flood of green armor and dark orange armor pressed the enemy in on itself. Aiya's heart sank. She looked to the others, unable to read the level of concern on their faces.

No one said anything as they were forced to watch the battle rage. It seemed to last forever, and Aiya stifled the impulse to run into the fray herself. *Please stay strong*, she thought. *Don't give up your ground.*

Eventually, the sun set too deep and twilight had taken over. It was nearly dusk.

Just as she thought she could bear it no longer, the fighting slowed, and both armies began parting down the middle. Aiya squinted her eyes. An orange-robed man on horseback was making his way down the line. He waved a large red flag to the side.

"Heavens dammit, does he plan to do this every night?" one of the Forgery Jodai hissed.

"What is that?" Totane asked.

"A call for an honor duel," Ueko answered, face contorted. "Sen's demanding a one on one match to the death."

# Words

"Little bastard." The same Jodai man stepped forward. He was a brawny man, distinguished and looking wise beyond his years, a horned helmet doming his head. "We've gone through the same routine the past three days. He's already taken out General Monoo and two lieutenants."

"We won't lose another," said a much younger, nimbler soldier next to him, brandishing a spear.

Aiya's extensive studies into warfare had still not prepared her for this. Honor duels were somewhat common in war, usually between two high ranking commanders towards the end of an important battle. It was a direct challenge, a test of courage and might. Though it was sometimes denied, this was seen as an act of cowardice that could tarnish a reputation. Generally, if the commander with the upper hand initiated, it was an act of mock mercy, giving their opponent a final chance to prove themselves. If the losing commander initiated, it was to buy time.

*In a battle between clan members, honor duels are one thing they can't deny.*

"*No, no, no!*" Hasa screamed. She bolted from her chair, falling to the ground, spittle flying from her mouth in tiny flecks. "He cannot be allowed! He won't again, he won't! I said no! Bastard! Insolence! Behead him and go on!" She gritted her teeth and panted like an ox.

"Calm yourself, Hasa!" Ueko hissed. She forced her daughter back into her seat, rougher than Aiya would have expected. She realized that Hasa was, in fact, insane. Clearly this was the reason Ueko was able to take advantage of her. The pieces were falling together. "Things will end differently this time. Lieutenant Toru, were you making an offer with that weapon drawn?"

The man gripping his spear answered, "Yes. If you will, my Lady, allow me to avenge the death of my fallen general, Monoo."

"It's brave of you, what you're doing," said the wise general, "but Sen is clearly not one to be underestimated. Blind anger won't win you this duel."

"Respectfully, General Honji, I don't intend to win on any pretense of rage. You all know as well as I the extent of my combat prowess. You believe I am second to only General Monoo within his army, but I would argue I was his equal. And I've watched enough of the boy these past few days to get an idea of his weaknesses."

Toru stepped forward to Ueko.

She sighed. "Fetch him a mount, quickly."

The Jodai behind her moved to do just that. Not a minute later, he was mounted and slipping on his helmet. Parts of him resembled the man from the Oshidai's fable of bravery who stood against the Sun Dragon.

"Toru." Honji stepped beside him.

"I'll settle this once and for all," the young man answered, and then he was galloping down into the field.

"He's being considered for the next title of general," Honji said, seemingly to himself. "He's sure to obtain it after this."

Aiya wondered just how good his chances were but remained silent. For Sen to approach the duel with no visible armor might as well be begging for death. All eyes remained on the field watching Toru passing through the ranks of men. The fighting had ceased completely. In this moment Toru was like a king, charging into the ferocious jaws of a monster. Sen couldn't be that dangerous, could he? The young lord certainly didn't have the mightiest stature.

Toru stopped short twenty feet of Sen and raised his polearm, a commander's weapon of choice. Sen threw down the flag and raised his sword, a bold answer. They stared each other down, rooted in place.

Finally lowering their weapons, the two men charged. Toru prepared a long jab from the left, but Sen had already knocked him from his steed with a powerful left blow. Toru tumbled off his horse and across the ground. He was on his feet before Sen's horse even had a chance to pivot back. He'd been stabbed, but it apparently hadn't gone too deep.

Sen came off his own mount and assumed a defensive position. Toru hesitated at this, clutching his side. Aiya squinted to see his expression. Toru took the bait and charged Sen, this time with more caution. He went for a wide upwards slash that would connect while maintaining a large distance between the two fighters. Sen ducked around it before Toru could react, shifting into his personal space.

Before Toru could bring up his knee into Sen's stomach, he had a sword going through his own. He doubled over, Sen withdrawing his weapon, spinning, and taking the lieutenant's head in one clean stroke.

The men around them erupted into a fury, but none dared move to stop him. Sen gathered up the head and held it high above his own, his soldiers cheering. After a few seconds he got back on his stallion and retreated.

As the sun dipped to its lowest point in the sky, the rest of his men were retreating with him, while Ueko's troops gathered up Toru's headless body.

"Empress' soul," Koji whispered. Aiya could hardly believe what she had witnessed. In two minutes, Sen had done in a commander who'd just been appraised as a general. The fight had been over before it had even begun.

Hasa was almost on a rampage. "We'll have your head! We'll have your head! Getting out of this won't happen! You'll only hold out for so long, before the entire continent...."

Ueko, this time letting her daughter be, stormed off into the main tent, composed yet livid. General Honji cursed and flounced after her.

Tsugo and the present Ginju looked at each other, unsure of what to do.

"Help the rest of our men set up camp next to Lady Hasa's troops," Tsugo finally said, then he followed Lady Ueko into the main tent.

Shuffling between relief and disbelief in their minds, they followed orders. Descending the hills, Aiya wondered how long the rest of the battle at Hijimata would last. They greatly outnumbered Sen's troops, and by Tsugo's own words, Sen would be at a staggering disadvantage come the next day.

As Koji galloped past her, "Hopefully we'll see a repeat of today's events tomorrow."

"Just don't let those western soldiers hear you say that aloud," Aiya replied.

They entered the hill's foot where arrangements for the night were already being assembled. Soldiers constructed tents and set sorted bundles of sticks from sacks into camp-fires. An air of satisfaction permeated the camp, from West Forgery to even the men of Agriculture. Aiya rode about, examining the camp layout and the efficiency of the men. She was curious about the mechanisms of war, feeling it was her duty from now on to learn them. She found Johori overseeing the far left side of the central division. General Mune of Agriculture directed the men, shouting as Johori mirrored him to a smaller degree, riding ever so closer to his men before making his commands. Aiya observed him, the flow through which the men were organized. A minute or two in, she rode close.

"It's no wonder Sen has lasted this long," she commented, "if his army fights as fearsome as he."

Agriculture soldiers coalesced here from all directions, creating a second half to the central division, or rather two-thirds, as they greatly outnumbered those of West Forgery. "He held the advantage in numbers up until now."

Fires lit up all around the camp. The day's visibility was declining rapidly.

"It's hard to imagine this in River. Causing all this de-struction, this death, for the throne. And yet this is how my father took rulership from his siblings. I could never do it against my own, no matter what."

"Such is the shadow of human nature. The empire is the embodiment of that, as we say."

A part of Erru society accepted this as the way things had always been. In contrast, not a story in the days of old embraced such selfish, gross accumulation of power. That dichotomy, perhaps a willful dissonance brought by greed, always remained distant in their minds. And yet, she had contributed to it herself. Her clan had resorted to intimidation, threat, murder, in direct opposition to the values so many of River held dear. The nobility really had strayed so far, and somehow she only now realized it.

Sitting near each other on horseback, a profoundly growing sense of familiarity cropped up between them. The precise moment Aiya had cast her first mote of trust upon him, upon Totane and Risako, even Tsugo, was oblivious to her. He'd transformed from malicious, to a dubious stranger, to a clear ally she could rely on, looking upon her with sincere eyes.

"Explain to me some of Agriculture's battle formations. If I'm going to be here, I want to understand our place on the field as much as you do."

"You're right about that, sorry." Aiya wasn't sure what he was apologizing for. "Follow me."

Johori pulled his reins, and together they galloped back up the hill. Forty feet from where they rode, a smattering of gold-helmed Jodai patrolled the crest, though Ueko, Hasa, and the rest of the commanders were no longer out in the open. They came to the secondary tent to the left facing the opposite hill. Aiya slipped off her horse and grabbed the tent flap, turning. Sen's HQ was a large singular tent, standing wide, gloomy in forlorn shadow.

Inside, across a number of beds and low tables, blankets and rope, water gourds and wine skins and an assortment of other items lay strewn. A high table at its center. The tent was reserved for Agriculture, though had clearly seen some previous use before their arrival. Tsugo and his officers busied themselves outside.

Her first impulse was to seek out any alcohol she could find, but she suppressed it.

The tables were meant to simulate the battlefield. A shallow grid was carved into the wood, accommodating pieces like cylinders topped with wooden spheres, coins, cubes, and an assortment of shapes and sizes, meticulously organized, though some took arbitrary positions on the board. Aiya had never seen one in actual use before. It resembled the game of Maton.

"I'm far from the strategist Risako is, but I've memorized all the basic formations and seen them in action during mock battles in Agriculture. No doubt you're aware of these: Hidden Arrow Formation, Low Tail and High Tail Formation, Boulder Formation, Shinti Formation..."

"Shinti Formation?"

"Ah," Johori flicked over a pawn with another pressed between his fingers, creating a sound like rolling dice on the wood, "The concept is exclusive to Agriculture, used exactly once during the fall of Ogasawa. It's not one we'll be able to utilize here. In battle, we would have ten units surround a large army from ten different points. The caveat is that they would have to remain at a distance, and the terrain should be varied so that some units could remain hidden. This all has the advantage of keeping relatively tight around the enemy force and being able to respond quickly to the enemy's movements. They would also have to have cornered the enemy and control the surrounding area. In truth, it would only be useful in the event that said army was powerful, difficult but on its last leg, with the off chance of receiving reinforcements. But, the name paints a fascinating picture."

"Just like the stories."

The name made sense, reminiscent of a legend more ancient than any other Erru tale. Aiya's mind stalled, recounting the story of creation.

In the beginning, the Great Spirits were the originators, the first of sentient life. There was only the earth, the simple-minded animals and nature, and the Ten Great Spirits known as the Shinti. They were natural beings of the earth whose names and features were not remembered, but who lived in harmony with each other and nature. After many eons of living among the abundance on earth's life, they desired something more honorable. The earthly spirits, the Kiru, were created in their own image. After them was mankind, whom some claimed to be the Shinti's greatest mistake. Nevertheless, mankind would best mother nature, more intelligent than any beast in the field, creature of the sea, or bird in the sky, yet also more numerous than the trees and seas of grass.

Only the Kiru could be in the presence of the Shinti, yet the Shinti gave preference to mankind. They taught them to survive and thrive. From living among them, the Shinti learned that with free will, humans would depart from them, from nature and what was good. Mankind was violent, like the animals, despite the capacity to choose otherwise. This disturbed the Shinti, and from war and atrocities committed by the many broken tribes of men, rose the abomination called Carnage, the literal manifestation of human violence.

The Ten Great Spirits came together to destroy Carnage and by consequence render mankind unable to commit violence, but they could not overcome him. They died, the essence of their souls banished to the spirit world and forming the ten domains.

Their daughter, who became the Empress, taught her most faithful select to draw power from these ten domains. The rivers, the mountains, the forests, the stone, the rain, the paths, agriculture, forgery, high noon, and twilight. These became the deities, each an essential aspect of civilized humanity. As the empire expanded, a new domain would be granted by the Empress.

"To think we wield their power," Aiya said. "And it's the Empress who blessed us with our abilities."

"I never liked stories much. I prefer more intellectual pastimes. Though, I like to imagine the Empress lost her way at some point. Perhaps she was not always so tyrannical."

"But you don't care about that, do you? What matters is that she's oppressing the Erru now."

Johori didn't answer, looking down. It gave the impression that she'd happened upon a tender subject for him. Mild concern touched her. She wished he would not always be so hesitant, that he spoke more freely to her.

"I still feel guilty about abandoning my family. Sure, they weren't the most upstanding nobles you'd ever meet. Far from Agriculture ideals. Even now, I feel resentment towards them, for who they were, and *what* they were. But, we were still kin. I allowed my father's death, and my clan's imprisonment. I willfully gave up my province to their enemies."

Johori met her eyes. "The fact you were able to do those things is admirable. It's, well, what I admire about you. And if they treated you as you and your siblings say, you should be proud of what you did. It's not easy to walk one's own path. To be honest, I envy you."

Aiya sighed. "You shouldn't."

After a moment, Johori said, "My upbringing was obviously different from yours. You can see that in my clan, for we do not carry ourselves like most others. I grew up seeing all the things my siblings saw. We witnessed the wealth, and poverty, of other provinces. I'm not like my clan. I've never been able to rid myself of the doubts clouding my mind. Doubts which pertain to the revolution.

"In Agriculture, we keep preserved the ruins of a couple burned villages, destroyed during empirical expansion. These sites serve as a reminder, because man has a tendency to forget, for history to repeat itself. The third or so time I visited them, I told Totane my feelings, that all I could see in the future was our lands burning up. Revolution is a perilous path. At least, that was what I intended to say, but it probably came out more than a little unclear, because I was frightened. Frightened of being called a coward, of holding everyone back. Totane saw I was scared, and he reassured me.

"But in truth, my soul could never support the idea. I learned the history of the Erru, the continent and my province, and the more I learned, the more I hated it. All I ever wanted was to live in peace with my clan, to see them prosper. I cherish my life, my province. I'm not self-sacrificing like the rest of Agriculture. I can't give those things up for the greater good."

"Empress' soul," Aiya said. She grew speechless. Like that, a barrier broke between them. His demeanor suddenly made sense.

"Just don't let Totane hear you swear by her name."

The tent flap came open. They both jumped, spinning to see who was intruding upon their intimate space.

Stepping through the tent, Lady Yomenuura Ueko turned her creased face in their direction, arms resting at her sides, taking in the scene.

"Forgive me if I trespass. My conscience is in dire need of cooling. I cannot help but pace and wander." Aiya watched her, strangely, with an air of caution. Ueko was an inch shorter than herself, dark hairs pulled back from a face that at once seemed both old and young. Her expression was in a perennial state of focus, and the woman talked at a confident, yet slow pace, leaving enough space for interjection, but with the implication that she would not be so forgiving if one chose the wrong words. "It is a sight to see for Tsugo to have herded all five of his children here with him. I'm aware that wars of inheritance are not par for the course in your province. Yet, you remind me of my own children."

Without warning, Aiya's insides began roiling. Something in the cool, indifferent tone of the woman's words had triggered her, and she grew livid. "You mean your own children which you killed?"

Ueko eyed Aiya as if reading her, studying an interesting specimen. "Given the worldliness of your father, I thought you to be the pragmatic type on these matters, even if you hail from Agriculture. It is clear that you do not understand the world, and a true shame Tsugo has raised you to be so naive."

"If it's realistic to murder your family at a moment's notice, I'll gladly be naive." Aiya squeezed a hidden fist between her hip and the simulation table. An intense loathing for Ueko arose, a hatred like that which she at many times in her life felt for her father. Here this noble woman, after having slain many of her own children, was now tearing her province apart to slay another, for the purposes of putting her incompetent daughter on the throne where she could be easily manipulated. All for Ueko's own gain. "I'd rather be that than heartless."

"Even so, here you are, helping me."

Johori tried stopping her. "Aiya, I-"

"My feelings lie separate from my duty. That is honorable. It changes nothing of the disgust I feel for you." Aiya kept their eyes locked. "My lady," she added, though the words made her sick.

"Then perhaps we are not so different," Ueko stated matter-of-factly before coming closer. Aiya fought the urge to step back. Her foot inched away, despite herself. Ueko stopped less than ten paces away, standing parallel to the table between them. She did not face them directly, instead craning her head and examining the canvas above. "I honored my husband's rule for an excruciating number of years before fate seized me this moment. Had I tried to take his rightful throne, his former generals would have sliced my ears from my head.

"So tell me, at what point during this battle are you willing to risk your life for my sake, for the completion of your father's orders, should it be necessary? Heavens forbid it. At what point would it be selfish to leave your mother to grieve over your death, brought about by conflict which does not concern you, but which you nonetheless seek to profit from? Assuming your mother will not consider her own economic gain to justify your death.

"The high nobility are not fit to live in squalor, not justified in simply seeking survival. We balance our power and wealth with duty. *That* is honorable. What I feel for my children is secondary. A High Lady may not fret over the wellbeing of her family the way a common mother might torment herself. The province is as much the offspring of my clan as my children were offspring of me. It is my duty that Forgery is overseen by its rightful rulers."

"You think your long-winded speech justifies your selfishness?"

Ueko faced her. Aiya thought she saw what might be the first suggestion of mirth crack onto the woman's face, but it was gone in an instant. "I seem to have misplaced your name."

She swallowed. "Tabeni Aiya."

"Aiya," Ueko tested the name slick on her tongue, "Look into the truest depths of your heart, and tell me if you honestly believe you will be your father's heir."

"If he desires it."

"Oh. You are a truly privileged soul. Blessed to the utmost degree. *If he desires it.* If I had waded through my life with that sentiment, I would likely be gathering dust at the farthest corner of my mother and father's keep, or perhaps dead in the earth next to them. I cannot fault you, however, nor be angry. You will not acquire power unless by taking it. Life can be likened to a web of conflicting interests, and there are points where force is necessary. That is the curse of mankind. Were you born outside of Agriculture, you might have stumbled upon this fact long ago. Of course, the neighbor's sword is always sharper."

Ueko moved to the tent flaps, exiting the way she came with an aura that commanded the air.

Tabeni Risako would have liked to think she was keeping her promise to herself. She denied that she had decided to break it from the moment the day had concluded, denied that she intended to see Gaku Hedi alone. She could not deny it any longer.

Ueoko and Tsugo's soldiers had set up camp together, though the men spoke little to one another. Its glow painted the grass stubble of the foothill in yellow-orange light, far below where Risako now trekked. Rations were passed around under the moonlit sky, mostly clear of clouds to reveal innumerable stars. Given their true motives, the Agriculture Jodai might not exude comradery with those of West Forgery, but some interaction could not be avoided. In war, there was no better way of getting close to one's enemy than to become their friend.

The faint glow behind her disappeared completely as Risako came to the far side of the hill. She approached the dark bulky form near the left slope, rubbing her arms from the night's chill. Gaku Hedi turned at the sound of her footsteps. Only his basic features could be made out, for neither of them carried a lantern. His forest-jade armor appeared black. The absence of his right arm was still evident. Risako smiled, and Hedi returned a faint one of his own. "We told each other this wouldn't happen. This battle should be the only thing racking our brains."

"Promised, in fact. We're terribly dishonest people," Risako answered, and she wrapped her arms around him. He wrapped his left across her back. The armor he still wore was cold, but his breath as he spoke into her ear warmed her entire body.

"Terribly dishonest. Unfitting for our rank. We should leave, resign from our positions in shame."

Risako leaned back. "You're the one with the formal rank. I'm just a noble woman who plays her part from the background."

"Please. You're in every meeting and public hearing in Agriculture. People know you and your position as Ginju. You'll probably be a general one day."

"If that happens, you'll be my right-hand man."

"Or left," he said with a grin.

Risako rolled her eyes.

"I got the chance to speak with one of our new allies last night. What can we expect of these foreign Ginju?"

Risako thought for a moment. It was true that Aiya and Koji had been ready to rip her head from her body three nights ago. They hadn't let their guard down after leaving Agriculture, understandably. Even now, she could not be sure of their level of loyalty to the cause. "I see something in Aiya at least, something I also perceived in Irashida. River sounds as carnivorous as they come. They have witnessed and understand the lies of the empire, its twisted sense of honor."

"Your tendency to be charitable notwithstanding?" She didn't answer, and Hedi brushed her face. "Only teasing."

She pushed her palms against his chest. "It feels wrong, what we're doing. As an army, I mean. We're helping fight the one person we're meant to keep alive, and we don't know exactly how long that will continue. In the meantime," she said, dejected, "we're sacrificing our own troops for a double cause."

"You're right," Hedi answered. "It feels wrong. But it is also a noble cause. We're just paying the cost for it. Our people understand that, which is why they're fighting their hardest while prepared to follow new orders at the drop of a feather. Be careful not to dishonor those who've already sacrificed themselves. We can't afford to be finicky."

Risako admired the strength in his voice, how quickly he was always able to address her concerns. He was a man who knew his purpose, indestructible in his resolve. "I had a terrible thought on the way over here," she said finally.

"What was so terrible?"

"Make me a new promise. One you can't break this time. Promise me you won't offer yourself to fight Sen. Nor will you allow yourself to be offered."

"What on earth would make me do that?"

"You wouldn't offer yourself for no reason. But Lady Ueko is clearly sick of losing her own high ranking officers to Sen. She might demand Tsugo tribute one of his own commanders instead. I know you'd take it if you thought it was the best move, or if you were taking someone's place."

Hedi didn't respond for a few moments. "In that case, Tsugo could easily decline. There's no reason for us to take those kinds of losses, especially in a battle for inheritance. You think I'd needlessly endanger myself like that in front of you?"

"No...I just want to be able to hold you at the end of this."

"I understand. I promise we'll make it out of this together. And now you have to promise me to stop worrying about my fate. We're revolutionists. We can't afford to worry about things as fickle as life and death. We just need to trust in ourselves, to look forward and fight."

The tear that rolled down Risako's cheek as he spoke could not be held back. She stepped back from him, admiring his sturdy frame as he gazed down into her own watery eyes, grateful for the fact that she was the one person he wanted to see during times like these. They gave each other strength.

"Promise me you'll put everything we're fighting for before me, Risako."

She nodded. "Of course, I promise. I live for the Republic, and for the Republic I will also die."

She'd die for Hedi too. She just wasn't sure which would come first.

"You wanted a private word?"

Tsugo did, and despite years as the High Lord of Agriculture, his mind before this particular negotiation would stop at nothing to sabotage the calm in his frame. Tonight presented an unsteady step toward the revolution he had spent his entire life fighting for. All those years leading, scheming, sacrificing.

Lady Ueko stood down the hillside opposite to the battlefield. Tsugo traversed the rough, steep slope, halting at a rocky patch. They each clasped flickering lanterns at their sides.

He would have to preface tonight's meeting in a way that would leave her open for future alliances. Ueko would be dead in the end, but whatever position they came in agreement upon would be eternal. A true leader of men was followed, adhered to long after death. The back of Tsugo's throat felt as dry as the ground on which they stood. He spoke.

"I understand the frustration with your daughter. My wife came into this world ordinary, but the functioning of her mind began to collapse about a decade ago. She went senile. Her clan's blood, unfortunately. I know, as you are likely aware, the rumors of your manipulation. I presume them to be true, so let's not insult each other's intelligence. I won't pretend as if I empathize with the pain of accepting her state, because I don't pretend you feel that pain, as I did with my beloved. I, however, can relate to the frustration that never ceases to eat at your very soul."

He paused, then continued.

"Those truly meant to rule prefer not to do so behind a veil. The delicate nature of your daughter's mind will someday draw your own into insanity."

"You make a wonderful speech." Ueko frowned, arms crossed in the cold breeze. "But I'm having trouble discerning the true nature of our discourse."

"I simply wanted to talk. Between two supreme commanders, we should have at least some rapport."

Tsugo's youth had been spent by his father's side on more diplomatic conferences than he could remember, following the final days of civil strife in River province. It had taken fifty years for the factions of the province to accept the ordinance of its High Clan. Alongside the empire, Agriculture had helped to instate the Takasa, for Takasa Sakumo had been a powerful and influential man, humble enough to repay a favor and ripened enough to remember more clearly the revered culture of Nirogawa. That, at least, was his father's justification, who had gone to painstaking efforts to ensure Tsugo and his brothers and sisters were prepared to take up his mantle.

He'd bring them along on his extensive diplomatic excursions, Tsugo first and foremost, as he was the chosen inheritor. Tsugo was shocked to witness the hereditary wars that generationally scourged the other provinces. Sibling resorted to killing sibling, should an agreement of an heir not be reached. When he first met Lord Sakumo of River, Lord Arusuke's father, he thought the man at first glance to be docile. Upon listening to him speak, absorbing the man's insight, logic and discernment accumulated over his many years upon the earth, he recognized the noble lord's quiet yet all-encompassing confidence, and with that confidence also came a certain amount of ruthlessness.

Statecraft in Agriculture was stressful, if mundane. Most were on the same accord. Nobles were like the mind and bones of the body, collaborating to keep everything in frame. Commoners were like the skin and muscle which allowed them to take action, to have resistance. Professions, trades, and establishments were all united for one cause.

Elsewhere on the continent, this was not so. Noble lords were hardened in a different manner, in contrast to the diligent physical training and rigorous study of statecraft their father had forced upon them. The nobility of the empire were  hardened by the unending vicious cycle, the contest for power.

Ueko watched him closely. She gave away very little in her posture, in the cadence of her voice. He was fifty, and she was ten years less, yet with twice as many lines in her face as he, perhaps bespeaking a long and winding tale of weal and woe. He considered each line a trace of wisdom on a woman who'd doubtlessly confronted and seen as much as himself.

"I understand Agriculture has waged no battles of inheritance for over a century, though you delight in involving yourself in such conflicts outside your borders. Chiefly, when River was a dogland. I haven't quite been able to determine why exactly you took interest in my own, nor why you seek a weapons deal in the first place."

"You assume our reputation as vultures who capitalize on foreign clan affairs. What you do not know is to what end we feast. I assure you, we have not lain dormant these past forty years."

"Likewise," she answered, "we were not twiddling our thumbs waiting for someone to come offering to save the day. I am always prepared, and I have many allies. Even as high as Rain."

Tsugo stepped closer, and the breeze which chilled their skin picked up, as if to ward off his impending statement. "But we came, and for good reason. It may sound mad what I am going to tell you, but you will hear me out. I want your daughter to join hands with my son, Totane. This union will tie Agriculture and Forgery together as one, with the intention that we will one day rule all the empire, bringing down the Empress and taking the Imperial Seat for ourselves."

For the first time, Ueko was visibly taken aback. If she agreed to his additional proposal, her subjects would unquestionably back her decision, diminishing the chances of revolt once Sen came into power. However, he couldn't deny, it was also insurance, in case of their failure at Hijimata, in case Sen so happened to be tragically slain. In such a case, the Republic would maintain at least some momentum down their current trajectory.

Ueko searched for the right words. Unable to, she resorted to the most obvious. "Are you mad?"

"You'd be wise to agree to this. The empire is slowly cracking, as we can all see. Provinces grow restless. Each one is tired of contributing our soldiers to the war effort against Tarshan, which has been stalled because of the conflict here. It seems the far north is reaching levels of conflict not seen since their adoption into the empire, which the Empress herself has been forced to attend to while you stall her efforts of expansion. How will you endure an increased levy by the Empress after the conclusion of your own internal affairs, as you clean up your ravaged province? This is an opportunity not to be missed. Your daughter's hand to my son will still allow you to position yourself as the authoritative figure of your clan. You can assume the title of High Lady until our offspring inherit our provinces."

He waited for her response.

"I-have no words for this. You are certainly a master at surprises, Lord Tsugo."

Before he could say another word, she was already making her way back towards the tents.

# Den

The main tent was a tiger's den of gathering officials. Aiya and Koji stood opposite from one another around a large circular table of stonewood. The table displayed a map of the hills and surrounding area, with figures and pieces that represented the armies. Totane stood next to Johori, Risako across from them beside the man who'd identified himself to Aiya as Gaku Hedi earlier. The rest of the Forgery and Agricultural generals stood between them all. Lord Tsugo was in the center to Aiya's left, and opposite him was Lady Ueko.

Like its smaller counterparts, the main tent held sleeping mats and other smaller tables of various instruments on top of them. The battle had raged a mere seven days, and yet to Aiya, these living quarters seemed a little more unkempt than the one before. It was a solemn and jaded atmosphere, but now that everyone had gotten a chance to gather themselves, the planning for tomorrow would begin.

All in all, there were fourteen of them cramped together under the canvas, the space full of musk and sweat. Including their two head commanders, Aiya, and the other Ginju, there was General Honji, General Masuo, General Fun, and Lieutenant Dasuke standing for Forgery. General Yko,

General Mune, and Lieutenant Hedi were with Agriculture. Hasa was noticeably absent.

There was an unwelcoming intensity to the small area they occupied. Aiya had ordered and executed numerous nobles in River, had faced her brothers on countless occasions, had gone toe to toe with Ginju that could recover from mortally inflicted wounds in mere seconds, but now, in this tent of officials, she found herself as nervous as an elk, hesitant to utter even a sound.

"Let us understand one thing." Ueko's gaze passed by everyone in the room, her cadence commanding their attention. When she spoke, others listened. "We've brought forth our best efforts in bringing down the eastern army. Masuo's division on the right has managed to push back Gheki's lines. However, Fun's lines have suffered too many heavy casualties over the past seven days, an unfortunate effect of losing Lieutenant Mushi on the first day. Because of this, Honji has had to send one thousand of his four thousand five hundred troops from the center to Fun's left army, creating an overall stalemate."

Ueko's hand moved on the map to show the positions of each player on the board. The more important the player, the bigger the piece. The two generals positioned to the left and right had smaller pieces than Honji's main army in the center.

"We began this war six months ago with ten thousand soldiers, Sen also managing to recruit ten thousand of his own. He's gathered a lot more support than I thought possible, directly under my nose. This represents about half of the available troops within Forgery province. The other lords are on standby, awaiting the outcome on this hill. Regardless, we arrived at these hills with seventy-five hundred troops, having lost a quarter of our ranks over the course of this conflict. Sen came with eight thousand, slightly outnumbering us. Over the course of this battle, we've taken a total of sixteen hundred casualties, while Sen has managed to keep his down to seven hundred.

"Thanks to the arrival of Agriculture, we've gained a massive numerical advantage over the eastern army. We estimate Agriculture casualties to be just fifty for the first day you arrived. At nearly sixteen thousand men, we more than double the number of Sen's troops. In fact, had you not arrived as the sun began setting, you almost certainly would have concluded this damned battle by the day's end.

"Nevertheless, tomorrow will be the end for him. This battlefield is his final frontier, the border between those who side with him and those who side with the true heir. The entire region west of here is my daughter's domain. While Sen has managed well with his impressive number of recruits, the east regions of Forgery are not nearly as well fortified as the west. Historically, there was never much need. If he falls or retreats here, the rest of the region will easily go down in just a matter of time, not to mention he will have lost the majority of his troops. This fact will devastate his reputation among his supporters and those who watch our conflict from afar, and they will come to our aid, because we will be seen as the clear winners. We will not give Sen a chance to pull the same stunt on the eighth day of battle."

A lump perpetually bulged in Aiya's throat. She felt as trapped as Sen, unable to keep her attention on the discussion at hand. Watching Ueko, her earlier words recurred again in Aiya's head against her will. *Then perhaps we are not so different.*

Aiya had let her father die out of loving duty to Ira. Their motives differed. She was driven by an urge to protect, while Ueko sought power. But Aiya had killed for her clan's power and used it for their corruption. Both of them put clan duty first, even if they believed their motives to be entirely different. Ueko was clearly a hard woman, willing to use any means necessary for her purpose.

*Damn, how foolish of us was it to kill Juso?* Aiya thought, bristling at the night's chill despite torchlight all around. Perhaps Sen would have managed victory by now had the general not been slain two months ago.

"Apologies for our blunder," Fun said, clasping a hand over a fist in front of him while bowing. The man's voice was far deeper than expected. He wore a gold helm that differentiated West Forgery soldiers from the east. "Lieutenant Mushi's units were unrivaled in offensive strategy, and as we know, offense is my biggest weakness."

"You're forgiven, General Fun. What's done is done. Warfare is about being prepared for these things, being ten steps ahead. What proposals do Agriculture's generals have for tomorrow's battle?"

Mune went first. "My division specializes in feints. If General Fun's army is struggling, then the enemy will fall to our deception even quicker. Allow my fourth company to be posted on Fun's front lines tomorrow, and we will draw at least half of Sen's right wing to their doom."

Masuo spoke up, a man with a small nose and particularly square face. "A sound strategy, except I doubt a feint on the left wing is the best option right now. Sen has opted for a completely defensive strategy this entire battle and only managed to inflict damage to our left because of Fun's aggressive tactics."

"Then I suggest we go into an all-out attack," said Yko. Next to Tsugo, he stood just as tall but spoke with none of the High Lord's polish. "No matter his strategy, in a match this uneven, he *will* fold. Even if he manages to hold off, Lieutenant Hedi's unit can go around his backdoor for an attack he won't see coming."

"What of Forgery Ginju?" Totane asked, turning the heads of everyone in the tent. He'd addressed Aiya's question for her, yanking her mind from her looping thoughts. He seemed to never hesitate in letting his thoughts and opinions known, operating with a deep personal distinction between right and wrong. "I suppose they are to stay out of sibling warfare just as it is in Agriculture tradition? Or has Sen managed to recruit them as well?"

Ueko eyed him for a minute, not answering. Finally, she said, "Yes, they will not be utilized in this particular battle, Lord Totane. No matter how dire the circumstances. We have certain ways of doing things in Forgery, of acting with honor, just as we have allowed our commanders to be slain in Sen's honor duels. So we will not resort to easily overpowering him with the likes of Ginju, just as you have chosen not to offer your own Ginju when you could render this excursion quick and painless."

"We figured if ten thousand troops weren't enough for the likes of one boy, nothing could be," Tsugo said. "Alas, before we continue forming our strategy, I think a more important prospect should be mentioned. That which concerns the joining of our two forces. Agriculture has long stood idle after many decades of securing the rule of other high families. Because of this, it may come to no shock that we stand before you. But do not be mistaken. We do not offer you our aid out of the goodness of our hearts. Like you, we feed on power and authority, for wealth and material gain. This is all but for one purpose.

"It is abrupt, but I sincerely ask that my request be deeply considered. I would propose that my first born son, Tabeni Totane, be joined together with your daughter, Yomenuura Hasa. I ask for her hand in marriage. This would prelude the merging of our two provinces together to become the most powerful in Egaisha. Think of it as the first permanent coalition."

The air turned heavy and dead. They exchanged looks, and Aiya could hardly believe the words that had just escaped Tsugo's mouth. Her eyes went to Totane, who stood flustered. He regarded his father, unblinking. Whatever replies the others could have made were lost. Was this the 'proposal' Tsugo had suggested at the onset of their journey?

Ueko glared at him as if she had been slapped in the face. "Right now, Lord Tsugo, is *not* the time to be making proposals such as that. Focus on ending this battle as quickly as possible, and that alone. Am I clear? We can discuss-"

"My apologies," Tsugo interrupted, an interruption that might have earned him a dagger in the face. His poise somehow equaled that of Ueko "My polite etiquette seems to have created a misunderstanding. I was not asking. It was, actually, a demand. We will come to an agreement before the break of dawn tomorrow, or I will be forced to withdraw every last one of my Agriculture troops before the battle begins."

Ueko almost fell backwards. Heat boiled the insides of Aiya's ears as she shifted in discomfort. Her eyes darted from one officer to another, to Risako, Johori, Koji, Totane. Commotion heard from the men outside the tent suddenly seemed to flush out, and somehow she was no longer cold.

"Understand me, Lord Tsugo," Ueko hissed, harboring every bit of composure to keep herself from shouting. "*Understand* me when I say this! Forgery values a friend, hates a foe, but a viper, one who whispers that he is a sheep in order to slither towards his way, he will never gain respect among us!"

Tsugo appeared unmoved. "My Lady Ueko. We're all vipers in war. Believe me, I have the utmost respect for you, and wish for your triumph. I also have a province whose needs I value far more. My original statement still stands."

General Honji slammed a fist onto the table, rattling the pieces. "Enough of this foolery! Your head should be on the chopping block right now for such disrespect!"

"Careful with your words," Mune warned. "We don't take kindly to threats towards Lord Tsugo."

Aiya desperately considered how she would apprehend the men if things got out of hand. *In war, the element of surprise may be your sharpest sword.* An old proverb. It was better to retain her disguise. Before any swords could be drawn, the commotion outside became a violent ruckus. Aiya swiveled towards the tent flaps. Men were crying out in alarm.

"What under the heavens is going on out there?" Yko said.

"What a timely distraction." Masuo forced his attention back to the men around him. "I really hope this isn't another one of your ploys of persuasion, because if it is-"

"Now you insult us," Hedi declared. "We provide aid on our terms alone. Don't assume we'd ever resort to that level of sabotage in the event we don't get our way."

Ueko said nothing, eyes locked on the tent's entrance.

Honji moved to the front of the tent as the noise grew louder and more chaotic. Closer. "We'll see just what-"

The man parted the flaps open with two burly hands, and no sooner had he done so did a sword become lodged in his left eye, traversing its way out the back of his head. Honji toppled to the ground, a look of shock forever stuck on his face.

# Hounds

I t was a suicide mission.

Hidesada Nanbu and his peers had taken it earnestly. They would die for Lord Sen on the battlefield, and they'd be grateful for it. They'd manage to secure for themselves seven heads in battle, so it was a shame they wouldn't live to be rewarded for it. Their families would be proud. Damn it all, they'd make them proud in death too.

Nanbu wore a golden helm, allowing him to blend in with the enemy. He'd pried it off a reeking head he'd severed himself, placing it on his own. That had been at the onset of dusk. Having come from the left wing division with the others, he'd slipped into the front lines of the center army and hid behind a wall of soldiers while switching helmets.

Then came the hard part. The men around him pretended to be alarmed and swung at him. An enemy soldier! They ejected him from their ranks as the battle came to a close and he'd barely escaped with his life. Or so their enemies thought.

Even though acting, they'd given him a blow to the elbow pretty good. The numbness still hadn't subsided.

His friends had, miraculously, pulled off the same stunt. Most of all he was glad for Mouri, who he'd come to love like a brother. Nanbu considered the two of them brothers, fighting by the other's side for years. Kagami, who he'd grown up in the same city with, though the two had never gotten close. Shoda, Junko, Kori, and Orin were men he'd not known prior to their assignment. But regardless of their past, he might as well lump them in as family now, because these were the men he'd die with.

Now they sat in the back of the enemy's camp closest to HQ, every soldier around them completely oblivious to the fact they didn't belong here. The sudden influx of Agriculture soldiers surely made that possible. Men and the occasional prostitute passed by the seven of them huddled around a fire, tending to their meager portion of broth with a little less vigor than the occasion deemed appropriate. Many danced to the sound of music, celebrating their assured success despite the loss of yet another commander. The sight made Nanbu hot, so he kept his eyes low.

Deception like this in battle was rare, and usually ended with failure before it even started. To hell with it. Failure wasn't something they could afford right now. The arrival of Agriculture forces had been the last thing they'd been expecting. A lot of the troops had almost given up hope. Better to die here around the joviality while making a difference than to mope back in Sen's camp.

"It's now or never," Mouri said, tearing half his bread loaf off with his teeth, discarding the rest. "Let's not be pussies about this."

"We know," said Junko. "Sure is a lot more difficult to think straight when you have this kind of pressure on you though, isn't it?" He eyed the people around him nervously in a fidgety motion.

"The more you think about it, the worse your anxiety will be," Kagami said. He finished his soup, looking like a prince with his dark hair tied in a short ponytail, even with all the dirt and grime on his face. The exemplary noble, appearance wise.

Nanbu locked eyes on Junko. "And the more you look around like that, the more attention we draw to ourselves, and the even shorter amount of time we have."

Mouri stood, cracking his knuckles. Balding and muscular, he had a friendly, almost boyish face, but to assume he had anything against violence was a terrible judgment to make. He did that part well, and that was why he'd volunteered for this part of the assignment. He'd always been one quick to act. "Let's get on with it then, shenshen. Who gets to be the lucky mark tonight?"

He looked straight at Nanbu as he said it. Nanbu scanned the area until his sight fell on an important looking man headed towards their direction, likely a squadron or unit leader by the manner others parted out of his way. He'd pass them and wouldn't expect to be ambushed at all. It would make for the best distraction, but also make it that much more likely they'd be chased down.

Nanbu nodded at the target. "See that man approaching us from behind? Junko, you fucking baboon, don't be so obvious! That man has to be the leader of a squadron or something, I'd bet it on the Empress herself. He's your best option."

"Say less." Mouri sat back down, waiting for the man to get closer.

Nanbu's heart was pounding heavier and heavier in his chest. The man appeared to slow his steps to a mere crawl. The fire seemed to grow angrier at his side. He came to a halt, and Nanbu feared he might be changing route. It was only a brief stall, however, and then he was almost upon them.

"Kori, Shoda, Junko and Orin, have my back. Kagami, Nanbu. Run."

The man came up behind Mouri, still focused ahead of him with a glowering face. Suddenly, with amazing speed, Mouri spun on him, sending a fist like a boulder into his face and knocking him to the side with a satisfying *crack*.

The man fell, grunting loudly as he hit the ground. All attention within a radius of at least fifty feet turned towards the commotion as Nanbu and Kagami jumped back.

"Four corners!" Mouri commanded, and the men around him backed up to create a small square perimeter around him.

"What the hell?" Nanbu shouted, parroting similar exclamations of alarm around him.

When the men realized it was a high-ranking soldier who'd been injured, they all cried out in anger. Then they began rushing them.

That was their cue. Nanbu and Kagami took off behind them, racing up the hill towards headquarters. Kagami raced behind him, and they refrained from withdrawing their swords in case they hadn't yet garnered any suspicion. *Unlikely*. Nanbu laughed to himself.

"I hope you're ready for this!" Kagami said, almost neck and neck with him. He glanced back to see the swarm of men joining the fighting.

"No idea exactly how we'll pull this off, but I'm ready!"

At the top of the hill, they met the expected. Elite guards were swarming around the tent. They looked confused at first but were quick to regard the approaching men suspiciously.

"Halt! What's your business?"

"What's the deal?" Kagami asked. "We just want a word with our commanders. Those Agriculture bastards sure made a rude entrance!"

The guards did not care to entertain any of it. They took two steps forward and warned them to stop or be cut down.

*Shit*, Nanbu thought, unsheathing his weapon. This was it. Thirty men outside the main tent. *That's an impenetrable wall if I've ever seen one.* "Split up!"

The two took sharp turns to the left and right. The guards followed only with their eyes, standing their ground. Nanbu rushed in to slice at the first guard. The guard parried, but lost his footing and Nanbu managed to take him down. That was pure luck. He wasn't so lucky with the next fellow, who sawed through his left arm nice and smoothly. Nanbu cried out, letting all his rage and emotions carry him. Using the few seconds the man's sword was buried into his arm, he cut him down too. He heard Kagami let out a gurgling shout, but he would not look over. Every ounce and fiber of his being was focused on this one task. He wouldn't fail.

*Mouri!* His mind cried out. He could only think about honoring his friend's death. The man who'd fought alongside him as children against bullies in the noble court. They'd trudged through hard times together as they became men, and their families depended on the outcome of this war. That was why it was no question that they'd support Sen when the young lord had offered them aid and glory in fighting for his rule. Mouri's family had hit hard times with debts owed on their land to the Yomenuura family. Sen offered to forgive them. Nanbu's own gambling houses had been in decline as well. No longer.

What Sen had done for them, they'd repay. Who was the rightful heir and who wasn't, didn't matter to Nanbu. Only that Sen was victorious in the end. Agriculture had made that difficult. Hell, from his own mouth, Lord Sen had told them slaying a general was their only shot at seeing the next day to the end. Nanbu couldn't fail.

Something hard knocked against his head, and he blacked out for mere seconds. He fell, and when he awoke, he saw stars. The world spun, but before he could recover an intense agony like he had never experienced exploded in his abdomen. He'd been stabbed. His stomach bubbled with pain like molten lava, and his muscles gave out. He looked ahead of him, the tent mere paces away. He'd never make it now. *I've failed.* The darkness enveloped him.

Mouri crested the hill to see his fallen friend, impaled by a spear through his gut. This didn't stop him. He'd soon have plenty of time with Nanbu in the afterlife anyway. Ahead of him, inside of the central tent, that was his stopping point. The others had managed to keep him alive with their four corners formation as they made for the hill. He should have died with them, but when the attacking soldiers stood back to allow an officer the privilege of killing him, they'd given Mouri just enough time to escape. It had been narrow, evidenced by the long gash on his leg which, if these guards didn't take him, his wound surely would.

Elite guards shouted for him to halt. He ignored them. They were coalescing in the center now, trying to form a wall. He'd just have to force his way through before the gaps closed for good. Ten guards stood directly between him and his prey. Ten men was the number it took to match his strength, and he'd not gained that reputation without merit.

Men dove at his side. Mouri paid them no heed. He prepared a wide swing and let it crash against those in front of him, bursting through their ranks. A spear entered his left arm. No worries, wouldn't be needed. A sword sliced at his abdomen, but he kept forward. His speed and size made him unstoppable, and just in time he closed the gap, the guards screaming behind him.

"*Haaa!*" he cried. Nothing could stop him now! Nothing and no one. Whoever was closest to him when he entered the tent would be the first to die. Then he'd take down as many as he could after that. For Lord Sen and his men.

For Nanbu.

The tent flaps parted just in time. A gray haired officer with a muscular body stood there, oblivious to his fate. This was the center army's main general. Mouri didn't care to remember his name. He raised up his weapon behind him before thrusting it into the man's left eye. It went in, breaking bones. His expression of shock was visible for only seconds before he toppled over, and Mouri knew the feeling of victory at last.

# Penetrate

Inside the tent, Aiya staggered back from the horrific sight. Koji started in unison beside her. As Honji fell, she caught the red silver glint of the sword deeply lodged in the general's face. His armor crashed on dirt, flying towards the simulation table before lying still and limp. Like that, he was dead.

Dasuke rushed towards his fallen body.

"No....Honji-shen!"

The guardsmen came rushing in from the other end, and in moments the stuffy room shattered into total chaos.

Aiya flinched, sharply drawing in breath. Ueko and Tsugo stood rooted, their voices stolen from them.

"Who did this? How did this happen?" Dasuke looked up to the guards in rage. "How was this allowed to happen?"

Before they could respond, he leaped up outside the tent and began yelling at the surrounding guards. "HOW WAS THIS ALLOWED TO HAPPEN?"

One moment General Honji had been a strong veteran of war standing before them, and now he lay in a pool of his own blood.

Aiya went numb, floating as if she were a spectator. Bodies in her periphery became invisible, and only the bludgeoned face of Honji remained.

With all the strength her mind could muster, Aiya tore herself from her sickened trance. She followed Dasuke outside, where a few other elite guards stood over the dead body of a rather large and muscular man. Dasuke was throwing insults all around when Aiya noticed, about twenty feet away, two other men lay dead at the top of the hill. Elite guards?

Johori moved in front of Tsugo as Masuo's blade flew in his direction from its scabbard.

"If you think to get out of this alive, don't be mistaken. We will kill you and every one of your soldiers down to the last man!"

"Move that blade one inch closer and your life will be forfeit," Johori threatened.

Fun moved in between them. "Stand down, Masuo. Look closer, these three men are clearly from Sen's camp. This must be that Aneken's doing."

Coming out of his rage, Masuo studied the burnt-orange armor they wore indicative of both East and West Forgery. Golden helms lay scattered near the heads of each of the men.

"The helms were stolen and used to sneak into our own ranks undercover. An unruly tactic as old as war itself. Somehow they managed to pull it off."

A guardsman fell to his knees before them. "My lord, we apologize for our egregious blunder! We will take our lives right here if we must!"

"Leave that for later and on your feet! Spread my order around the camp that we are to enter night watch formation!" Ueko shouted, causing them to stumble back up. "We've got a war to win first. Sen is going to die regardless."

Honji's body had been dragged outside the tent for all to see. He was a grisled mess. Aiya's throat clenched. Ueko grabbed and held Honji's head with one hand, sitting on her knees beside him and looking over his corpse. Slowly, she began stroking his scalp. There was nothing to be done, no one daring to speak.

"Leave us," Ueko said, not looking up. Aiya studied the others and then turned to Koji, who was equally perplexed.

"Leave us until morning!" Ueko hurled her burning hot stare at everyone before her eyes landed on Tsugo. Eyes that nearly seemed to gleam.

Tsugo nodded and turned away. Shortly after, the rest of them started to do the same. Aiya was shaken from her trance, if only by their head commander's sudden outburst. Even one as cold-hearted as Ueko could experience tender emotions, could perform dojetsu, honoring her subordinate with her grief. She would sacrifice sleep and remain at his side until sunrise. It was an honor performed by head commanders and reserved for the highest of generals in war. Watching her cradle Honji's head, Ueko's small frame appeared vulnerable, even fragile.

On the way back to their tents not a word was uttered. Between the Ginju, no one knew what words to say, or if they did, how they might say it.

*Even one such as Ueko honors others besides herself.*

Aiya entered Agriculture's HQ and laid down on a mat in the far corner of the room. She thought about how well their situation bodes for Sen, even if it only left Ueko one general short. Head resting upon the firm mattress, she found herself fearful of falling asleep alone. No, she was being silly. She was a Ginju, the most fearsome of all. And yet, tonight, her own mortality was forced into view right in front of her. She couldn't defend herself while sleeping, nor from any surprise attacks. Ira's words from the Year's-End Festival returned to her with ominous clarity: '*To think, we're almost like the Kiru compared to them, and yet we can be disposed of by the same illnesses as the unblessed. The heavens surely mock us.*'

What was more was Tsugo's demands of marriage. That had been almost equally unexpected. Almost. There was more to this battle, to this war, and to their cause backing it that she could not anticipate. She felt once again like a child in the noble courts.

Some hours later, she slept.

From afar, Koji caught a strikingly pretty woman watching HQ at the foot of the hill. She wore a tight robe cut short above her knees, barely discernible in the darkness. The clothing of a camp prostitute. They locked eyes for the span of a few seconds before she briskly walked away. Koji followed her, almost stumbling down the hill. By the time he made it down she was ready to disappear into the clusters of camp tents. When she didn't stop he called, "Hey, you. Halt!"

She turned to glower at him.

*What's her issue? Could I be intruding on something?* Koji thought.

"My *name* is Kefa, and my services are finished for today. And I don't see how it can still be stiff after seeing that." She pointed to headquarters.

"I saw you staring at me, so I thought something was up."

"Something up?" the woman raised an eyebrow. "I was just curious like everyone else. Why did you feel the need to chase after me?"

"You're the prostitute who was assaulted the other night. I heard about the incident and some people pointed you out earlier today."

"Are you asking if I'm alright? I'm genuinely amazed that two nobles have so much care for a lowly person such as myself."

They looked at each other for a few seconds before Koji diverted his gaze elsewhere.

"So you were looking for service. I'm generally not a fan of potential clients who beat around the bush, but it beats being assaulted any day. Find me in the morning before dawn and I'll be all washed up, and at your service."

She said the last part with particular grace then turned to go.

"Look, I'm usually not one to be indirect. I'm here to ask...why do you still do it?" Koji asked. "Your profession, I mean. I don't mean to press, and I know it's only a means to get by. I mean, nobody exactly chooses what they do.

Sometimes you're forced to do things. Still, haven't you ever wanted something more normal among common folk? A home, a husband, children?" The thought of his father forced the respectability of such a thing from his heart, but then he remembered Kisane and Asaya, and longing warmth came rushing back.

"Normal does not always mean good. There's nothing moral about bringing children into a world like this. No, I've come a long way from where I was, and I don't for one second want to go back and live a more 'common' life. My reasons are my own."

She seemed to be about to turn again, then said, "Don't assume I'm at all a good person though. No matter their status, nobody in this world is who you think they are. Even your own mother."

"My mother definitely isn't great. I had the privilege of understanding that from a young age."

"At least you know the truth about her," Kefa answered as she departed. "And hopefully yourself."

Koji watched her disappear around the tents. He felt almost hollow, unsteady. He realized he was *unsure*, anxious for what the winds would toss down on them from here on out. He hadn't written any poems since the day Ira had collapsed.

"Couldn't sleep either?"

He turned to face Risako walking towards him, a mere ten paces away. "Following me?"

"Don't flatter yourself." Risako stood in front of him now. The fires of camp reflected off her face, fires that should have been put out by now which fed off the sullen atmosphere. "And no, I couldn't. I'm not sure how many of us will."

Nothingness passed between them as Koji strained his head toward the stars. "Why do I get the impression that you're the responsible one out of your siblings?"

"Perhaps it's the mutual respect we've come to share for each other. Even if Totane is the oldest."

She was as any other noble, yet shared more with Koji than most he had known in River. She was a Ginju like him, but she was also, to some extent, an adhesive between her two siblings, even her greater family. He examined it in the way she carried herself, the slight aura, still in its infancy, that emanated from her and enticed acknowledgement from those around her. "We haven't known each other that long, but I think perhaps you are the better version of myself." He raised his eyes to HQ, then returned them to her. She could see Honji's death had shaken him as much as herself. "I understand Ira puts the trust of his heart and soul into this Republic. When he wraps his mind around something, there's no undoing it. I suppose I am in part responsible for that." *No, that would be taking far too arrogant of me. It is only because of Ira's immutable spirit.* For some reason, his mind took him to their entanglement at their old estate. Aiya had somehow learned to retain alignment with the river at full strength for several minutes. She'd sparred with the very girl in front of him, who might be considered both of their equals. It hadn't been enough. His sister had struggled the most, lost to the darkness of the river, and became weakened by it. Had it been a real fight, she'd no doubt be dead. Of this, Koji was certain. She would never admit it, most of all not to Ira. He suspected he was the last not to have his image of her tainted in some way, at least that was how she saw it. Regardless, none of them were safe, her most of all. "Even Aiya is at least enticed by the idea. Whether we can bring it into fruition or not, my only concern is to see them both alive and well by the end of this. My full loyalty is for them alone."

"That much about you is obvious," Risako replied. "If it's any condolence, my hope is to achieve our cause through little violence. This does not have to be the war we think it does."

Koji raised an eyebrow, then adopted a small grin. "Well, I don't feel it's my place to call you naive just yet, but that may be where you and I differ. Even so, I can't deny my envy that you can believe such a thing is possible."

# Alliance

Aiya woke at dawn to the busying in Ueko's camp. For Sen, the night would have been welcomed indefinitely. Before the sun had peered over the horizon, West Forgery was already packing its tents in a fury. A stewing bloodthirst hung in the air. The Jodai were ravenous, ready for slaughter.

A ghostly mist formed dew on the grass, while cotton masses of clouds rowed overhead. Halfway through dawn, the east's formations were set. Aiya raised a hand to block the increasing flood of sunlight, gazing upon the enemy. She noticed his soldiers did not move with the intimidation their enemies expected. General Fun made his way to the front of the central division's lines. The plan was to execute a full force frontal assault and have units from either side cut through the left and right division, taking Sen from behind while applying pressure on all sides. The loss of Honji had affected their troops' morale, but it had also served to strengthen them with anger. Whatever Sen had hoped to accomplish with the move had backfired. *So they believe.*

She hadn't noticed Tsugo nearing her. "You're still holding out hope. I can see it in your frame."

The wisdom in his eyes and matching height revealed something like a thinner, kinder Shozhu, what Shozhu might have been in another life. "You're right. I guess it's only because I have no other choice. It's a foolish hope."

"Foolishness is good. Retain that quality in yourself, you'll need it if you plan on changing the world around you. Don't give up, and you might be surprised by how the tables can turn."

Aiya squeezed her fist, strangely helpless. *Heavens*, she prayed, *give Sen a way out. Just a little longer.*

Just then, she spotted Sen in his robes riding through his ranks.

*When did he...?*

She hadn't seen him coming from HQ. Had she missed that, or had Sen joined his ranks before the morning began? Sen slowed as he arrived at the center of his army, grinding to a halt as he looked up at them from his position.

"What is he doing? Throwing himself in the middle of battle isn't the same as an honor duel!"

"Perhaps he means to throw us off," said Tsugo, though even he did not sound sure.

Sen remained, barely space to make him out between the other soldiers. The confusion he'd brought upon those on the hill was quickly disregarded. "The boy chooses to die with his men, like one of them," said General Masuo. "*Heh.* At least he has that much honor."

Lieutenant Dasuke sneered.

Tension rose between the two waiting armies until it burst, and the two forces charged at the decree of their generals. Thousands of men came rushing at each other, intent on murder. Spears flew, swords clashed, and the previously tranquil land transformed into a breeding ground for flying spit, blood, and death. With that, the second day of battle began.

Aiya and the rest of the Ginju observed the battle play out from the hill above. They all had switched into the burnt-orange armor of Forgery. Next to them were Tsugo and the same guardsmen, who had gone stiff. Ueko assumed the same position as yesterday, next to her daughter. No one said much. The death of Honji was still fresh on everyone's minds.

Ueko had remained in her sitting position, tending to Honji for the entire night. The other Forgery generals had not taken his death any better, and Aiya hoped the exhaustion would somehow interfere before Sen could be taken down. It felt bizarre that Honji's death was, in reality, a good thing, that the brains oozing from the loyal man's face were cause for celebration, but none of Agriculture commented on it.

"How much longer must we suffer this nonsense?" Hasa asked, to no one, or perhaps everyone.

Ueko didn't answer as Hasa pounded her fist on the seat. Aiya shifted uncomfortably.

"Die already! Useless! Surrender, *swine*. Die like Yahida and Hasu, scum!"

The battle beneath was unfolding as expected. Their opponents were like hens for the slaughter.

Soon, however, Aiya noticed something strange. Eastern forces were gradually being pushed back, but Ueko's men were not making much progress forward. Then, it turned out, they were not being pushed back, but instead pushed into themselves. More and more, they became tighter and the charging men's progress came to a crunching stop.

"This could be it," Johori said, stepping forward in alarm. The deep urgency in his voice aroused Aiya's nervousness. "His lines are collapsing in on themselves."

"No," Aiya replied, watching closer. It was half a plea, half an observation. "They're not collapsing. They're not even moving anymore...."

"It's a defensive formation," declared Tsugo.

Sen's army had compressed in on themselves, arranging their ranks in a criss-cross pattern formation. For every man with a forward facing shield, the one behind him stood with his shield facing right or left, while the Jodai behind him would have his facing forward. Aiya traced the pattern through the entire army, and suddenly the entire hilltop realized this was part of Sen's strategy.

Ueko's advance came to an abrupt halt. Sen's forces were holding their ground. Every once in a while, they would briefly push the enemy out and then fall back in line where they stood before. It was clear: the wall they formed around their entire ranks was impenetrable.

A wave rushed feebly over Aiya, one she at first did not recognize, then understood it as relief. Not only was the battle being drawn out, but the human stronghold was resulting in far fewer casualties for the Forgery lordling. Fewer deaths of good men. Men who surely didn't deserve the same fate as the nobles of River who had defied her father.

"How did they set that up so fast?" said Risako.

Tsugo pinched his beard. "He must have had this planned from the start. He knew with our arrival his time was limited. Now he means to stall. It is still simply a matter of time before he falls." He turned to Ueko, who'd become mute while she concentrated on the field below, giving Aiya's silent pleas at least some measure of hope. "Of course, I haven't forgotten, or retracted, my original stipulations, my lady."

Ueko faced him, the first time she'd moved the entire day. Aiya was not sure she could have held those hard, piercing eyes as long as Tsugo did. "You are a testing man, Lord Tsugo."

She turned to Hasa, who, unblinking, zoned in on the battle below like a hawk.

"Hasa, dear, how badly do you want this foolishness to be finished with already?"

Hasa, without turning, said, "I want it over, mother. We all do. Sen is a disruption to the entirety of Forgery right now. He *dares* challenge me as heir."

"Indeed, for that he must suffer. What would you be willing to do to make that happen?"

Hasa looked at her. "Anything, mother."

Ueko stepped back and gave Tsugo an expectant look.

"I am humbled by your presence, Hasa," Tsugo said, giving a bow. "Agriculture and I are in full support of your efforts against your brother, and we greatly cherish a union between your province and ours. Therefore, I would ask for your hand in my son's marriage. The bond you two would share would be the progenitor of an alliance between

Forgery and Agriculture, and becoming one, we would stand as the strongest province in all Egaisha."

Time ceased as Hasa mused over his words. "You're proposing a marriage between your eldest son and me? How does that get rid of Sen?"

Hasa's sudden ability to articulate knocked Aiya off guard. Her entire demeanor had transformed from the frothing creature she had been before. Now she stared with eyes that held complete reason within them.

"Think of it as your repayment for our aiding you in this battle. Not only will it guarantee continued good relations between our provinces, but it positions both of us for even more power in the future."

Hasa watched him for a minute. "This is certainly unexpected. I assume that what you really desire is my mother's consent."

"You are the true ruler of Forgery, Lady Hasa. I by no means want to rush your decision, but such a thing should be discussed before we strip Sen's life away."

"Why didn't you bring this up earlier? It sounds like you are trying to force my answer. We have no business with Agriculture in the future. Our weapons deal will be enough."

"Now, Hasa, consider the advantage. Your marriage will benefit you." Ueko stepped in between the two.

"I assure you, my lady, I only want what's best for both of us. I want us to come together willingly, to strengthen each other."

"If I must." Hasa turned back to battle. "What. The. Hell. *Is that*?" Hasa was back up screaming again as their troops below struggled to advance even a foot.

This formation Sen had thought of was actually stopping their advance. *But for how long*? The sun was still rising, which meant they had all day to hack away at it. Her underarms grew moist.

Watching the battle from above was exhausting. Ueko and Tsugo both continued to make calculations and alternative battle plans with the other commanders. Aiya could only watch and listen, unable to offer true insight on the matter. Most of Ueko's troops were committed to the assault, while a smattering of small units held back directly beneath them as they observed from HQ.

As the day progressed, Ueko and Tsugo's forces made marginal progress towards penetrating the formation's center where Sen stayed guarded. Clouds covered them overhead, shielding them from the sun. A few made solemn remarks about a possible Wailstorm.

"Placing himself in the middle of battle at the start was a move based on pure intellect," Risako said. "Had he stayed positioned at HQ, we definitely would have breached it by now and taken his head. We'll have to take down at least half his soldiers to have a chance at getting him, and that formation is rock solid."

Ueko and Hasa lost their minds. More than once Ueko had to stalk off as Hasa entered into another fit of screaming rage. Sen's resilience was proving to be detrimental for his sister, and Aiya wondered if she'd be the cause of her own death. The rest of them were becoming more uncomfortable as her fits grew more animated and depraved. She spat, blew snot from her nose, threw things at the battlefield, then finally attempted to snatch a guardsman's sword for herself before taking off with it. The Jodai caught her swiftly and Ueko had to restrain herself from strangling Hasa where she writhed in the Jodai's arms.

The long day finally drew to an early close as the gray sky grew darker. Aiya supposed they had maybe an hour and a half before they'd be forced to retreat in the darkness. Rain clouds set in like a wide blanket, rendering the sun invisible for hours now. The fighting grew more intense, though they'd only taken out a tenth of Sen's troops. Sen's forces reacted far more sluggish compared to the start of the day. Tsugo mused they'd only have one more day in them before they'd collapse from exhaustion.

Aiya started. Sen waved the same flag from the day before, both arms swaying back and forth above his head, its red color dark and muted. His troops didn't budge as western soldiers continued batting their swords against his shields, but Sen waved his flag on.

"*NOOOOO!*" Hasa screamed, while the Jodai next to her grabbed her and covered her mouth.

"This chickenshit performance must end," Ueko said. She turned to Tsugo and searched him for a long while. "Lord Tsugo, I've accepted your request for my daughter's hand, along with the other terms we came to agreement on before your arrival to these hills. Two of my finest generals and three of my lieutenants have fallen to Sen's tactics. I have come to the conclusion that we have put too much on the line."

"What are you trying to say?" Tsugo asked.

"All my best commanders are dead, save General Fun. I respectfully ask that you send one of your own officers against Sen to take his head."

Aiya started. Despite the raging battle below, the tense atmosphere crumbled, becoming deathly still. Aiya hadn't foreseen this. Not to mention that the task Ueko was asking for was required of Hasa. Surely Tsugo would refuse.

"Will you honor my request?"

Tsugo thought for a bit. Aiya held her breath.

"Totane, show your future wife what you are capable of."

# Fight

Tabeni Totane felt an overwhelming wave of nausea, anger, and anxiety rush over him all at once.

Anger for the fact that Ueko had the audacity to suggest their own tribute, anxiety for pondering how he might handle this predicament, and nausea at the thought of what would happen if it went wrong.

"Show her why Agriculture has thrived for as long as we have," his father demanded.

Totane's eyes fell on Hasa awkwardly. She weighed him closely for the first time with great interest, inflicting him with a rare sense of intimidation. A thick layer of disgust ran like sludge down his insides. Her eyes seemed to peer into, no, *through* his own. She and Sen both had the eyes of their mother. Totane gained his senses and went to bow.

"My Lady, allow this to be my first honorary act in your name which may persuade your heart." *And let's hope you die of a stray arrow first,* he finished.

Hasa turned back to the battlefield. "Go," she said.

Totane turned to his father and nodded before giving brief glances to his siblings and the River Ginju. A guard pulled a horse forward for him.

"Do you really have this much faith in him?" Ueko asked suspiciously.

"Ueko-shen, would I send out my own son to die?"

Totane felt ten pounds heavier settling onto the horse. Suddenly the battlefield ahead appeared more chaotic, more violent. It seemed closer than ever before. Totane felt his hand on his scabbard which, for the first time since he'd set foot on these hills, was slick with sweat.

"Totane," Johori called from his side. He looked over to his brother and sister and saw remarkably unconcerned faces. If they believed in him, he'd believe in himself.

Without a word, he nodded and raised the reins on his horse.

"Totane," Aiya said.

He glanced at her face too. Too much concern.

*Dammit, don't make me more nervous than I already am.*

"Sen's a dead man," he declared, with as much contempt as he could muster.

He reined the horse into a trot toward the battlefield, absorbing the blast of cold wind down the hill. It felt good against his profuse sweat as his insides warmed by the second. The men on the battlefield had ceased fighting and were watching him as if he were the Empress herself. Totane could make out Sen's face more clearly now. It was a determined, bold face. His ally was being forced to challenge him, and Sen accepted that challenge running towards him with open arms, dropping the flag to his feet. A subordinate came and quickly retrieved it.

Totane kept his focus on Sen as he rode through the ranks until the two were but twenty paces apart. He came to a skittering halt while noticing Sen's hand had yet to brush his weapon.

*How was this supposed to work again?* Totane grew slightly flustered. He couldn't help but think he'd forgotten some essential element of this timeless tradition.

Sen didn't let his focus slip for even a moment. Totane cursed. Gray clouds brooded above, foreboding thunder sounding in the background. Their stare down was going longer than it had between Sen and Lieutenant Toru. Finally, the Forgery lord's hand went to his sword.

"Agriculture's aid will surely be appreciated by Forgery for generations to come," he said.

Totane looked him up and down, parsing through the words. *It seems he's being subtle*, he thought. Did Sen understand this situation, throwing in a reminder of their alliance? Could he be oblivious, fearing for his life?

Totane cursed again, drew his sword and held it up to his right side. Sen did the same.

"I don't doubt it," Totane replied, and the two charged.

Totane was as skilled as the best Jodai warrior without his Ginju abilities; with them, he'd make minced meat of Sen in seconds. *No, this is perfect*, he thought. He couldn't kill Sen, but Sen could certainly kill him. Though it would surely blow his cover under Ueko's eyes, if he intended to stay alive afterwards.

He realized the obvious option. He'd only injure Sen and force Hasa to do the honors. That was when they'd make their big betrayal and he would save Sen at the last second, creating an opening for him to slay his sister.

Totane swung back his weapon and prepared to cleave Sen in two from the neck up. Judging from the skill Sen displayed in previous fights, he'd dodge it.

*We didn't come this far to see your death! I didn't train all those years and become this strong merely to kill the likes of you! So don't you dare die!*

The two men closed in on each other, and the clash of their swords rang loud in their ears. Totane's sword was nearly knocked from his grip. He barely managed to hold on as his steed skidded to a halt and turned around to face Sen again.

*What in the hell is that power?* He raised his weapon in front of him, amazed by his opponent's blow. Sen had already recovered and was making for his second attack. He wasn't a large man, slightly shorter than Totane himself, but he packed the strength of an ox.

Their horses rushed each other again. Now they were within arm's reach. Totane jerked the reins to the right, creating a bit of distance at the last second. With his left hand he made for an upwards swing. It would slice Sen's right side from hip to shoulder and leave him dead from blood loss in seconds. Sen mirrored his move and avoided the attack, then sharply spun back on Totane and came straight for him from his right side.

Unprepared, Totane barely had time to block Sen's sweeping attack. He caught it with his own upturned blade, allowing them to glide off each other. Sen sliced clean air.

The collision left Totane alarmed and breathless. *He's incredibly fast!*

The Forgery lord was easily in a class of his own, standing head and shoulders above almost all the opponents Totane had ever fought. Almost.

Injuring him without relying on his deity's power was now a difficult conundrum. If he did decide to draw it, he'd rise too far above Sen in martial might, and any delicate blows he might use to simply break a bone or two would require utmost precision in the heat of the moment.

Totane changed tactics and aimed to carve through the meat of Sen's leg. A familiar sensation of exploding pain in his abdomen staved off his otherwise perfectly timed strike. He jerked forward, his blade narrowly missing and swinging into empty air. The motion threw him off his horse and he slammed into the hard earth, tumbling but managing to keep hold of his weapon. Celestial bodies and flowing patterns swirled through his vision, flashing hot red.

He lurched back into an upwards sitting position, hoping to the heavens he wouldn't be stampeded on. Sen remained on his horse, merely feet away. He wasn't watching Totane or coming in for a finishing blow. Instead his head jerked around the surrounding men, who had resumed shouting in angry voices.

Still confused, Totane's hand went to the searing pain in his stomach. He felt tender warmth and wetness. It came away bloody. Looking down, he saw the arrow that had burrowed straight through his stomach and felt overwhelming nausea.

*It's fine*, he thought. *Concentrate*!

He silenced out the escalating noise around him, focusing solely on his throbbing belly. He did not focus on the pain, but acknowledged it. He was aware of his injury and of the life leaking out of him, but he was no longer in his own body. He floated away further and further, until all he perceived was the life force within himself in its constant 'change'. His organs, tissues, and bodily fluids in constant movement, at work within themselves, like farmers in a field. They gave, they took, the leaking contents of his stomach like spilling water against his ragged breath.

Agriculture, the art of cultivation, gave him life. It granted all life, sustained it. Totane, one with his deity, became like a god of the Tarshani religion, with the power to bestow life and smite it out. Power surged through his limbs and head. The muscles and organs torn by the arrow knitted themselves back to their natural form, and when he opened his eyes-turned-green, his vision was no longer blurry. He was no longer at the feet of his steed either, but on the back of his horse as the soldier who rode it in front of him made his way through the ranks of increasingly riotous men.

"Lord Totane, are you well? Can you hear me?" the Agriculture soldier asked. Totane did not recognize him and reasoned he was a foot soldier who had thought quickly and gathered the both of them on top of Totane's horse, fleeing the scene. Totane sat behind him, unbothered by the bumpiness of the ride.

"Yes, I've healed myself." He looked back to where he and Sen had been fighting, but the large circle of space was no longer there. Only chaos.

"Where's Sen? Why has the fighting continued?"

"That arrow wasn't some freak stray, it was aimed at you from one of Sen's soldiers, my lord! Doing so, they broke the one rule of an honor duel, and now any soldier will take Lord Sen's head! He's gone to retreat, now that his formations have broken and we outnumber him so drastically!"

*An eye for an eye*, Totane thought, considering he'd just been sent to kill Sen by his own mother. "The Oshidai spoke of this, didn't he? Sen's getting his own turn of chaos."

"Right now's not the time for talk of religion, my lord. We may have been forced to advance into the second stage of this war. Lord Tsugo would demand our speedy appearance at once."

# Chase

J ohori watched his brother being carried back uphill. The guards gathered around as the Jodai soldier made it to the hilltop and trotted into their ranks. Totane appeared as he always had even as he seemed to be fighting off death: a warrior of awe and inspiration, sitting as straight as his body would allow on top of his horse. Johori's brother jumped down, holding two halves of the arrow in his hands that had been shot through him. Pain contorted his face, but Johori knew better.

Ueko all but lunged beside him.

"You shouldn't be standing!"

Totane was slightly bent over, still clutching his abdomen smeared with blood. "I'll live, it was only a graze. Sen's signed his own death now, that's all that matters."

He was a convincing actor. Watching Totane limp as if he was still wounded, Johori could have been fooled into having as much concern for his brother as he did for Sen. But Sen was in immediate danger, and the roar of men on the battlefield had never been louder. No matter how many opponents he'd defeated before, no one could triumph against fifteen-thousand swords.

"It seems Sen has begun to retreat, Ueko-shen," a guard pointed out.

Ueko's arms were crossed. "Then this stalemate has come to an end."

Tsugo tended to Totane, holding him up steady and begging him to stop and rest. Totane shook his head, fake grimacing here and there. "You've done your part, Totane, now you must be laid down!"

He led Totane to Agriculture's tent, giving the rest of them a brief look that told them to follow. Johori looked at Risako, saw that she had already begun moving, and followed his father to the tent. He heard Aiya and Koji follow after him. Johori prayed, although he was convinced Ueko was fooled by their act.

Johori focused on Totane's back, hunched but still bearing the weight of their cause, the cause in which any who claimed themselves a citizen of Agriculture gave their lives. His brother would do anything for it. Such was the strength of his conviction, a strength which Johori had been denied at birth, a piece of themselves his siblings had inherited, but which he was forever missing.

He'd grown up seeing many of the places and things Totane saw in their youth. Hokoto and Deba. The destitution of Stone and the wealth of Sanaba. Worst of all, the savage exploitation of their mother. Yet, in his heart, Johori carried a heavy burden of doubts, invisible to his siblings, yet crushing on himself. He'd contributed to the revolution, but deep within him, his only concerns lay with the simple progression of living, ensuring his own people were happy, safe, satisfied. He'd told Totane so, once after they witnessed the burned villages for the first time. All he saw in their future was the burning up of their rebellious land. Revolution might not be the wisest path. A path of tragedy. That was what he intended to say, but none of it came out so clear, such was his fear. Fear of being called a coward, of holding the revolution back. Totane just took his concerns as nothing more than youthful apprehension, hugging and reassuring him.

The zealotry of his brother and sister ran deep, and so he would never dare express to them his true feelings. Even if all he ever wanted was a wife and security, he still found himself following, his pensive gaze always at their backs.

In the past few days, however, he'd tasted an unusual deep relief from his heartfelt troubles, particularly on the previous day after the day's battle had ended. Shamefully, he still clung on to the hope that something *more* might emerge from this battle, something to satisfy his selfishness, more fulfilling than Sen's victory which would only lead them into a revolution that would surely end with the lives of many loved ones lost.

Truthfully, he desired the security of his province, his clan, and a woman to share it with. He looked to Aiya behind them, unable to move his eyes. She met him with a look of concern. Even that look on her was enchanting. He turned, staunchly keeping his blush hidden.

*You have to enjoy the life you live before it's gone*, General Yko would tell him sporadically through a fit of coughs, lifting his smoking leaf with satisfaction. Johori often wondered if such words were no more solid than the smoke Yko recited them through, how sincerely he could honor his own desires, and those of the Republic. An impossible task.

They entered the tent. Once they all were in, Tsugo let Totane free and turned around, facing Johori, Risako, Aiya, Koji and his firstborn son. They stood around their High Lord whose focused eyes passed over them briefly. There was an intense air of finality between them feeding into a dark intuition that made Johori sweat.

"It's looking bad for Sen," said Tsugo. "This is the final stage. We will allow the High Lord to escape. He is sure to flee to his fortified city, and once we arrive there, we shall turn on Ueko's army."

"We can't wait that long," Aiya interjected.

Johori turned to her, piqued by the boldness in her voice.

"I've got a feeling Ueko will send special units after Sen, the ones she's seemed to have kept to the sidelines for the entirety of this battle. She won't chance his escape, even if it's unlikely. It may not be optimal to play our hand at these hills, but if you send the five of us out there now, we can get Sen to safety while our forces put a stop to Ueko now. Sen still has over six-thousand men, so our casualties might be higher than if we waited, but they'll still be low."

*Of course, escaping from six-thousand swords with the aid of Ginju and another army would be much better odds*, Johori thought. *So she's been paying attention.*

She was savvy. Intelligent. A Ginju. Johori's chest fluttered.

Tsugo only smiled.

"Well said, Aiya-shen. You'll cut Sen a path to his stronghold. Go after him, fend away any pursuing troops as soon as you are in his vicinity and not a second sooner. Agriculture troops will be alerted before you make your first strike. At that point we shall quell this battlefield."

Koji nodded, his face hard. "It's the soundest plan to me."

"So this is where Hijimata ends and the real battle begins," Totane said. "We'll protect him with our lives."

Johori steeled himself for what was to come. After this, there would be no going back on revolution.

Aiya saddled herself on her horse, brushing at a raindrop plopping against her forehead. The first one today. Though hard to tell, it was four past noon, and the slight breeze had become considerably colder. The clouds above rolled in with menace now.

Tsugo approached Ueko's back, who fiercely watched the battlefield, limbs twitching at nearly every utterance from the commanders around her. She turned to face him before he'd gotten five paces within her reach.

"Lord Tsugo. I must ask that you not be angry with my previous request. How is your son's condition?"

"He demands to ride back out to battle. He placed his honor on his vow to see Sen dead and please Lady Hasa. Even I cannot reason with him."

Ueko pursed her lips. "I suppose I cannot blame the young man," she replied. "Nor will I stop him. I'm not sure what he is to possess his level of ability, but he fought Sen better than any of my commanders. Regardless, Sen was able to slip through the pandemonium unscathed. I've sent the Haaku and Dasuke units after him. We won't allow him to revive himself in the east cities and drag this war out even longer."

*She's a shrewd one, as I anticipated*, Aiya thought. Ueko had chosen to send her head-retrievers before informing Agriculture of her actions. Perhaps it was unwise to allow a foreign province, even an ally, claim of her own son now that he was within reach. *We can't gain your full trust with just this battle alone. But I'm one step ahead of you.*

Aiya kicked her steed forward in her forest-jade armor, looking down at Ueko. "We *will* take Sen's head."

Ueko looked her up and down. "With no helm?"

"You'll see that the strength of Agriculture is unmatched. Totane is the least of Sen's worries."

Aiya looked down to the battlefield below raging like a current, observing intently. In under a day, she'd allowed the carnage to become more palatable, burying her disgust and stomaching the necessity of their great sacrifice. In its place, she'd gained a budding awareness for the formation of tactics: intricate, subtle and swift. She focused on the heaps of soldiers clambering in the middle of the field, a point which every man trudged and hacked his way towards with his sword or spear. Sen was there, fighting desperately against the men at his back. He cut his way free from the crash of soldiers, forming a path of escape. The heavens bestowed them with only a short window to save him.

"I'll have him drawn and quartered! I'll have him hanging by his toes until he begs to be on the chopping block!" Hasa was screaming behind them. Totane coolly bore the pain of his injury with stifled grunts and a forceful limp, vowing vengeance on Sen under his breath.

"Our unit will join yours," Aiya declared. She faced Ueko again, meeting her face, her unbreakable posture. Every fiber in Aiya's being wanted to deny the woman her proper deference. Still, though she resisted at first, she performed a reluctant bow in Ueko's direction. "It will consist of me and my four siblings. You have our word that this battle will conclude  before the sun rests."

Ueko crossed her arms, nodded, then quietly reassured her daughter that Sen's time had come, that it was only a matter of time before his head would be at her feet.

Aiya turned back to the battlefield, realizing how much hatred she held for Hasa too. Ueko, along with her final living daughter, represented all the worst things in the nobility. Greed, pride, callousness, cold indifference, wrath. All the worst traits, and none of the admirable.

From the side, Koji's horse stepped in front of hers. Hands bunched into white knuckles, his body was still and rigid as she'd ever seen him.

He couldn't stop her. She wouldn't abandon her instincts, not when she knew that Sen needed her. She wouldn't abandon those like him. She wouldn't abandon her duties.

"I'm going, Koji. I'm leading this."

Pulling his reins, he backed out of her way.

Tsugo stood beside them at the edge of the hill. "Follow the units of Haaku and Dasuke now. You've been handed the fastest horses in this army. Give chase, and don't let Sen get away."

His eyes were dark as he spoke. The severity of the situation settled firmly onto Aiya's shoulders as she looked far off into the distance. Nothing but a deep gray sky lay beyond it.

"Understood," she replied, and then they were off.

The rush of cold wind down the hill was invigorating. Aiya was as nervous as she was excited, unsure whether the butterflies in her stomach would make her sick. Memories boiled up from a time when she raced not to save, but destroy. *If I can save Sen, perhaps those days won't matter anymore*, she thought. And, maybe, she'd become honorable. Finally, she would be *worthy*.

They approached the center division. With every gallop of the horse, Aiya braced herself to bat down enemy soldiers with her weapon. Over five thousand men were at Sen's back, and about a hundred at his neck, giving chase as he retreated towards his HQ. Aiya weaved her horse around the soldiers at the outskirts fighting for entry into the chaos. Because Sen had abandoned his HQ, Ueko had not considered it worth the effort or manpower it would require to capture, instead focusing her entire force at the center where Sen lay dormant. If he returned there now, he'd be free. This was a chance to prove herself, to put her abilities to the test for the greater good.

"You know, I'm glad this part finally came around," Koji yelled from behind. Totane led them with Aiya just trailing him.

"I couldn't agree more," Risako shouted. "Everything here depends on our performance. Let's not screw things up from here." As soon as she finished, they broke into the ranks ahead, western soldiers parting for them. The smell of mashing bodies and blood was powerful. There was no use talking against the level of noise, so they simply rode on and kept their attention ahead. Bordering the fast diminishing eastern grounds of the battlefield, they caught sight of the tail end of one of Ueko's units breaking through Sen's army.

The men beside Aiya yelled commands to not allow Sen's escape. *He's broken free, and now he's on the run. Heavens, please, let him make it.*

It was drizzling. With rain, his running would become harder, but so would their chase. Aiya glanced around her. The five of them were closing the gap between themselves and the special unit ahead. *Let us get ahead and catch up first!*

She and the Ginju were within the unit giving chase now, the men galloping fiercely on their horses and thirsty for bloodshed. Totane informed one of them that they'd been sent by Tsugo and Lady Ueko to help give chase. The man informed him they were the Haaku unit, and Dasuke was a little further ahead.

Aiya knocked away a spear aimed for her horse's side. They were on East Forgery's side of the battlefield now, most of its men keeping enemy Jodai at bay while their lord made his way to HQ.

As her fresh steed rode through the Haaku unit with relative ease, Aiya squinted at Sen's back.

"They're gaining him!" Totane shouted.

She'd caught up to Dasuke's unit now, Johori and Totane at her sides. Ahead of them, nearly a hundred paces from the opposite hill, a retreating unit of fifty men surrounded Sen as he fled. Twenty of Dasuke's riders were attacking them from behind, and six men were managing to break through the flimsy barricade.

"Those men can't fight Sen alone!" Aiya shouted, despite her alarm. They would at least slow him down, and then the rest of Dasuke's unit would rain their swords down on him.

"That's Lieutenant Dasuke and his best guard there! They're bound to kill him!"

*Not the answer I wanted to hear.* Aiya slapped her reins against her steed even harder, to no avail. They wouldn't make it in time. She looked towards Totane, who returned it, equally hopeless. A deep sense of loss filled her like a dark cloud over her mind. She wouldn't accept his death, not this time.

Shutting her eyes, Aiya allowed herself to fall back off the horse, letting go of everything. The river was her, and she was the river.

She landed perfectly on the ground, ignoring the cries of alarm, ignoring the men and horses stumbling over her. Aiya looked up, inhaling, then bolted forward. Soon she was caught up to Koji, Totane, then passed them.

She ran into Sen's group of soldiers, knocking two of Dasuke's men off their horses. Sen's men gawked at her with alarm. Steel whizzed by, but none managed to land a hit on her. In front of her, Dasuke and his five men had caught up and were now attacking Sen himself.

The officer and two of his men cornered Sen mid-flight, attacking him from three directions at once. One of Sen's guards prepared to fend off the enemy on Sen's left side, but the man flashed teeth like a predator, turning and readying himself to cut the defender down.

Aiya burst forth, batted the man's sword out of the way at the last second, and kicked his jaw in, launching him off the horse and cracking his bones against the hard earth.

The rest of them–Sen, his men and his pursuers–came to a skittering stop. None said a word. Officer Dasuke started. "Y-*you*...in the air-"

"What is she?" one of Sen's soldiers asked amidst the trembling stares.

"What's the meaning of this?" Dasuke demanded.

"Listen, I'll say this only once." Aiya raised her sword up at him. She'd thrown herself into the fray. There was no way to back out now. "Lord Sen is the rightful heir of Forgery. This army, *his* army, will surrender now."

Dasuke considered her for a bit, turning to the others. "I see...."

"So you understand that we're under order from Lord Tsugo himself." A dangerous glare played on Risako's face. "Surrender now. We won't ask twice."

Dasuke's bewilderment slowly left him. His features spread until they made out a satisfied grin. "What a turn of events. No, *you* should listen. Even if all of you here were to turn on the lady Ueko right now, it wouldn't mean shit for Sen. We sought out more allies than just Agriculture."

Aiya's face twisted in confusion. Just then there was a roar from Ueko's HQ. All at once, they turned in horror to see a new army rushing over the hill behind them. Large swathes of light purple armor ran down it with the raised banners of Rain province.

# Doom

"You're finished," Dasuke declared in triumph as their new arrivals piled over the hill.

Aiya's life nearly escaped her. Legions of new troops, at least twenty thousand, stormed from high above them. The fighting had come to a standstill, gazes held captive on their encroaching fate.

*This is it*, Aiya thought. *Our entire plan down the drain. We're going to die.*

As the stampede drew closer, Ueko's troops resumed killing, cheering in victory. Sen's troops had their last grain of morale stripped away and were dropping like flies. Agriculture troops fought clumsily or stood petrified, unsure what to make of the sight. Aiya looked to Sen who stared back. She saw no fear on his face, but his concern was obvious.

"You played your cards at the wrong time," Dasuke said, holding out his sword.

"You're wrong there," Koji said, "even an entire army is no match for Erru like ourselves." He held his chest out as he said it, leaning into the fear all the myths of the Ginju offered.

Dasuke eyed him. Finally, he said, "You're not the only special talents on this battlefield." He turned to his men, and shouted, "This is our victory! Hold these traitors off and die honorably! We're all heroes here, forever to be remembered in Forgery's history as the brave men of this war!"

Aiya was still rooted in place as Dasuke's men shouted in response and charged their enemies.

"This can't be real!" Aiya screamed as she dodged Dasuke's horse, cutting him across his waist and spilling the man's guts.

"They're not stopping," Koji said, "This is pretty fucking real!"

"Fortunately they don't know Agriculture is the enemy just yet!" Totane slew two guards–aiming straight past him for Sen–at the neck. "Lord Sen, this is your chance to retreat! We'll hold them off long enough for you to escape."

Sen remained for a few moments, wide eyes making him look flustered.

"GO!" Totane repeated.

Finally, he nodded and turned to leave. The opposing Forgery soldiers continued their chase and Aiya's attention slipped, giving them almost enough time to slide past her. She had the backs of two skulls bashed in before they could make it.

She looked to see Sen in retreat along with his fifty men. Her heart calmed a little. In front of her, Agriculture troops had begun to turn on West Forgery. Rain was entering the battle, coming in fast, while more of Ueko's soldiers stormed towards her like boulders.

All she could take notice of was Rain. Thousands of men from the Empress' home province, where the capital resided. The Empress didn't rule the province, only the capital city, but she might as well, for Rain and Sanaba were near synonymous. Why were they here at Ueko's side?

Aiya occupied herself by cutting down any enemy soldier stepping within a few paces of her. Ueko had surely figured out Tsugo's game by now. It was them and the remainder of Sen's troops against her and twenty-thousand fresh men. Sen had retreated, but now they had an entirely new problem on their hands.

A man came for Aiya's side, spear pulled back and pointed at her skull. Aiya cut through his elbow with a single stroke, slamming a fist into his face before his severed arm hit the ground, still gripping the spear. His body flew into another soldier with such force that the man was knocked a few paces backwards.

Rain was upon them. Koji advanced into the fray and took out glossy-armored men left and right, too quick for them to react. The remaining three were not persuaded into backing down, even as blades nicked their bodies. For every man they killed, another took his place.

Skywater fell harder now. It was still a light pour, lured out by twin flashes of lightning.

That cold, creeping sensation returned to her, as her vision dimmed.

Not this time.

As her spirit overflowed, she recognized her subconscious drawing of the river. Deeper than that, in a moment of unnatural self-awareness, she peered into her core and understood *why*: *All the times I've lost control, every time I've failed, it's because of my fear.*

Pushing away black bubbling fear from her vision, Aiya took control of the flow of the river within her. It was as Koji had told her many nights ago at the Takasa estate, what he'd always told her: her alignment with their deity was perfect. So perfect, she'd made a habit of drawing too much of the river, without notice, exacerbated by fear, a subconscious attempt to compensate, impulsive. No more.

She'd been going on for five minutes now, fighting presently and cutting the excess flow of power in her. In her was a surge of adrenaline, a mixture of excitement and fear as the enemy continued their onslaught.

Agriculture soldiers fell next to her as Rain joined the mix. One Forgery soldier accused another of being a traitor, to which the man responded that the west were the real traitors. He was cut down for that.

"How long can we keep this up?" grunted Koji.

"We should number around sixteen thousand or more with Sen's troops!" Totane replied. "Against their twenty-five, we'll last as long as we need. Just hold the line here so that no one advances. All our soldiers have already begun funneling the enemy to we Ginju, so we just need to play our part!"

Sixteen against twenty five weren't the best odds, but Totane's confidence held Aiya's hope. She caught a dagger coming right under her chin from the corner of her eye and ducked at the last second. She jumped backwards, bringing her own weapon down on the man's shoulder. She figured she'd aimed improperly as her blade slammed down on the edge of his shoulder plate. She sliced off a chunk as he leapt back out of her reach.

A Jodai of Rain, also with no helm. Eyes a light purple. His hair was white blond, and in his rigid glare was a challenge.

"You missed me," the man said. He wasn't much older than her.

Aiya scrunched her face. "You say it as if you are disappointed to live five seconds longer."

Aiming to catch him off guard, she rushed him, sword positioned to stab him through the gut and out the back. To her surprise, he used his two daggers to successfully block her attack. She gritted her teeth and shook as he struggled against her own force. Her eyes slowly widened with dumbfounded realization.

*There's only one way he's able to stand up to me! He's a Rain Ginju!*

Smiling as if he read the thought on her face, he shoved her back. She let him, then spun to the side as he lunged for the kill. As her body came back around to face him, she brought her blade down to cut at the shoulder again. This time she followed his movements. He tilted the angle of his shoulder down, allowing the blade to slip off again. Their feet slid against the muddying ground, both of them quickly resuming fighting positions.

There was a pang of something familiar inside her. A mix of shock, nervous energy, and excitement. Unlike normal soldiers, Ginju posed a threat. Neither she nor he could be careless. This wasn't training, but one of the rare times in their lives where a fight meant life or death.

A true chance to prove herself. She'd just have to do better this time.

"It's been five seconds. Why aren't I dead?"

Aiya admired that. "We are a cocky bunch, aren't we? It's about time one of us was humbled."

Then she was at his left side. He was caught off guard, alarmed by her speed. She circled him as he tried to follow. Changing course, she went straight for his back. She'd have him separated from the waist down.

He'd kept up, and a backwards kick to the face made it obvious. Pain exploded in her cheek as she soared almost ten paces back. She recovered from the ground quickly. Ignoring the flourishing pain in her face was difficult. The boy rushed her, both daggers held at either side.

Doing the best to stabilize her spinning world, she met him head on. He brought one dagger back, keeping the other forward. She recognized the form instantly. *A three-point attack. He's created an illusion of an opening, hoping I'll try to skewer him through the stomach from my right.* He was smart, and a quick thinker.

Luckily she still had her feet on her side.

As they closed in on each other, she raised a leg and sent the most powerful kick she could muster for his left shoulder. She squinted through watery eyes as her foot made impact with his armor and he let out a grunt. She'd re-arranged his form so that his body stumbled for balance, twirling him to the left.

Using her momentum to spin the other direction, her swordpoint became destined for the middle of his back. She leaned in with all her might, determined not to be thrown off.

Her blade slipped through his back without any resistance, her opponent skipping away with quiet steps. Her blade plunged into muddy soil.

*What...?*

She looked up to see him fine, kicking mud off his boots and staring down at her angrily, like some especially tenacious prey.

"By the heavens," Aiya whispered. She'd been directly above him, *seen* the blade plunge into him. Yet it hadn't made any sound connecting with his armor, his flesh. There wasn't any blood, and now he stood in front of her unscathed.

Suddenly she realized the fighting around them had ceased. In its stead, the Jodai observed their skirmish in awe. Two more Rain soldiers, one female, sat on horseback at the edge of the circle the men had formed around them.

"This must be what Dasuke meant by other 'special talents'," Risako remarked from Aiya's side.

"So he's a Rain Ginju," Koji said, "and from their self-important stances, I'd bet those two on horseback are his kin."

"Just when things couldn't have gotten any worse," groaned Johori.

"You'd be right about that," the white haired boy responded as the other two jumped down. The girl, likely his sister, sported long black hair and the other boy was built heavier and more masculine, with a messy mop of hair that didn't at all suit him. The two pulled twin daggers out that looked sharp enough to slice through steel.

"You're outmatched," Totane said as if giving the most nonchalant warning. He unmounted from his own horse and unsheathed his sword.

The white haired boy turned with a scornful smirk. "What of it?"

The girl lunged forward, daggers prepared to sting. Koji went to engage her, catching one dagger with a sword while Johori caught the other. Risako and Totane blocked the other male Ginju as he rushed towards Aiya. She was nearly caught as White Hair sent a dagger across her vision. She ducked, connecting her fist with his stomach. White Hair doubled over, Aiya wheeling around him and kicking him down on his stomach.

Johori had dropped his weapon, grabbing hold of both the girl's wrists. Koji went in for the swing. Aiya raced over to finish her off. Koji's sword traveled across the air and into her neck, then right back out. There was no spray of blood. Her head didn't roll. Aiya blinked twice.The girl was suddenly free from Johori's grip. She wasted no time stabbing him through the neck. Aiya pulled back her sword as she came up on the girl and went for her leg.

The girl noticed and dodged just in time, barely avoiding an impaled leg. The blade tore through flesh on her outer thigh, this time drawing blood aplenty.

The girl's dagger hilt smashed Aiya's forehead and sent her hard into Koji. She collapsed with her brother to the ground. Her cheekbone pounded. She helped Koji to his feet, the Rain girl limping back so that she, Johori, and the pair of River Ginju formed a triangle. The flesh on Johori's neck was sealing itself as he righted himself, coughing up gobs of blood.

"They're phasing through our attacks," Aiya said.

"So this is the talent of the rain." Koji held out his sword as White Hair angled towards them, nose bloodied. "Can you keep going?"

"I could go forever. I feel so light now that I don't have to hide from Ira!"

Across from them, Totane grunted as he was kicked backwards. The third Rain Ginju started. Risako came in, sending her first blade through his body. He phased through it, and a split second later Risako had slammed the flat of her other sword against his jaw. The boy screamed over an audible *crack*. As he fell, he rebounded and delivered a kick to her ribcage that sent her back.

"She can heal from that," Koji said. "Not so sure about your partner."

The girl smirked. "Serves him right. That was long past due."

"Focus on our enemy, bitch," White Hair snapped. He shifted to the right a bit.

Aiya and Koji touched backs, saying nothing but feeling everything the other thought. *So their ability has limits. And we certainly have better coordination than them.*

Who would make the first move? The battlefield had turned into a stage, and with them, their audience held their breath. This was the scene of a lifetime, of three lifetimes. What these men witnessed was history, a fantastical fight out of legend. Aiya released air then filled her lungs again. She would make sure they were not disappointed.

Agriculture moved first. Totane and Risako dashed for the muscled boy from opposite angles, crouching low as he held his weapons high to cover his jaw. Taking advantage of her diverted attention, Johori rushed the girl, his wound now closed completely. He moved considerably slower, almost sluggishly. The girl prepared for his oncoming strike while keeping her head on the swivel. Aiya and Koji kept their backs pressed and shuffled their feet so that they switched places. White Hair's steel met Aiya's, and he grimaced.

"You don't phase through when our blades touch." Aiya said, grinning. "That means only your body can phase, and only every so often."

White Hair's eyes flickered between her and his injured teammate. His mistake. As Koji pushed off her towards the girl, he launched Aiya further into her opponent. White Hair fell back. He splashed onto the ground, Aiya's sword still pushing against his, one hand on her hilt and one gripping the other end. Slowly, it slid up his daggers, towards the edge of his blades where it would fall and slice into his face.

"Best to drop your weapons," she warned sardonically, shaking. He gritted his teeth in response. His strained arms looked ready to collapse. Aiya's blade grinded halfway up his daggers. She'd overpowered him.

His eyes flicked behind her, then back on her, suddenly dark brown in color. His face relaxed, his arms suddenly giving in. Her sword glided down the daggers and made for his neck. Aiya gave in to the blade's trajectory, welcoming her opponent's end. There was a *splash*. Half of it plunged into the mud below.

Muddy water splashed onto her face as she stared into the ground for precious seconds. She sat there on her knees, bent over with a palm pressed against the wet earth. Her other still gripped her weapon's hilt. White Hair wasn't there. Her mind took its time to comprehend what she had just seen. Or rather what she hadn't.

The only thing remaining was her bent over in empty mud, the sudden image of his blade plunging into her neck setting her mind off in panic. She pulled her blade from the ground and swung it at the space behind her, striking empty air.

To her horror, White Hair stood a few feet from the girl who was struggling against Koji's blade, an inch away from her demise. White Hair's own blade was blood soaked, plunged into Johori's stomach. Johori's eyes bulged.

White Hair pulled his other dagger through the side of Johori's neck, then rammed it a few times into his side. Johori grunted in pain, unable to move.

"Die," White Hair told him, kicking Johori to the ground.

# Ambush

The clamor around Aiya was silenced.

There was only the tumult of rain, and the swift jabs of White Hair's daggers in and out of Johori's arms, neck, face, and torso. White Hair had him pinned down as he worked on brutalizing his body.

Aiya jerked back to reality by the sound of Johori's gargled screams. She didn't know when she moved, but she landed with her sword inches from White Hair's spine. He realized her far too late. The only thing that saved him were his sister's daggers, and her boot which she sunk under Aiya's ribcage.

The pain barely registered as she stumbled back. Before Aiya could recover, Totane grappled with the girl. Johori managed to push White Hair off him by some miracle, allowing Koji to barrage him with a fury of attacks.

Aiya scrambled to Johori, whose form curled up, clutching his sides in agony. She fell to her knees in front of him as he moaned in pain. Long, deep gashes spilled life from his body. The wounds weren't closing.

Hooves behind her pounded. Her head whipped backwards to see Lieutenant Gaku Hedi on horseback with six men approaching them fast. The men around them, she registered, had resumed fighting.

Hedi's spear crossed the air as he came up on the female Ginju being handled by Totane. She freed herself from Totane's grip at the last second and jumped back, the spearhead nicking her shoulder.

Hedi skidded to a stop with his men behind. He overlooked Aiya kneeling above Johori.

His mouth seemed to work for words, but his eyes were glued to the trembling body. "My lord...."

Aiya searched over Johori, unsure of what to do.

"This ends now!" Hedi yelled. He'd caught every Ginju's attention. "The five of you, follow Sen and protect him at all costs! We'll handle the rest from here!"

Aiya immediately tracked the Rain Ginju, all of whom looked worse for wear. Their faces, beaten with one case of a bruised eye on the muscled boy, and their armor was considerably battered. They also showed no signs of backing down.

Risako stepped back from her opponent, who barely kept himself up on one knee. "Are you out of your mind? This is a battle of Ginju, it must be seen to the end!"

"These are Tsugo's orders," Hedi answered. "We can handle ourselves from here. These Rain scoundrels look like they paid an arm and a leg fighting you off. I'd say they'd be risking everything if they continue."

White Hair scoffed. "You'll die here."

Hedi stared him down a long moment, facing fearlessly an opponent who would easily tear him limb for limb without a second thought. "I think we both know you're potentially putting your province in a vulnerable situation, being that you aren't exactly replaceable. Furthermore, I think even you don't want to continue this." He turned to Risako. "Sen must be protected by any means. A straight path from the other side of that hill will lead you to the city of Tsuisaka. It's his most fortified zone in East Forgery. We'll take out as many here as we can, and you'll figure out the rest with Sen. He shouldn't be too far ahead."

Risako gave no response. She gaped at the man, a deepness in her eyes that made her look stricken.

"Is he alright?" Totane called, still in fighting stance. The female Ginju pulled her attention from him to Hedi, to Risako, then back to Totane. Totane searched Johori's unmoving posture, wide eyed. "Johori, why aren't you saying anything? Get up!"

Johori only murmured in response to Totane's shaky voice. His wounds had healed marginally, but he still lay in an expanding puddle of his own blood that had made its way to Aiya's knees.

"Why isn't he responding?" Totane demanded, louder, more aggressive this time.

"His wounds aren't healing," Aiya said, mustering all the volume she could. He lay in a fetal position, shivering like a lone wet dog on the street.

"Why aren't they?" said Totane.

Risako landed beside Aiya, right above Johori's head. "Johori, get it together! Get up so we can go after Sen!"

"I don't think he'll be moving again," the Rain girl testified.

Totane lunged at her, sword ready for contact with her ribs, stopping short of it and instead sending an iron fist into her lips. She fell, quickly righting herself before his sword came down on her. This time she diverted him with her daggers. "At least he'll die with some measure of honor."

"Totane, enough!" Risako called. "Our job here is done! We need to get moving to Sen! Help me sit Johori up!"

Totane spat at the girl before backing off and rushing to his brother. Johori's breaths were shallow now, rainwater running down into his nose and open mouth. His eyelids were loosely shut. Were those tears or raindrops as he tried muttering his last words?

Aiya almost didn't catch sight of the dozen West Forgery men charging them from Hedi's left. They'd somehow broken through the ranks, coming to finish her injured comrade. Their faces were angry, wild in triumph. An especially courageous bunch.

"Shit!" Aiya exclaimed.

Totane met the frenzied attack head on, hacking down one man after another. He screamed, taking off an arm, fingers, severed kneecaps, separated a head from its body. The attackers tried to disperse but were unable to keep up with both his swift blade and his seething rage. Two at a time, they died.

"Why aren't you healing yourself, Johori?" Totane shouted, catching a spear in the back. It barely broke skin, and in return the Jodai man wielding it had his skull broken.

Aiya twirled around, bashing two Rain soldiers across their helms with her sword. The men around them screamed as they scrambled for the fallen Ginju. They appeared to see a chance, an opening. They were mistaken.

Aiya watched White Hair gather up his fallen brother, whose jaw had swollen to the size of an apple. The two escaped into the advancing frenzy of soldiers. The last of their opponents slowly backed away into the flurry of men until she disappeared, alone.

Now it was the four of them. Aiya cursed, looking back to see Johori's body had gone limp. Risako, in the midst of taking off the top half of a man's face, looked back too. She didn't look at Johori, nor Aiya, but behind Aiya.

Agriculture troops in all directions began swarming them. The troops slayed both Rain and enemy Forgery soldiers in their way, surrounding the Ginju and Hedi's men, locking them into safety.

"Fyujin unit under General Yko's command!" their commander shouted. "We're here for your swift retreat!"

Risako yelled, "What's the status of Lord Tsugo?"

"Lord Tsugo gathered twenty men around himself right after you all joined the battle. When Lady Ueko saw he'd betrayed her, a skirmish broke out and is now at a standstill. Both now await the outcome of this battle."

Risako looked down.

"So if we go, Lord Tsugo will have lost," Aiya concluded.

"We still have plenty of men to put up a fight here. If worse comes to worst, we will surrender and spare at least some of ourselves. We will give our lives to protect our Lord. At this point, however, it is imperative that Sen becomes the victor. The entirety of Agriculture depends on it."

Koji stood next to Aiya, placing a hand on her shoulder. "I think we'd better get going."

They watched helplessly as Totane stumbled forward and fell next to Johori. His armor was mostly broken, cracked and stained all over. A cut remained drawn across his cheek. He lifted Johori into his arms and embraced him, kneeling with his face in Johori's shoulders.

The three didn't interrupt. Aiya thought she heard Risako whimpering softly. She felt a hundred times heavier, barely able to keep her head lifted. With all the strength left in her, she looked to Koji. He offered nothing. The cold rain fell without rest.

A man behind them brought horses forward, keeping a timid grip on the reins. "Your mounts, my lords."

On the horses were packs with extra provisions. The soldiers around them kept the enemy at bay while Aiya peered up at the Ueko's hill. She could see clusters of men but could make out no features that might reveal where Tsugo was or the state he was in.

"Totane, we must go." Risako's voice was shaky. She hugged him as he said it, but only for a few moments before rising and stalking briskly towards the horses.

Totane sobbed, his face contorted in anguish. He got to his feet, lifting Johori with him. "We're taking him with us."

A single tear fell from Aiya's cheek, splashing on her mudstained boots. She climbed her horse, watching Risako help lift Johori onto Totane's. Aiya was unable to settle in on her own steed until his body was strapped sideways and secured onto the animal's back. The battle raged on around her, but it felt as if their own battle was about to start all over.

Hedi exchanged a few words with Risako which Aiya couldn't make out. In front of them the men cleared a path for them to ride. Hedi took his hand from Risako's shoulder, then faced the rest of them.

"General Yko and four of his closest guard will accompany you! We will rendezvous again soon! Now go! We'll make certain you're not followed!"

General Yko led the way, and the nine of them still living sped off, their soldiers blocking the way of the enemy. An arrow whizzed past, prompting Aiya to draw power from the river.

Once they escaped the battlefield onto Sen's domain, they rode their horses uphill, Aiya fighting with everything in her to not look back. *Your mission isn't complete yet, but it will be, Ira.*

They crested the hill, stampeding past Sen's abandoned headquarters, empty and silent like death. Soon they were traveling downhill, and in the dimming light Aiya could see nothing but distant plains, forests and dark gray skies.

# Legends

The first cluster of trees was not far off from the Hiji-mata hills. The terrain in front of them was lower in elevation but still full of inclines that slowed their trot. The rain continued to fall yet failed to wash the mud stains from their clothes and armor. General Yko still led in front about twenty paces ahead, his elite guard posted at the back.

Aiya felt numb. She kept her horse at a steady pace beside Koji, Risako doing the same with Totane directly behind Yko. She was saying something to comfort her brother in his silence.

Aiya glanced at Koji, disoriented by the situation. Every step of the hooves below was becoming maddeningly un-comfortable.

"This is more than I imagined we'd face," Koji said. "Es-pecially this early on. First Ira...."

"I–didn't believe this would happen, that one of us would end up dead. Maybe I just didn't want to believe," Aiya blurted. Her voice moved like a boulder in her throat.

"Feels like Kawanura all over again."

Sunlight filtered through clouds had almost completely dissipated while forest covered the plains as far as she could see. A few minutes passed before they brought out lanterns from their packs. She looked back to the soldiers behind them and eyed them until one of them awkwardly trotted forward.

"Yes, my Lady?" the man asked. His helm was embellished with small dangling gold coins, and his ears were pierced with jade.

"Not likely, but have you any idea how large the nearest city is that Sen is going to?"

"From the information I received from Lord Yko, Tsuisaka is smaller than most notable eastern cities. It won't have the defenses you'd expect of a city ruled by a lordling."

"Sen's sure to have fortified it significantly since this war started though," Koji mused.

"I would hope so, my lord."

Her horse blew snot, catching Aiya off guard. "That's all I wanted. Thank you, soldier."

"Fuda, my lady." He made a curt bow and turned his horse around to regroup with his comrades.

"Guess we should start learning names," said Koji. "We are citizens of Agriculture after all."

She'd hardly given it thought, hardly accepted it. Somehow, she didn't feel she was, as if it was a thing unearned.

Aiya looked into the sky, wishing her heavy clothes weren't so drenched. The trek into the forest brought their group more huddled together. The thought of being ambushed by the Rain Ginju crossed Aiya's mind, though she chided herself for dwelling on something so unlikely, if at all possible. Part of her, however, wished for it, to finish what they had started sooner rather than later.

General Yko informed them that their trek would not last longer than two or three hours. The trees shielded them from the downpour somewhat, though the chill of the air hadn't warmed. If she ever returned to River, she'd not take its muggy winters for granted.

In the meantime, there was little to distract herself from Johori's limp frame flopping against the restraints on the back of Totane's horse. She made sure to keep her distance. They'd only known each other for a few days, but Johori's death still seemed wrong, surreal. An event so sudden it seemed not to fit, a cruel trick of fate. He hadn't chosen it freely as their faithful Jodai had, who threw themselves willingly into the fray. She could not mourn his passing, but knowing the grief set upon his brother and his twin sister left her deeply dismayed.

In a way, his downfall in particular was most disturbing. Risako was smart, refined, leaving Aiya intrigued. Totane was almost defined by his valiance, and still both shared their father's capacity to inspire her through their own passion, though Johori had always seemed to burn with less of it. He was more reserved for reasons that had once been unknown to Aiya. After their conversation in the tent, however, she viewed him differently. He was more thoughtful, a torn figure treading with cautionary wisdom, who wore a mask of bravery to honor the hopes of his clan, even his entire province, and yet in the end, it was he who was sacrificed, taking his fears with him.

Risako turned and looked Aiya in the eyes, making her fidget.

She averted her gaze, her posture softening. "This is the cost of revolution. Now both of us have suffered greatly for it. Always stand on guard, and don't think for a *fucking* second that you're invincible."

Aiya and Koji said nothing.

Risako's gaze went back over Johori's limp form. "The amount of damage he endured was too much, too quickly, for him to heal fast enough. I assume there's also a limit of power you can draw from your deity: too much and the mind reacts poorly. That probably explains why those Rain Ginju could only phase through our attacks every so often."

"Empress' soul," Koji cursed. "Speaking of them, it's clear that cunt Ueko had a real reason for not sending Forgery Ginju against her son. She'd rather use someone else's."

Totane turned to him. "Swearing to the Empress only gives her more power over our own minds."

They were all silent for the next twenty paces.

Aiya wondered if the Forgery Ginju were even on Ueko's side. But then, clearly, they weren't sided with Sen. If it came down to it, chances were they'd be Ueko's last resort. The odds of the four of them taking down six enemy Ginju felt slim. Furthermore, this war was showing to be more than a simple contest of strength.

"A Wailstorm is on its way," Yko said. "I can feel it in the air. It will slow down Ueko's approach. In the meantime, there's a concept I want to share with you two. A concept that is one of the pillars of the Republic's beliefs. Do you know the number of factions in Egaisha?"

Aiya and Koji looked at each other. "Factions?"

"Yes. How many factions do you think exist?"

Koji scratched his chin. "In terms of parties in conflict? Ten? The ten provinces?"

"Those are the first ten. But you must also take into account two others. The Imperial Seat, or the Empress. Though she is the sovereign, her rule is not as absolute as you think, otherwise the empire would not be facing outbreaks of civil unrest and outcries against expanding taxation. Every province is rife with disruption, and the Empress can only be one place at a time. There have been those who have rebelled and disobeyed in the past."

*Which is supposedly the origin of Wailstorms*, Aiya thought.

"So what's the final faction?" Koji asked.

"Think about it. There are the ten provinces that make up the empire, the Empress herself, and the ones who are the outsiders."

"Tarshan?"

"They have yet to be absorbed into the empire. The twelfth blade is made of those who oppose the empire and everything it stands for. They too exist in the spectrum. You have those who oppose the empire, us, versus the Empress herself, who embodies it. All other factions are neutral, allowing change to happen around them however they may. Yet they still participate in our current society with contempt, because no man or woman possesses what they truly desire. We use that contempt to sway them to our side, and the more factions we have with us, the better chance we have at victory. River, Agriculture, Forgery, Rain, the Empress, and so forth. The passive aggressive relationships between these factions are like Jodai encircling each other with blades pointed in every direction, eyes locked and seething with hatred and greed. The Republic makes the twelfth blade, held with just as much contempt as the others."

"So, Forgery is the first of those we're bringing to our side," Koji said, "but how will we get the rest? The states closer to the Imperial Seat have existed in the empire for the longest. I doubt they dislike the current system very much."

"A very true observation. We won't be able to sway them all to our side, but, fortunately, our strategy doesn't require it. We only n–hush."

He didn't need to tell them, as their attention had already been stripped from the conversation. Was it a noise they'd just heard? It was hard to tell. Aiya looked around, as did the others.

"Did you hear something?" Yko asked.

"Could have sworn I did," Risako said.

Suddenly the air around them was frigid. The pitter-patter against sticks and leaves faded from their senses, their horses coming to a curious halt. There was a certain stillness that everything took on, as if frozen in time. In the background, there was a shuffling noise, like sweeping piles of leaves, though it faded in and out as if it were tickling the imagination. They listened, puzzled, unable to determine whether their ears should be given any credibility.

An unexplainable yet familiar fear blossomed within Aiya. She turned to Koji, who, for the first time in a while, looked confounded with that same fear. They didn't have to say it, their minds had both jumped to the same conclusion. Their worst fears as Ginju, straight from the stories. They'd all come to a stop, Risako and Totane looking just as frightened. They'd be of no help to the soldiers watching them.

Without warning, as if materializing from nothing, there was a spirit, stepping out from behind a tree in front of them. Aiya nearly lost her breath. Its features were a strange mixture. The torso, arms and legs were that of a man, naked and adorned with beads of various shapes and colors around its neck, while the head was that of an ox. The spirit was large, dizzyingly tall, its horn tips putting it at twenty feet, reaching into the branches of the trees. Its majestic form pulsated, fading in and out as it walked, going from a pale transparent green to a green deep and tangible, its footsteps sending winds whirling around them wherever they went. Aiya's hair flew back in the breeze, the air around her even colder against her soaked body.

It was a moment straight out of legend. There was a nostalgic air around it, something that seemed very familiar. Aiya wanted to reach into the chasm of her memories and grab it, whatever it was that seemed on the verge of being pulled from its depths. Admiration, respect, wonder, and terror swirled within her. The spirit did not give off a hostile aura as it lumbered across, paying them no heed. Indeed, Aiya felt more mystified by its presence now than fearful. It was rare one actually saw a spirit. More often than not, stories of encounters were assumed to be the tall tales of those who received too little attention.

The spirit stopped and turned, its presence undeniable. Those still, unwavering eyes fell on her, subdued her in place. With aching intensity, they bore into Aiya's soul. She sank into them. Absorbing pools of black, eyes that belonged to a more docile creature. Sacred. Divine. This encounter was primal, a relic of a great and distant past, eons forgotten, merged with *her* era. Aiya felt a powerful urge to fall to her knees in reverence, to keep herself from desecrating the scene with her unworthy gaze. She looked on.

*Blight....*

She became more aware of the space within her own mind than she had ever been. It had been filled with something just then, just a wisp. That something, a thought perhaps, had not been her own. She had no idea where it had come from, looking to see if anyone else had heard. Koji commanded his horse to take a few steps back, his teeth chattering.

The spirit seemed to cast a spell on her and the rest of her unit, one which was ineffective on horses. The beasts were as calm as they'd ever been, peaceful in fact. Yko and Totane's horses attempted to move towards the spirit, repeatedly reined back in terror.

*You are a blight...on this earth. You* taint *the world.*

The words were clear this time, and then she knew the spirit was speaking to her in her mind. Its words were raspy and sharp in her head, leaving no room for thoughts of her own. She was frightened and confused again, but couldn't pry her eyes from its gaze, which now appeared solely focused on her.

As if by some miracle, the creature finally turned its head, lifting a leg and taking another step forward. Winds like hurricanes whipped through their manes, hair, and clothing. The horses turned their heads to watch, unperturbed by the icy gusts. The spirit became more faint, almost imperceptible once it was behind another tree, its back turned to them. Aiya released the tension in her muscles, relieved, and as it faded away, she wondered if a Ginju stood any chance against such a thing as that.

# Lord and Lady

The forests went on for many leagues before clearing up, vanishing into more hilly plains. By now the rain had slowed to a light drizzle, leaving enough clarity for them to spot the small city lights in the distance about a mile away. The city was surrounded by walls but looked only slightly larger than a big town in River.

Their horses were exhausted, moving at a slowed pace. The animals seemed to have entirely forgotten their last encounter, but for Aiya, it was still fresh on her mind. They'd all been shaken, and no one said much since the spirit passed. None took it upon themselves to break the silence.

Had they, in fact, emerged from some kind of hallucination? Spirits were widely believed to exist, but for one to claim to have seen one up close and personal, *that* was rare, almost laughable. Spirits existed in the minds of the Erru as explanation for the unexplainable, giving reason where there often was none. It resolved the bump in the night, the freak accident that the child survived, the sickness that ran through a family thought to be a curse. Therein was the reason they were feared among Erru, foremost to Ginju; they were truly unexplainable.

"It's okay, girl, almost there," one of the men behind them cooed to his horse.

Aiya kept her head on a swivel, making sure nothing and no one snuck up on them again from any direction. It was all grassland and trees for leagues around, and they were growing ever blacker.

"You're only going to make yourself more nervous doing that," Koji said. "We'll be fine, the city is right ahead of us."

Aiya frowned. "Sounds like you're saying that to comfort yourself more than anything."

His face was crossed. "I'm saying it so you stop making everyone so fucking nervous with your constant fidgeting. That's what we're in a group for. Understand?"

She kept her furrowed brows on him but said nothing. The others continued their march in silence, until they were finally in front of the Tsuisaka city walls. The stone rose to a height that was anything but laughable, rising thirty feet above ground. Outside were a few dozen men posted along its base. A few more patrolled the top of the wall. A slight tension stalled the air as they got closer, though the men likely knew their alliance.

A soldier demanded they halt at about a hundred paces away from the city. Yko stated his name and their relation to Lord Sen. The guards allowed them closer and began to unlock the huge doors of oak. The doors creaked loudly as they opened, and Aiya could feel the brittle bones of the city as they did so. Such a place like this was well fortified for its size and the short time frame Sen had to reinforce it, but against a sizable army with skilled commanders, how long it would last in battle was questionable.

They stepped off of their horses, relief flooding through Aiya's system. Risako helped Totane lift Johori's body onto the ground. Totane kneeled next to him, holding him up by the back of his head. He stared for a long while and said nothing. Risako pointedly kept her back turned, head down.

"We'll have to burn him," the man said. "An unfortunate mandate during times of war, when we don't have the luxury of immediate burial."

Totane nodded, leaned down to kiss Johori's forehead for the last time, and stood. "He's been dead for a few hours."

The man nodded, and two of the soldiers on watch came and gathered Johori up. Aiya felt her stomach churning and forced the entire scene out of her sight.

Outside of the continent, they might fool themselves with the hope of seeing loved ones in another form. But the Erru accepted that there was no reincarnation, only heaven, hell, and the storms.

Those who opposed the Empress joined the storm upon death. In the days of Nirogawa, hell was thought to be the destination of all souls, a freezing cold valley that cleansed itself through dissipation. The Valley of Zakura, before it had been infiltrated by demons. Those who were good in life, who followed the virtues of the Oshidai, earned their privilege to read the scrolls containing all their good deeds and happy memories as their souls disappeared. Those who were not were forced to read of their bad deeds, and to relive their worst memories up to their final moments.

The man then led them in, past dozens of guards lined at the inner gates. In the cold dreariness it was a sort of eerie sight. The streets were completely bare, no sign of citizenry or life. It was quiet, almost as quiet as their trek over here, and the air was empty, devoid of any smells of food and bustling warmth.

The paths cut neatly through the austere network of buildings, indicating a city that had been grown artificially, as opposed to the natural flourishing from village roots over the decades. Everything here was more spread out so as to admire the clean open road. The man leading them took a single turn around an area of foliage before stopping outside a large house that rested at the city's center.

No guards were posted outside its doors.

"Wait here," the man told them. He walked up the steps and knocked three times, then went through the door anyway.

The clouds had run dry by now, though the nine of them were still wet and Aiya found her hands chapped from the cold. She did her best to control her shivers in front of the others. The man was gone for a couple of minutes, and with every passing second the group grew more and more irritated at being left in the frost.

"Heavens, I've had enough of this damned weather," the man named Fuda hissed.

"Hush!" Yko barked right as the man returned. He held the door wide open, ushering them in.

"Inside, my lords."

They shuffled up the steps. Inside, Aiya was caressed back to warmth as she took in the sight before her. A functional room, spacious, like everything in this place. Small charcoal braziers in each corner. Eight men sat around in a circle with dark faces. An extra brazier was being shared between the men. Sen, propped up on a pillow, was the center of attention.

Compared to Tsugo, even to her father, he was so young.

They took the empty spots made for them, Aiya adjusting her blade as her ass hit the hardwood. She'd been a little clumsy about it, hoping Sen hadn't taken notice. Koji sat to her right, the rest of their party lined beside him. Their guards took their place in the back of the room. Settled in, the silence was deafening. She caught a whiff of distinct body odor on the man to her left. Finally, Sen cleared the air.

"This day has been challenging. Before I begin, I would like to say that I am humbled and deeply grateful for the assistance of Agriculture. Like you, I had no way of knowing my mother was conspiring with Rain, and, without your aid my head would have been hanging as an ornament in my sister's tent right now. Still, you bore the brunt of their attack. I understand one of your brothers was lost to our opponents. It might not mean much, but for that I offer my grievances."

Under the crackling of coals, their lips remained pursed.

"It is in the unspoken laws of the Erru people, to a great degree in Forgery, that in the event offspring fight for the throne, they must be the ones to take their siblings' lives. Because of this, I'm not angry that you played your part in deceit, killing my men. I did the same. Nevertheless, our battle isn't over. I was hoping I would not be forced here, but it has inevitably come down to it. We've spent the better part of a year fortifying the east, at least those cities that fight with us, but it won't matter much with my mother having the upper hand. First, I'd like to be enlightened on the events of the battlefield before you escaped here. What is the status of Lord Tsugo?"

Yko bowed. "Still engaged with the enemy, Lord Sen, but our militia is always prepared for these situations. We'll have him escape with his life, even if it costs us all of ours, just as your men did for you."

Sen nodded before continuing. "In the meantime, we must use every moment of opportunity to prepare for Ueko's second attack, while she prepares for the oncoming storm. She and Hasa have gone too far. I swear by the Empress, they'll both receive justice. Rest assured, Hasa's head will be an ornament at my feet soon enough. She will suffer more than all of you today."

So this was the young man her father had turned away on that fateful day that seemed so long ago now. He was proving to be far above the type her father had labeled him.

"Nevertheless, the citizens of this town have mostly been relocated to other areas, leaving the entire city functioning as barracks. We number a mere three-hundred strong. Sadly, that's the remainder of my men. We'll have to gather the rest from neighboring cities before the storm hits."

An old lord, hair gone white with eyes that drooped low, sat a few seats away from Sen and croaked, "Well, I haven't had the pleasure of being in a situation as desperate as this in over twenty years. I must say, in all my lifetime, this has to be the one occasion where I've actually looked forward to a Wailstorm."

"In my short life, this may also be the only time that I've looked on a Wailstorm with gratitude. Lord Aneken, my

Agriculture friends." He gestured to the men around him, introducing each. "Your names?"

Yko introduced himself first, Aiya last. She tried not to stumble over her words, breathing a short sigh of relief when she was done.

"We'll save further introduction for later. As I said, the plan is to gather soldiers from our neighboring lords. Or rather, we will recruit them. Might be the better word, considering they declined to partake in all this once before. And since we're short on time, we won't waste any that we have left."

"Commander Gheki is already posted with the men outside the east gates," a scraggly haired, younger lord proclaimed in a bow.

The rest of the men began laying out the defensive positioning of the city, debating over their strategic advantages and disadvantages.

"Lord Jesu will not hand over a single troop, dimwit, he might as well be skipped!"

"That spineless bastard won't lift a finger against us, it's Komei we should be concerned about."

It was moving so fast Aiya had trouble focusing.

"Enough, we'll get them to cooperate whether they're feeling it or not," Sen barked. "Now I'll be needing a few extra horses." He turned to Yko. "How much rest do you and your people require?"

"None, Lord Sen," Yko answered. "We're eager to do what is necessary to end this, sooner rather than later."

Sen nodded. "Meeting adjourned."

The men around them rose and left the room, the cold rushing in through the open doors. Yko and the five of them sat there for a moment, uttering not a word. Aiya was about to ask what was next, when Totane spoke up.

"That's it. Just like that, we're moving forward."

"Totane–" Aiya said as Risako ran her hand over his shoulder.

"Times of war seldom respect your time to grieve, my lord" Sen said. He stood, faced them, and came forward a few paces. "I'm sorry for your loss. I can't understand the bond you had, but a few of my beloved ones were lost to me as well in all of this, so I can conceive your pain. You three are welcome to rest in this room for the time being, until after the storm has passed." His eyes landed on Aiya and Koji. "You two, on the other hand, will come with me."

Aiya and Koji exchanged glances.

Yko pressed on. "Lord Sen, as I said before, we didn't come all this way to rest. We've come to finish what we started, not to sit here on our haunches!"

"I admire your sense of duty, but as we discussed earlier, everything is already in place. There's not much else to do until after the storm hits, so for now, you wait. Besides, the two of you are all I require, my River lord and lady."

# Wind

Totane hardly registered the *thud* of his shoulder plate colliding with another. He hardly registered the swift *scuff* of rotating feet, the rough hand that took hold of his shoulder, nor the fury in the Jodai man's face who–for one reason or another–had taken offense to him.

He was yelling something, but Totane only saw past him. Outside the central meeting hub, Jodai walked swiftly about without much chatter. His surroundings appeared ghostly, callous, the ground like mud in which he was eternally sinking. He judged that it would take an eternity to digest the roiling heaviness invading his insides.

"Still won't answer me, huh?" Flecks of spit fell across the man's goatee. "What, think you can walk around bumping into others around you? You believe you're some Agriculture king? We allowed you on these premises, but that doesn't mean you can act however you please!"

Totane saw the man's eyes were wild with anger, every portion of his face animated with warmth and passion. How full of life it was. How fickle life could be.

The man gritted his teeth, growling. He relaxed his grip and gave Totane a hard shove.

Forgetting himself, Totane saw red. Instinctively, he released himself, letting *agriculture* take his place. Taking a step forward, he stared the Forgery soldier down. "Don't mess with me."

Yko intervened, firmly grabbing Totane at both his shoulders. Then he rounded on the Jodai, hovering inches above his face. "You, soldier, have just committed the greatest blunder as a resident of a war camp. Becoming physical with a standing officer! As an Agriculture officer, I should and would be right to banish you into the coming storm, right now!"

The man lost all color in his face, backing down. "I'm sorry, I didn't know–my good sense has fled from me. Forgive me my lords, my brother-in-arms perished just this morning."

"Enough," Yko barked. "You'll spend tonight in solitary confinement where you can get your head straight for tomorrow's battle."

Two Jodai stepped in to lead their comrade away, while Yko moved Totane under the corrugated roof of a beige building. Totane watched him fidget in place with troubled hands tugging at his lenin belt, breaths raspy against the cold. He peered up into the endless sky for so long that his mind seemed stolen away by the heavens, and Totane wished he could be up there with him.

"I saw your eyes. You were planning on killing that man."

Totane licked his lips against the cold but didn't answer.

"I'd prefer not to confide this, Totane-shen, but there's nothing I wish I had more than a smoke right now." Yko's face fell back to the earth, face twisted and distraught.

"It wasn't supposed to go this way," Totane said. He felt if Johori was here, he'd have something better to say. He might have been quiet, but Totane believed it was because his mind worked on a deeper level. If he'd only shown more of himself, crawled out from his shell from time to time, he might have found he had a knack for delivering dignified speeches as skillfully as their father.

Yet here he was, the one who'd survived. By-the-books Yko, for the first time in Totane's memory, slouched in front of him, shedding a tear. In that moment, Totane turned numb, all feeling leaving him, as his mind and body worked to fathom it all.

Yko stood up straight and diligently wiped at his face, a dutiful expression set upon it. "I'm grateful Lord Sen had us stay behind. I needed this moment."

Risako appeared at Totane's side. Her armor was as battered as Yko's, a bloodstain still smeared across his left cheek. No evidence she had wept, except she held the most dejected expression. Had his sister not pried him from the battlefield, he'd have continued slaughtering until his death, and then would have taken the Rain Ginju with him. Risako had always been in more control of herself, and he couldn't understand her ability to be so calm.

He needed to get rid of this heavy feeling within him if he was going to continue.

"I can't banish the thought," he started, "and I don't know if I should be ashamed or not for it. If father goes, and us too, come tomorrow, will mother...understand?"

Risako was taken aback, frightened by the thought, but gave it no further consideration. "Of course she will."

He watched her. "And, is that a good or a bad thing?" That, she couldn't answer. "We aren't invincible. You were right about that. Are you prepared for what that means?"

"If I still have you."

Totane turned and faced the best man he knew. Yko might have been decades older, but Totane felt a greater connection to him than anyone outside of his clan. In him was the wisdom of his father and the strength of Totane himself, three times over.

"Yko, show me the meditation again. The breathing one."

Yko came and placed one solemn hand on his back and spread the other across his chest. Fresh tears welled in Totane's eyes, but he blinked them away. Yko spoke softly. "Let your breaths pass through you like the wind. Let them become the wind, and rest assured that they will carry you to the right place."

Totane exhaled, stilled, then took in another large breath. Minutes passed. The heavy feeling became a little lighter, just a tad more bearable. He wasn't sure when it would come crashing down on him again, but this was enough.

"I'm going to send him off myself."

Risako looked stricken. "Totane, don't."

"I'll be back shortly." Before she could protest more, he was already plodding towards the city gates.

He walked as if a ghost, reminiscing on the time he'd spent with Johori: at one time they'd been boys, then at some point they became men, but they'd always been brothers. Together, they'd learned what it meant to lead, memorized the names of many Agriculture citizens, common and noble. Johori was always better at remembering.

The guards let him outside the city without questioning. A small bonfire roared merely dozens of feet from the city walls, and the soldiers there nodded to him as he approached. Even from afar, Totane's nose wrinkled at the fetid smell of burning flesh. Johori's body no doubt burned black in that raging fire, creating the most sickening sight he'd ever witnessed.

This terrible thing was what Risako had tried shielding him from. He squinted his eyes, forcing himself to take it all in. He wouldn't let this happen again, not ever. Hasa would be lucky to have her body burned with her head intact. Sen was going to live, and so too would the Republic. *I will spare no enemy.*

A guard handed him a stick out of the three gathered piles next to the bonfire, all of varying sizes. In his hand, it felt just right. He tossed it into the all-consuming fire. Wherever Johori was now, Totane hoped he would accept it.

They'd never fought each other outside of training, as was custom between brothers growing up. Totane couldn't imagine it any other way.

That made it perfect, then, that Johori had died fighting by his side.

*Farewell, brother.*

# Decision

By the time Sen's small army began moving, the winds had picked up considerably, and the drop in temperature felt ominous. Marching with three-hundred men was far more easily managed than ten-thousand. Aiya and Koji rode with Sen at the front, the soldiers behind them fresh as a new spring day. They hadn't been involved in any of the fighting. Aiya hoped they wouldn't have to before the storm hit.

Such a remarkable turn of events, to ride next to Sen in his plight.

"Let this be a reminder that spectating undecidedly in a conflict never turns out well in the end," Sen said, not bothering to look at them. "We must all choose sides, eventually."

Aiya could see the cities lit in the distance, but from here it seemed they were moving at a snail's pace. Fortunately, their lanterns were closed, rendering the gusts a non-issue. Marching at night required far more awareness of their surroundings, notwithstanding the threat of being ambushed.

Despite limited visibility, Aiya took in the expansive darkness around them, and imagined for the first time in many ages just how large the continent really was. "I see you remember our encounter in River." Shame flushed her insides.

Sen nodded. "How could I forget? One of my closest commanders left the place in two."

"The way I recall it, that was the unfortunate consequences of his own doing," said Koji, then added, "My Lord."

Aiya shot him a fearsome look, unsure of whether he saw, then said, "We're deeply sorry for the loss of one of your commanders, Lord Sen. It was the poor decision of our father that led to that. He was not one to give a hand easily, and sometimes he relished in the suffering of others."

"Was? I assume he's no longer with us."

"Yes. It's a long story."

"Not one that affects our current alliance," Koji said. "Forgive me if I came off on the wrong footing. All this traveling has had a bad effect on my temper. I got the impression that you felt we were to blame."

"It is no matter, your sister did a better job on Dasuke," Sen responded. "Now listen. The two of you, Aiya and Koji, will be an integral part of this short expedition, my main points of persuasion. For that, consider us even."

The Forgery lord didn't explain how or why that was to be the case, though Aiya figured she could guess.

The first city took them in without impediments. It was slightly larger than Tsuisaka, having developed more naturally. Sen's soldiers were left outside the gates. Sen, addressing his men's concerns briefly, entered with Aiya and Koji alone. The three were led by a couple of Jodai and the city lord's brother, who repeatedly gave his 'sincere' apologies for any inconveniences during their travels. Residents stood on either side of the street, watching them pass by. They whispered amongst themselves, not daring to speak directly to Sen or his company. There were commoners and nobles, dressed distinctly different just as in River, and Aiya was again reminded of the vastness of the world.

They arrived at a small shrine house surrounded by miniature gardens and entered, their guide closing the door behind them. The walls here were graced with incense, five soldiers posted alongside them. A table in the room's center, and behind it, their host. The three outsiders situated themselves in their seats.

"Thank you for coming, Lord Sen. I've heard of your pressing matters." Lord Jesu smoked on a roll of fatabi leaf, the creases in his forehead swelling as his face lit up in a grin. He removed it from his mouth and ashed it on the table.

"Lord Jesu. How are you?"

"I could be better, but I can't complain. I didn't expect you'd show up again so soon."

"Unfortunately, events have not unfolded as planned. I was forced to flee the battle at the Hijimata hills."

"Unfortunate indeed! I hope you understand how deeply crossed this leaves me. Your sister is the last I'd expect to take up the mantle as heir! So, what can I do to help?"

Sen paused. "All we ask for is nine tenths of your available infantry in the city."

One of the guards in the room sneezed.

Jesu took a long puff of his roll, lighting the ember on the opposite end. He exhaled a plume of smoke into the air, coughing and setting the roll down. "Yes, well, I regret to

inform you that concerning this war, there won't be any involvement on my part. Just as I told you in our last meeting."

"Surely we can come to an agreement."

"Well, you see, with your current situation, you've already
garnered the aid of Agriculture, so I find my aid is unnecessary."

"Agriculture is fighting a losing battle as we speak. My
sister has been bolstered by thousands of additional forces
from Rain province. Once Ueko's army arrives it will be too
late if you don't act now."

"All the more reason to not get involved! What can my
men do? You have to understand, I'm only looking out for
my own city!"

Sen shut his eyes for a moment, rubbing them and gritting
his teeth. "You choose cowardice. You know damn well
you'll be kissing my mother's feet for the rest of your life
after this. Have you not a shred of self-respect?"

"That, along with a peculiar sense of self-preservation.
Take them away." Lord Jesu got up and hurried to leave as a
guard came and grabbed Aiya's arm, his other reaching for
Koji.

Aiya spun from his grasp, got behind him and brought his
face down onto the table. Hard.

Jesu stopped in his tracks. "What is this?"

Other guards stepped forward to handle them. Aiya and
Koji swiftly delivered kicks and jabs to their non-vitals. The
men collapsed, failing to detain their guests. The door to the
room opened again, Jesu's brother standing behind it with
three more guards, flustered. "In a shrine?"

"Your involvement is not a matter of choice, Lord Jesu," Sen said. "I am prepared to do whatever is necessary to win this, and I don't take kindly to those who get in my way. These two are Ginju from the land of River, the only insurance I had when I walked in here. So please believe me when I say I'll have them kill as many of your men as needed, your precious pawns of protection, should you choose not to cooperate. Of course, I hope it does not come to that."

Jesu snickered. "And why should I believe these two little runts can take out over twelve-hundred men at my beck and call?"

Drawing on the river, Aiya grabbed the edge of the heavy wood table. She lifted it from the ground with a single arm, her muscles straining as she moved it. Everyone jumped back as she flung it towards the door, almost hitting the guards. It cracked against the stone wall interior, the fatabi roll landing off to its side.

Jesu was backed against the wall, murmuring something as he examined them in fright. The guards twiddled cluelessly.

"I was prepared to make an example out of a few more men, but your quick thinking just saved us more time. And manpower," Sen said to her.

Aiya blushed, running a hand along her lower back. She might have overdone it.

Sen turned back to Jesu. "So, what is your decision?"

They approached the next city boasting fifteen-hundred strong, or somewhere near it.

Aiya wasn't sure whether to sympathize with their new manpower, or Lord Jesu, for that matter. The Jodai were essentially captives, though they assimilated quite easily. Perhaps Lord Jesu had acted selfishly after all. Perhaps, sometimes, it was also necessary to rely on any means necessary for one's cause. If that meant a future where wars of succession ceased to be, perhaps one where all warfare was eradicated, then so be it.

Conversation was deathly sparse in-between, and Aiya was glad for it. An oddly uncomfortable nervousness cropped up whenever Sen looked in her direction.

When they arrived, the city's troops were already posted outside its gates. An army about half the size of their own. Aiya felt her palms sweaty, but the city lord rushed out to meet Sen before they'd even made it a hundred paces outside the gates. The man bowed and profusely offered words of praise, and Aiya was shocked to find that he was turning over his troops without putting up so much as an unkind word. Sen assured him he would be rewarded for his loyalty and sent him away. Eight-hundred men were organized into their army before moving on to the third and final city.

"That man was an ass kisser, known for kissing the asses of other lords," Sen explained. "He maintains his riches that way. His estate is nothing but a relic of what it used to be, holding onto the last bit of remaining wealth his once-great family owns. Hence why he is so keen on pleasing me."

Word traveled fast across cities within the same province, and the man also hadn't wanted any contentions with Sen's bodyguards.

The last city wasn't so far away, which Aiya silently gave thanks to the heavens for. Sen explained that the final lord was his old mentor, a man who'd been welcomed into their estate many times and had taken a personal liking to Sen. For the first time, perhaps since before the battle of the Hijimata hills, a tingling sensation prickled in Aiya's stomach and chest. It was a feeling of hope.

"I wonder what ever happened to Shozhu," Koji told Aiya, and she gave him a confounded look.

"Why are you thinking about that of all things right now?"

"I dunno, it just popped into my head for some reason."

"Well, I'm sure we'll know eventually. Personally, I wouldn't mind if we never saw or heard from the bastard again."

The final lord, Lord Komei, also had his soldiers posted outside his city walls when they arrived. Something seemed a bit off about Sen as they approached. A dip in the shoulders, maybe? Curiously pursed lips indicated his intense concentration. Aiya watched him closely once they stopped, awaiting for Lord Komei's arrival.

Komei's men swaggered slowly on horseback towards them. Komei led them, a man with ample facial hair. He was cocky-looking, and he knew it, carrying himself like an open book. He smirked, his Forgery robes longer than would be expected. "Lord Sen, you've arrived."

"Master Komei."

"Your turn of harmony seems to have slipped past you."

"Let's skip the small talk. You know why I'm here."

"Yes, my beloved apprentice, always the serious type. I know why you're here, what you've brought with you, and what you picked up along the way. And also how you got it." His eyes brushed past Sen's right, then over Aiya. The air had suddenly become more stiff, their proximity from one another tighter, slightly dangerous. "River Ginju, huh? You've done well for yourself politically too. Unfortunately, well, you won't want to hear this, but what worked on Jesu and Taru won't work on me."

Sen was quiet for a bit. His silence was near suffocating. "And why would that be?"

"Simply put, you're doomed. It was already a close bet between you and your sister, and I must say I was shocked to hear you'd managed to drag Agriculture into it. I applaud you for that. But Ueko, she was always one step ahead of you. Have you truly resorted to using Agriculture and River Ginju now? Sen, you should be ashamed."

He turned to go. Aiya was shocked when Sen said nothing; their men from behind sat in equally stunned silence. The truth had unfolded: these lords were not beholden to him in any way. With no familial authority to fall back on, true violence might become necessary.

A few feet into his retreat, Komei turned. "Oh, and if you are planning on attacking, I trust you know that I will bring down this entire city if I must."

Sen said nothing, and Aiya could see him twitching in his saddle as he stared coldly into Komei's eyes.

"I serve Ueko, Sen, as I always have. You shouldn't have forgotten."

Komei galloped away.

"So that's it, we're just gonna let him go?" Aiya demanded.

"Leave it," Sen said, in a tone so stern she hushed at once. "There's nothing we can do, we'll have to make do with our current numbers. The storm is approaching faster than we predicted anyway."

"Two-thousand troops, gone," Koji said.

"No," Sen said. "They were never ours to begin with. We still have decent numbers. Pray to the heavens for the best."

Facing the wind as they journeyed back proved incredibly unpleasant. A few men complained of the cold behind them, quickly silenced by the more hardened of their kind. The glimmering sense of hope from earlier wilted into a heavy black ooze that hung from Aiya's insides. She constantly fought to keep it from festering into despair. Morning fast approached, making the empty fields visible once again, and Sen said little until they were halfway back, Aiya waiting for his anger to burst into a tirade.

"Don't lose hope," he said to them. Aiya didn't know how to respond at first.

"Seems a little hard. After you told us he was your mentor I expected that to be the easiest grab," she finally said.

"Don't expect things to come too easy either. Not in times like these. Anyway, it's...complicated."

"Yeah, we've learned nothing ever happens as expected a lot lately."

Sen's eyes fell on her feet, then rose to her face. "You said your father had passed earlier. Forgive me if it's an intrusion, but is that the reason you're here?"

"Summed up, you'd be correct," she said. "Agriculture, and our brother, our third blessed sibling, are the ones responsible for saving us...and also for forcing us into all this. I guess you haven't heard of recent developments in River because of your predicament."

"So you're not here by choice?"

"Well, not for the reasons you'd expect. What Tsugo's told you about his grand plan, you're just the start. Even after winning this, I don't see how it will change the grand scheme of the empire. Hell, I'm not sure if I'd be sane to think it would. But, we still chose to come along for the ride."

"You won't know. No man could foresee the outcome at the Hijimata hills, nor how many troops we'd recruit before this Wailstorm, nor the outcome of this civil war. But we *believed*. You fight, whether you know the end result or not. Something Lord Komei taught me, believe it or not."

Aiya studied him, taking in his words and posture. He was a true man of principle. She saw him extend his arm, reach for a further part of his rein and tug on it. As he did so, his long sleeve slid up his arm, revealing a strange sight. His skin was darker in some spots, malformed. She quickly recognized them as burn marks.

Sen looked at her, saw that she had noticed them. He said nothing and made no indication that he was bothered by it. Instead, he told her, "Don't settle being complacent, especially if that complacency is an illusion." He turned to Koji. "Same to you."

As they approached Tsuisaka, the winds only got colder.

# Return

Her first Wailstorm had been fourteen years ago. At least, that was the first storm Aiya could remember. At age eight, however, her memory of them became more clear. She was a timid little girl staring out the window at the tempest, facing it with wonder, and, inside, a small, healthy dose of fear.

Wrapped up in that fear and wonder was a peculiar feeling of amazement and insignificantness, the sheer power of the gales pounding the Takasa castle frames, creating the illusion that they might be under attack. The landscape outside had changed, shrouded in surging mists below a bright gray sky. So bright that it was almost white, and somehow more vivid than the cloudy congestion should have allowed.

Then there was the wailing, the reason they were named Wailstorms. Indoors or out, wherever one went, followed the sound of a wailing woman. Long, deep cries of despair, perhaps over a lost child, taken by frostsickle. Yet the wails were muffled, blotted out by booming, thundering winds.

The storms were unnatural, a disturbance on nature itself, and as the cold seeped in, for the first time Aiya connected the stories of the Empress' first wrath to the spectacle taking place before her. Wailstorms always brought cold, no matter if the sun had beat down on them with its heat in the hours prior. The Empress must have been a cold person for her to have brought this about, recurring every so often. Was she angry right now? Did she spawn them on a whim? It seemed unnecessarily cruel.

Irashida and Koji stood far back from the window, huddled with Kisane. Irashida had gone out before in this weather, catching frostsickle. Their father reprimanded him heavily for it. Worse for Ira, the apparitions and chills were enough for him to stay as far away from the storms as possible from then on. He'd whispered the apparitions caused by frostsickle were like the silhouettes of people, except they were a blinding white. They were very tall, and large. They could be seen pacing or drifting about, and sometimes they couldn't be seen at all.

Koji always had the better sense not to adventure out into the storms. Aiya never liked them much either. She also was not sure the Empress was fully responsible for them, though she couldn't put into words why. She was a Ginju, being taught the ways of the river through daily meditation, and though she was early in her training and had yet to even begin aligning herself, meditation taught her to recognize the forces of the world that were larger than life. This storm was larger than any of them, beyond their understanding, even as Ginju. Like the spirits of legend that struck fear in men's hearts, except it was so much more gargantuan that it made even them seem inconsequential. Immortal Empress or not, Wailstorms seemed to be the only true thing that kept a watchful eye from corner to corner of Egaisha.

It was Second Day in the second week of Fenn. Aiya sat in the corner of the central hub next to the charcoal brazier, staring out the window into the mists. She appreciated the warmth while admiring the storm for its raw power, the foreboding eeriness of the drawn out wails. Both for what it was and what the passage of time that allowed its arrival meant. The officials present chatted quietly in the background, but Aiya was eager to keep to herself in this small corner of hers. She hadn't realized how tired she was, but anxiety was keeping her up.

She hadn't noticed Koji sliding next to her. She didn't avert her gaze for a while, content just to have him by her side, regardless of his musky odor. His presence, the crackling charcoal and the boisterous winds had an oddly calming effect. It was only right to soak it up while they had the chance.

Koji leaned in close, whispering. "Tell me why I have a bad feeling about Irashida."

His face was droopy, tired yet restless, the most he'd ever been. A flash of anger crossed his face. He was no doubt troubled by the fact they'd allowed Ira to push himself, or perhaps because Ira had chosen to do so by his own violation. That anger mirrored itself in Aiya, simmering in her stomach. Koji often had that effect on her. "Don't say things like that Koji. You're homesick."

"Yeah, I suppose I am. You know, something in me wants to be out there right now, in the storm."

"Really? Not you of all people."

Koji shrugged. "Ever since we passed that *thing* in the forest. Remember back when we were younger, and I went out during that Wailstorm on a dare?"

"And you ran back in because you were scared of catching frostsickle?"

"Haha, smirk all you want, meathead. Catching what Ira had can hardly be called brave. But I remember it so clearly, the feeling of being one small person, or like an animal. Like a rabbit or something, trapped, even though I was out in the open. I felt so small, so insubstantial."

"I get exactly what you mean."

"I was terrified when you were facing off against the Rain Ginju."

"You don't have to worry about that anymore, Koji. I simply thought of protecting you and Sen. Then I was able to overcome myself."

"Ever since the forest, I can't stop thinking about *it*. About our lives, our pasts and futures as Ginju. This freak storm. I don't know." He placed a hand on her knee. "I'm sorry for snapping on you earlier. You were as freaked out as the rest of us."

"If you want to make up for it, show me your little book. I want to see your latest drawing."

He leaned back a bit, shaking his head. "If we get through tomorrow, maybe you can see it as a reward."

"Mhm. You don't really draw in it though, do you? Don't give me that 'what do you mean?' face, you look constipated.

I see you writing words in it sometimes, and your drawings haven't gotten any better over the years. I've, uh, peeped a few times too."

"You what?" He exclaimed. "Well, guess I can't get mad..."

What secrets could he be hiding from her? "Are you writing poetry? What's to be ashamed of? Intellectual pursuits are the pride of the nobility! You could bring to life our stories of heroic battles or lament on the honor and tragedy of combat–"

"It's not the kind you think." He sighed, cutting her off from saying anything further. "Listen, I'm glad we joined this Republic. If we get through tomorrow, you and Ira will have won me over. I'll need to make him promise, no more enemies to friends situations. My brain can't handle it."

She leaned in and embraced him. It caught him off guard, but she didn't care. "This battle has been hard on you Koji. Let's not think about the past or the future. Like Sen told us, we just have to know we'll send that bitch Ueko's head rolling. Like you told me, we march and we fight, as Ira would expect us to do. He's never given up on himself. We're Ginju after all."

Aiya passed out from pure exhaustion, waking two hours later. Koji was nowhere in sight.

Totane and Risako rested next to each other as Aiya awoke, though Totane began to rise right as Aiya was leaving the conference room.

"You should...keep sleeping," Aiya told him in the doorway. "You'll need the rest."

"Don't coddle me, please," Totane said with a grimace, stretching.

Aiya stalled, careful to give him space, but not wanting to leave the air hanging. "They're serving rations outside."

"Thanks, I'll be out once Risako is up."

Outside, the sun showed itself again, warming the air to a mildly uncomfortable chill. Soldiers roamed the streets in orderly fashion, despite the air of uncertainty. Once the storm passed, Sen wasted no time. Scouts were sent out of the city to determine the status of the opposing army and their proximity.

Rations were meager, a bowl of rice barely the size of her fist. After eating her share, she decided to walk around the city. It was so clean, so organized, Aiya couldn't imagine it devolving into a warzone. The southern quarters had less soldiers on patrol, and after about ten minutes of walking through it, she realized there was nobody around her. The streets here were abandoned, or at least Sen saw no use for them at this time. Still, something was off.

The south city wall loomed about two hundred paces away. She stood in an area with sparse architecture, almost as if this part of the city had yet to see completion.

She walked aimlessly, getting close to a round building in particular when she spotted something. Her face pulled into curiosity before confusion, then disgust. An arm sticking out from behind the corner of the building.

Her eyes squinted as her stomach dropped. She slowly moved to inspect it, gasping at the dead body laying behind the bend. A Jodai man lay face down. Aiya's mind entertained the idea that he might be sleeping, but she'd come too far for that. Turning him over, she saw he was young, face undisturbed, as if resting, yet his neck was smeared in blood, carved from one end of his chin to the other. His armor was still glossy, so his death hadn't been the result of some skirmish. The deep gash had not allowed him to scream, or live long.

She moved to notify someone, then stopped. A presence in front of her. She didn't look but rolled out of the way as a dagger sunk into the dirt behind her. Facing forwards, she came to face the three Rain Ginju from the day before. White Hair, his sister, and brother. They stood only a few paces from their victim, and not far from her. The other male Ginju bled through the patches on his jaw, which was still crooked as the last day she'd seen it. Aiya took the chance to look around her. No one.

"Caught us just in time. But you're all alone," the girl said, taking a step back. Her limp was gone, with effort.

"How did you get in these walls?" Aiya shouted, realizing she didn't have her sword on her. A foolish mistake.

"I'm sure you know the answer to that," White Hair said, a cocky grin teasing his cheeks. "Not hard to figure out."

"Seems you forgot something," said the girl. She unsheathed both her daggers, White Hair holding up the one he still had. "Dekuri's terrible aim may have just bought you a few more seconds."

Aiya considered grabbing the dagger from behind her and running for aid. If she led them into the heart of the city, they'd wreak havoc, massacring soldiers until the other Ginju intervened. Then again, two of them might easily run around her while she engaged one. She'd have to hold all three here for as long as possible, find a way to attract the attention of the others. "Have you forgotten what happened last time we fought?"

"A pitiful bluff," the one named Dekuri said, taking a step forward. His brother took one with him, though he didn't try to speak past his bandages. Dekuri smiled, clearly enjoying this interrogation. "I'll take this one, Shoba."

Heart pounding, Aiya stalled. "Where are the Rain troops? You three can't be here alone."

"Pitiful last w-" Dekuri started, and as he did Aiya watched the girl lift her daggers and slide them across her siblings' throats. Before they could react, she ran them through their necks, drawing thick rivulets of blood. Wide-eyed, the two collapsed, making futile gasps for air.

Aiya's arms shot halfway up then became stiff as if they'd forgotten how to function. She tried mouthing words but found none. The two writhed on the floor, looking up at their sister, who looked down on them, no remorse in her.

Aiya stepped back from the scene as the girl kneeled down to them and cooed Dekuri to sleep. When the girl looked up, eyes a light purple, Aiya turned and ran for the dagger, grabbing it and spinning to face her opponent.

"Relax!" the girl told her. "I mean no harm."

"W-what is this? What the hell is this?"

"I know I'm your enemy," said the girl. "Consider this my token of goodwill."

"Why did you just kill them?"

"It's personal," she answered. "Long story short, I've been waiting for this moment for a long time. I can't have imagined a better opportunity. You and me, we tried killing each other at the Hijimata hills. Because of me you're alive. Let's call us even."

Aiya tilted her head in confusion. "You...are you asking me to let you live?"

"I only ask you to shelter me from Rain for now, for the time being. Trust me, they're just as much my enemies as they are yours. After this battle is over, I won't bother you."

Aiya stared her down for a moment longer, shook her head, and charged.

The girl backed up, then, when Aiya was on her, passed through her. Aiya turned and stuck out her dagger, hoping it sank into flesh. The girl hadn't stopped until she was fifteen paces away on the other side of Aiya.

"Stop!" she exclaimed. "I mean what I say! It sounds bizarre, but unbelievable as it is, I'm only asking that you trust me until this battle is over."

"Shut the hell up!" Aiya growled. "Earlier, we were at each other's throats! Why should I let you live?"

"Because you need me," the girl replied.

Aiya breathed heavily but didn't respond.

"Hasa is coming as we speak, and she's coming fast. You'll want every arm you can muster."

Aiya examined her, considering. She was disgusted just looking at her, but then, the girl had a point. They could use her, and whatever reason she had for it, murdering her siblings was a benefit to them. What could her past be, that she could so easily take vengeance on whatever terrible thing they'd done?

She turned to the bodies of the girl's siblings. Along with the murdered Jodai man, it was a grisly sight. "Are they really dead?"

The girl waited to meet her eyes. "Yes, they are."

"Kick them."

The girl inched forward, then back. "You want...proof?"

Aiya stalked over to the bodies herself, planting a foot in Dekuri's face. She lifted her leg again and came down hard. The feeling of her foot against his dead cheek was sickening. "That's for earlier," she said.

She turned back to the girl. "Walk in front of me." She held up her dagger.

"Even if I were to turn on you, you're faster."

Aiya was standing a mere five paces from her now. "And you can phase through objects. I'll stay this far from you until we get to everyone else. Walk."

The girl did just that. They spent the next ten minutes or so in silence, Aiya's nerves fraying by the second. She couldn't believe what she allowed in front of her and considered simply killing the girl. Even holding Dekuri's dagger nearly sent her into a fit of revulsion. Aiya kept pace as they came into the populated area of the city. Patrolling Jodai noticed the spectacle and began asking questions. Guilty, Aiya denied comment and ordered them not to mind.

Sen was the first to spot them directly outside the conference room, mid-conversation with one of his subjects. He stopped, staring. The murmuring intensified.

Totane and Risako exited the building in unison. Seeing the pair of them, Totane made no hesitation before snatching the nearest Jodai man's sword and leaping for the girl.

"Wait, Totane-"

Aiya didn't get a chance to finish. Totane was already throwing a flurry of swipes against the girl, who was retreating into the crowds. Some ran out the way, aware the two couldn't be contained, while others stood their ground, petrified.

"Totane, listen to me!" Aiya went to grab Totane, but he slammed his shoulder into her. She caught it, and before she knew what was happening, she was pinning Totane down with Koji and four Jodai men. Totane tried wriggling free, cursing both them and his target.

The girl stood in front of the rations stand, its line now evacuated.

"Relax, Totane!" Aiya yelled. "You'll get your chance with her, but first...just...calm down!"

Totane finally got hold of himself, ceasing his struggle. He buried his head into his arm, screaming. The Jodai men took the opportunity to back off, exhausted but relieved. Koji looked to Aiya.

"What the fuck is she doing here?"

"I'm as clueless as you are, believe me." Aiya hopped off of Totane as Risako ran for him. He slowly gained control of himself, looking at Aiya with disdain.

"I'm so sorry," Aiya said. "I found her with the others-"

"Others? They're all here?"

"Yes. The other Rain Ginju, they killed a guard at the southern edge of the city. I stumbled on him and out came these three." She gestured to the girl with a hand. "I thought they were about to kill me, but she," Aiya pointed to the girl, "she...slit their throats. She killed her comrades right in front of me. I tried to kill her, but apparently she thinks she can help us now."

Risako looked from her to Aiya in disbelief. "*Help* us? Is this some sick joke?"

"His mother and sister are almost here," the girl said, pointing to Sen. "If I wanted to cause you harm, I could have done it ten times over and retreated already. I'm trying to help."

Risako, who carried her blade, drew it from her scabbard.

"Enough!" Sen exclaimed. All eyes went to him. Aiya wanted nothing to do with this situation anymore. "This Rain Ginju wants forgiveness. I find it hard to believe, but in this dire situation, I'm willing to listen. What is your name?"

The girl swallowed, then answered, "Renna."

"Renna. And you say, how far are mother's troops?"

Before she could respond, they heard shouting from the tops of the city wall. The guards were suddenly worked up, their voices sounding haunted. "Rain and Forgery troops sighted! Enemy troops in the distance! Forgive us if we're mistaken, but...they seem to be accompanied by the Empress herself!"

# Confrontation

Empress Isao Naji did not take kindly to roadblocks. That was all she considered this conflict, a block in the road. Tarshan was the real objective. Tarshan, with their wide ships, masters of sea warfare. Tarshan, whose tactics somehow proved superior to her own. She picked at a string in her cuff. Silk should not thread. It seemed, however, that everything frayed eventually.

She could not break the *flow*, but it had been generations since the empire had struggled to hold itself together like this, long before she was even born.

Still, she was weary of these locals impeding her advances, stalling her with their inconsequential concerns. They complained when she reprimanded them, and complained at her favor. They did not understand their place.

She despised civil wars, every wretched one of them.

"They're lining outside for us, Your Sovereign," Shige told her. She saw them lining outside the city, formations and all, scuttling into masses, much like ants.

The army around her and Ueko's thirty troops took position. They'd arrived a thousand paces outside the city, poised to end this silly spectacle. The Empress refused her palanquin. She'd meet the perpetrators of this prolonged battle on her feet, little did they deserve it. She would humble them. Naji looked over the opposing army for a long while. "I assume the one at the front is the young Forgery Lord. Who are those four behind him? They have a knife pointed at the back of Renna."

"Those are the Ginju he rallied, Your Sovereign," Ueko answered. Naji always took interest in looking upon her. That hardened face, hair pulled into a short tail fitting for a High Lady. In the rare times she came into Naji's presence, there was a distant yet undeniable kinship between them, a spiritual one. It was difficult to identify the feeling, but Naji supposed Ueko was the closest experience to guiding a daughter of her own. *This one is me in another life. I could have been her.*

"Agriculture seems to have been given two more than me, Sovereign," Ueko continued. "Rain was able to take out one of them at the Hijimata hills, but it seems they've managed to return the favor twofold when we sent their Ginju to scout out the city."

Naji did not betray her relaxed, observant expression. "They'll die soon enough, and in the meantime, you should concern yourself elsewhere. I will return soon to Sanaba. I've wasted enough time here already."

Two Ginju had been slain by none other than Ginju from yet another province. How many provinces were involved? Large swaths of the southern empire might be at risk of a great outbreak in war against one another, and if Ginju were being relied on, that was an unsettling thing.

She should have intervened far sooner.

Ueko believed in her immortality, trusting her Empress to stop this skirmish with the snap of her fingers. She certainly would.

Naji took three deep breaths and calmed herself. No matter, this would all now come to an end. Ueko would be placed on the throne and expansion would continue. For Naji, it would be remembered merely as a simple diversion. *Her* empire would never fail.

"Mother's coming forward with Hasa." Sen sat tall on his horse, the only one on horseback among the seven of them. A young general named Gheki, who happened to be the youngest general Aiya had yet seen, stood by his side. Risako, Totane, and Koji stood around Aiya, who still held her newly claimed dagger at the Rain girl's back. Each possessed a sheathed sword, bracing themselves.

Aiya didn't know where Sen was looking. She couldn't make out anyone in particular but the woman trailing towards them in impossibly long robes. They looked to be robes of purple silk brilliant in the noon sunlight. As she came closer, Aiya saw the woman's hair was long too, entwined in a beautiful style over her crown of amethyst. Through her robes ran large swirling patterns, discernible even from this distance, dancing in the sun's beams.

The Empress. She'd come marching for Ueko, just as she had the Warlord Kozuku at the birth of the empire. Surely, the Sorceress of Storms had come to settle things here and now. She'd come to destroy. In all her life, Aiya could not recall a single moment where her stomach had plunged to lower depths and fear had slithered throughout her entire frame, binding her, making her small, feeble, constricted.

"Two-thousand men." General Gheki's voice faltered. "They've brought less than we'd expect."

"Father gave them the hard time they deserved," Totane answered.

Aiya's knees grew shaky.

Gheki shook his head, dull-faced and serious. "These might be the Empress' personal guard. Their armor is a slightly different hue. They're Rain Jodai either way."

The Empress didn't stop, and neither did her army. Sen's men raised their weapons in the most terrifying display of courage Aiya had ever witnessed. The Empress was actually here, and she wasn't stopping.

Just when Aiya thought they had only a few moments to live, the Empress came to a halt. She stood a mere ten feet from them while her army stood back another forty. Posted beside her were both Hasa and Ueko.

The Empress was beautiful, slender, and her aura repressive. Her skin shone smooth like the finest porcelain. The Empress did not appear especially strong in physique, yet her presence alone overwhelmed Aiya's senses, as if her clothing had been drenched in ice cold waters, slowly weighing her down.

Was her reputation alone responsible for such a feeling? Aiya looked to the others, who also appeared to struggle against some unseen force, postures going stiff. The Empress was a conqueror, the one who brought subjugation. A woman out of dreams, who quelled any reaction or response any of them might have. As soon as she halted, Aiya's head turned to the clamor behind her, watching all the soldiers who'd hurried to bow. "Your Sovereign!" the men shouted.

Aiya was suddenly sinking into the ground, unable to bear the weight of her own body.

Totane rushed to grab her shoulders and pulled her up. "STAND!"

She looked wide eyed around her. Every Jodai remained bowed. Renna was coming out of her own bow, looking to her and Totane.

The Empress raised an eyebrow that dried up Aiya's throat like baked soil. The voice that came from her luscious lips was sweet as honey yet venomous as a viper.

"What's wrong, young ones? Are you feeling nervous?"

There was no response, the air around them suffocating. Aiya tried backing away, unable to stand her presence. Totane held her firm.

"We will…NEVER…bow to you!" Totane shook.

The Empress smiled.

"Neither will I," said Sen. "I sacrificed much to be in the position I am in now, and I will sacrifice more. As have Agriculture and River, who are with me. And if I am forced to take you down with my mother, so be it."

The soldiers around them began muttering to themselves. "Fool, she calls the storms!"

"Forgive us, Sovereign!"

Aiya shook with the realization that this was the true moment for her decision. The Empress herself stood before them, the immortal ruler of the land. Sorceress of Storms. Running to her feet now would surely save her and Koji's life, if the Empress didn't decide to kill them first. Still, she could run, and give them a better chance for their survival. She could instead honor Ira's will, her promise to Totane and Agriculture. She could honor her vow to protect Sen. Would she abandon him now? There might never be a better opportunity.

She remembered River, when she'd allowed her clan to be subjugated and humiliated by Owa. With astounding clarity, she saw what the Republic fought against. She would never allow herself to become heartless like Ueko, to be as cold as she herself once was. She would not turn on her family again. She would protect not only Koji, but Totane, Risako, Tsugo, Sen, until death do them part.

She held firm, and stood. There was no going back.

The Empress looked down to Renna.

"You stand with them too?"

Shaking, Renna slowly raised her dagger toward the Empress.

The Empress smiled. "So you will all die, and East Forgery will be severely punished. The families of every Jodai, commander, Ginju, lord and lady in this region will feel my wrath. I will erase you from memory, destroy your bloodlines from the earth. Three times for speaking out of turn."

"She caused the Wailstorm," one of the soldiers shouted. "You're doomed!"

Ueko and Hasa were white enough to have seen spirits. Aiya almost wanted to throw up. She steeled herself, cementing her resolve. If this was the person that truly stood against her and her siblings, Aiya would see her as the final and ultimate challenge against her strength. She would become the impossible and kill this person, the Empress herself, if that's what it took to overthrow her.

"This conflict lies between me and my sister. I challenge her to an honor duel to settle this once and for all." Sen's voice was unfaltering.

The smile on the Empress' face spread, ending with laughter. "I have the final say in this matter, silly pig. You'll be flayed before you die, and your legacy will become like dust. Yes, Forgery has fallen far out of favor. But your worst blasphemy today is your lack of faith in me. In my power."

The Empress called forth a man from the army behind her. The man was dressed in all white robes with a veil covering his face, clipped to show only his mouth. The hood of his robe was tight around the head, and the long veil was buttoned with gold beads to the sides of the hood hanging to his chin. Aiya's heart raced. The man stopped before the Empress. Without turning, the Empress raised her arm behind her and held out an upraised palm.

"You are Ginju, powerful Erru indeed. But what you don't understand is that I am the one who created you."

"Created us?" Sen said.

The Empress put a hand up to the small curvature of her mouth, holding in laughter. "Haven't you noticed why all the Ginju you've known are in sets of three? You were told you were chosen, blessed by me. The only ones in your clans capable of wielding great power while the rest grew up and took care of political work. In reality, you were chosen because you were the only ones capable of learning to be

Ginju. I gave you the ability to see and contact your deities. For each province, I gave access to a separate deity. The deities and the Shinti are one and the same, whom I alone have full access to. Three children, of any current ruler, are chosen by their parents and blessed in each province, an impartation of my power."

The Empress' eyes fell on Koji in particular. Then to Aiya. Her knees almost gave out, but she stood. "I remember your father, Arusuke. Rest his soul. He was one of the proudest men I'd ever known. It made him a great ruler. However, he couldn't bear to stand the thought of you two being more powerful than he. I know because he secretly despised the idea of bowing even to me. That's why he chose for you to come from commoner blood. Your mothers were present for each one of you on the day of blessing. Wrapped in hoods and baggy clothing to hide their identity. Your father didn't want to be disgraced himself, but for you...

"Poor child, don't look so surprised. You were still given your deity. You still boast power few men and women ever comprehend. At the center of the deities is wrath however, wrath that mere mortals as yourselves dare to look at them, to take a glimpse of their glory. That's why when you access enough of this glimpse, they can come into contact with you, and attempt to hurt you. This is why they become ugly. Your mind understands you are under threat, but not quite why.

"But I have access to all of these deities, and I see them for what they truly are. They have given me many servants. I'll leave one with you as a reminder of my sovereignty, since every one of you is unworthy to be in my presence. Behold, for you will perish, and shortly after so shall my servant dissipate into the breath of the earth, and thus this skirmish shall be forgotten to history."

There was a loud *pop* from behind the Empress. Heads turned this way and that, and a few men yelped. Even Totane took a step back. Then they heard it again, and again. More popping sounds, until they realized it was coming from the man in white behind her, the Empress' hand still upraised and spread out directly towards him. His body squirmed and convulsed as he let out increasingly intense grunts of pain. He did not ask for it to stop.

Aiya gaped, seeing the man's body had become bloated, almost ready to burst through his clothing. After what seemed an eternity, his body expanded three times its size, then even larger. He became a mix of mismatched limbs, jagged bones, and red-green scales. A monstrous hand clawed at the earth, raking up tufts of grass and dirt, as the formless creature let out an ear-splitting screech. Finally, it began to take shape, drawing up to stand on its haunches.

Her stomach plummeted.

There was no mistaking the beast. Thick whiskers at the end of its snout. It's lizard-like appearance, complimented by hundreds of tiny spikes along its head, its muscular frame, and the long, scaly tail.

The man had transformed into a dragon.

The Jodai men were backing away and yelling obscenities before it even roared. When it did, they lost all courage. Aiya had to clamp her hands to her ears, the sound rattling her skull.

It finished and looked on them, hungry. The Empress was already ambling back to her army, who didn't dare step any closer. Hasa and Ueko ran ahead of her, shrieking.

"Retreat!" yelled a Jodai man. He didn't have to tell them. The formations they'd made were ruined, half the soldiers trying to get back into the city.

"We will *not* retreat!" Sen commanded, rearing his horse. "Stand your ground! We are warriors, Jodai and Ginju alike! Nothing will take us down, so stand your ground, damn it!"

"Empress' soul," Aiya whispered.

The rest of the Ginju drew their swords as Aiya did the same. Renna turned for the first time, both daggers at the ready. "Guess you're glad I'm still here now."

Aiya couldn't take her eyes off the creature. It was straight out of legend, forty feet long and unmistakable. The dragon, with the cold and calculating eye of a reptile, was here before them. It existed.

And now it charged them. One daring glance back revealed only a third of their forces still in formation. Aiya braced herself, gritting her teeth. Her grip on her blade was ironclad.

"Get Sen to safety!" Totane screamed, then met the creature head on.

Totane prepared a stab but didn't get the chance. At ten feet tall, the dragon was as wide as many men. One swipe from its claw nearly tore Totane in two. He managed to dodge at the last second, its nail digging across his chest and spraying his blood on the dirt. Totane tumbled into its hind legs.

The creature would have rounded on him, but Risako was at its other side. She jabbed an elbow and was smacked to the side in return.

Aiya joined them, dashing between the creature's feet and bringing her blade point into its belly. The tip barely penetrated. She was almost crushed, knocked to the side before she knew what was happening. The *smack* of its backhand left her stunned. Her body hit the soggy ground hard, rolling to a rough stop.

Ignoring the stiffness in her right shoulder, she threw herself up to see Koji whacked by its tail with blazing speed. Koji cried out as he tumbled over the ground. Totane slashed its hind leg. Risako went for its groin.

Aiya returned to slice its neck, scraping away scales with repeated swipes, shoulder muscles burning as she swiped her blade back and forth, keeping her feet in motion. She showered in red. Its jaws came down on her. It might have taken her entire arm in its jaws had she not released her weapon, retreating twenty paces back.

*So fast*! She thought, finding she didn't need to realign herself. Its tail whipped around in a frenzy, the only thing she'd ever seen move as fast as her. The dragon was equal in speed, and greater in strength.

More shouting.

Mid-stride, Aiya watched around her with awe as the Jodai soldiers charged the creature. The men roared in unison, their battle cries almost matching the dragon's. The transformation in demeanor took Aiya aback. Swords and spears made for the creature, who reared its head and waited to kill. In unison, these men stampeded to their death.

Aiya joined them as the creature raked the life from the Jodai with its claws. It trampled one, then mauled three, thrashing against the swarm. Amazingly, the men didn't retreat. They continued to pile against it, hacking at its scales, cursing and dying.

Cocking its head back, the beast filled its lungs, sucking in air as its red-green scaly chest expanded, leaving its head out of reach. Perhaps instinctively, Risako and Totane fell back. The Jodai men weren't so lucky. The dragon swung down its head, releasing a burst of icy breath from its jaws.

Glistening cold plumed down on them, coating the field in thick frost. Its breath spread rapidly on every soldier in its vicinity, cutting their cries short. Left in their wake were rigid bodies, frozen stiff in mid-flight. One by one, they fell to the ground, cracking or shattering like toppled statues.

*Empress' soul, even agriculture couldn't heal them from that!*

The attack had deterred some soldiers, who ran for their lives. Their comrades rallied them to fight on.

Renna zipped past Aiya and leapt at the creature. It turned in the nick of time. She brought two daggers back as the dragon knocked five men aside, then swiped as Renna came within reach. She should have been ripped in three, but she passed through its hand unscathed, bringing the daggers down on each eye and raking them down before tearing them away. The creature shrieked, entering a blind rampage.

Aiya looked to the man next to her, realizing it was Fuda, who'd been with her to witness the forest spirit. He was locked in a perpetual motion of back and forth, grip firm on his sword, yet unable to charge the creature. He muttered something under his breath with bulging eyes.

Aiya pried the sword from his hands and rushed forward. Had they a thousand men, they might stand a chance. With only three hundred, if that, men would continue to die, and they'd only be closer to defeat. Fortunately, they didn't have to rely on Jodai.

Aiya sprung. She soared twenty feet in the air, plummeting towards the creature. Behind them, the Empress' army was marching away, turning their backs on the scene and all its futility. The Empress hadn't even considered their deaths worthy of being witnessed. Merely empty, foregone conclusions that would be lost under the dust of Ueko's feet. Or so she believed.

Aiya landed on its back and held onto a protruding spike, her skin prickling at the cold mist slipping through the layered scales. Sections of its back had begun to mist away as well.

Aiya buried her sword near its spine. The weapon sunk inches into it. She didn't stop. Aiya held on more tightly than she had ever held on to anything before, plunging her weapon in and out as the creature flailed.

Her armor became soaked in metallic-smelling blood. She buried her sword a final time, halfway into its back before the blade broke. The creature scraped ground and air, movements turning more erratic, then slowed. It used its last remaining effort to topple over in an attempt to crush its assailant. Aiya pushed off, letting herself crash against the earth.

The dragon was crawling now, groaning through its slightly parted jaws. Totane, Koji and Risako stood back, ready to further bloody their weapons to stop its advance.

The Jodai around them kept a distance of at least fifty paces. Dead or dying soldiers littered the ground around it.

The creature no longer moved. Its murderers gave no reaction at first.

Then a cheer erupted from the men, one that might rumble through the entire continent. Somehow, they'd slain this mythical creature and still drew breath.

Aiya was still catching her breath as Renna rushed the dead creature, assaulting its face with her daggers. Aiya huffed as Koji went to her side, grabbing her shoulders and yanking her from her violent outburst.

"It's finished! Enough, it's already dead!"

Renna finally pulled her daggers back, dropped them, and fell to her knees. "Damn you," she told it. "And damn the Empress."

Its eyes were still, stab wounds no longer seeping cold. Only leaking chilled blood. To see the mighty creature dead before them...this was surreal. The servant of the Empress was dead, finished by Aiya's own hands. In a way, the Empress had been defeated too. She should have swelled at her accomplishment. But she was too tired to feel it.

Aiya started. Looking back, the Empress' army was off in the distance. She'd left them to deal with the creature, confident they'd meet their end. But Hasa and Ueko were nowhere in sight.

"Where's Sen?" she blurted out.

The other Ginju looked towards her. Aiya surveyed the battlefield, noticing that Jodai were in action again, yelling to rush to the young lord's aid. She spotted Yko galloping on horseback away from the city. Aiya ran towards him, cursing herself for getting distracted. She ran until she caught up. "Is Sen safe?"

Yko didn't pry his eyes from his front. "On the opposite side of this field, behind the city! Hasa went after him with a large group of men as soon as the Empress and her army went away!"

"How many men did he have with him when he fell back?"

"About a dozen men! Hasa, probably thirty or so!"

Aiya sped up and rushed past the Jodai scrambling to Sen's rescue. She imagined Hasa's men on Sen like dogs, and ran faster. Aiya squinted her eyes in exhaustion, her hand going to her chest. She rounded the city walls, unsure of how much longer she could go. *Not as well rested as I thought....*

There was screaming. Her alignment was beginning to falter, but she made it to the other side before she released herself from the river deity. She stumbled into the middle of the chaos.

Hasa's men outnumbered them two to one, but their enemies weren't the ones screaming. Flames licked the soil and men around them. They flailed as they burned, the heat palpable even twenty paces away.

Standing in front of them, Sen blasted flames in every direction.

Aiya was taken aback and shook her head as if to clear it. The sight remained.

That couldn't be Sen burning those men with flames that came from nowhere but his own body, could it?

*Sen, he's a Ginju.*

Hasa was fleeing on her horse in the distance.

"Oh, no. Not...happening!" Aiya shot up and chased after her. Sen's men trailed behind her but made no progress. They looked back to see Aiya approaching, but she had already passed them. Hasa turned and squealed, terror-stricken, when she spotted Aiya gaining on her.

Pushing through the strain on her body, Aiya came beside Hasa's horse and lunged. She delivered a roundhouse kick to the animal's snout, snapping its neck. Hasa flew hard into the field ahead of her as the creature crashed into the ground, lifeless.

Aiya fell to her knees, watching Hasa who was limp on the grass. She wondered if she was dead. Hasa lifted her head and moaned. She'd likely broken a few bones. Grimacing, Aiya trudged over to her. A breeze had picked up as Hasa began crawling forward, trembling in tears.

Aiya stood five paces away at her side. Hasa growled.

"Baboon! Filthy *swine*! Get out of the *wayyy*!"

Sen appeared behind her. Hasa noticed and turned her head back as far as it would go. "Bastard," Hasa spat.

His face betrayed nothing.

Hasa began squirming in an attempt to move faster. Her voice cracking, she pleaded, "I'm sorry, brother, I didn't mean it. I'm sorry, so sorry. Please let me go."

Sen walked casually over to his sister. He didn't say a word. Reaching out to her, he held up a palm and spread out his fingers. Flaming tendrils leapt from his hand and danced across Hasa's lower body.

Hasa screamed and writhed in agony. She was unable to stop the flames.

"Forgive me! FORGIVE ME!"

The pungent odor of burnt flesh filled Aiya's nostrils and made her sick. Sen didn't give into his sister's pleas, only watching her suffer. Hasa wailed as Sen stood calm, almost as if in deep meditation. He basked in it.

Slowly, he moved the flames up her body. He seared her lower back, then upper back before finally moving onto her shoulders. Hasa lied there, barely managing a croak. Her face twitched. Sen took his sword from his sheath and raised it. He closed his eyes, taking a deep breath. Then he brought it down on her neck.

Like that, in one clean stroke, he had her head. He kneeled next to it for a long moment, head down. He was sweating, clear beads falling from his face onto the ground. Finally, he grabbed it by the hair, held it high above his own, and screamed in victory.

# Epilogue

I rashida lay in darkness. It had been that way for a long time. He woke confused, unsure of where he was. Raising his head slightly, he squinted his eyes. His skull pounded. He turned from side to side. Not much could be made out in the room that he was in, save for a walking cane in the corner illuminated by pale moonlight.

He slowly wriggled his arms from under the sheets, stretching and taking in a deep breath, remembering now that he'd woken here before. He must have passed out. It almost seemed like a dream, so long ago.

The door to his room slid open. The sudden brightness of two lanterns made Ira's eyes water. He turned to see a man and woman enter. The man was portly, his long gray beard falling over his gray robes. He was bald on top, likely in his late forties. There was a smile plastered to his face. "There you are, lordling! Finally awake I see!"

"How are you feeling?" The woman asked. She was slender, twenty years Ira's senior. Her thin red lips looked sweet, her robes a dark pink.

"I think...I think I remember. You two," Ira answered. He had a hard time forming the words. His speech was slightly slurred, as if drunk on rice wine, and he had to speak slower to concentrate on getting the sounds right. He stretched one leg. Ira tried stretching the other. He realized he couldn't.

The man saw him getting worked up and came to his side, placing a gentle hand over his shoulder. "Relax, Irashida. It's alright. Calm down so we can explain."

"Why can't. I move *myyy* right leg? And, where's Aiya and Koji?"

The woman sat down at the edge of the bed. "Do not fear, Irashida. You had an episode that left you unconscious the past four days. Your siblings went on without you, but rest assured they will be returning. That said, you've unfortunately suffered a stroke."

Ira looked dazed, unable to comprehend her words. He had to look down at his bedsheets to make sure his leg was even still there. "Stroke?"

"Unfortunately. You had a seizure, and apparently you have a history of illness. How often does this happen?"

"O-once before. Usually I...just have *smaller* episodes where I'm, uh, lightheaded. Too dizzy. to. move."

"That may be the culprit. You suffered a massive stroke four days ago, in which you lost control of your right leg and some of your ability to speak. You displayed this two days ago, but you passed out again after a half hour. Your condition usually runs in a family."

The man squeezed Ira's shoulders. "You've been in good hands. With time and work, these things may return."

Ira dropped his head into his palms. "*Whaat*, now?"

"In the meantime, there's much to do. We have a job for you of course, an honorable duty that will give you something to do as you learn to get back to normal. Everyone has their place in Agriculture. We aren't without our own many issues. Financial roadblocks, debts, and civil conflict are not below us. Of course, this won't stop us, you'll see. The revolution must go on."

# My Thanks

T hank you so much for reading! If you enjoyed this book, please consider leaving a review on Amazon (and even Goodreads). Sign up for my newsletter for updates, sneak previews, and so that you don't miss the next book, A Reign of Heavenly Fire, coming soon!

# Acknowledgements

T he saying is true. Writing (and more importantly, completing) your first book is hard. Completing *any* book is a feat. Twelve Blades in Contempt is a project of many long days and nights, many highs and lows, an accomplishment that would have not been possible without the contributions of my first editor, Angela Taficante, whose insights into Japanese Culture and progression-style fantasy greatly aided the world and its characterization throughout this novel. I also have to thank my first editor, James Eelbode, whose deep understanding of the writing craft developed my ideas further than I could imagine. My second editor (and beta reader), Tiffany Munro, deserves accolades for her enthusiastic involvement in this series and her genuine eye for detail. My cover artist, Giaphox, and my typographer, Gabriel Akinrinmade, are to thank for this book's downright incredible cover. Map designer, Endi Oblak (Štrigunart), did amazing work bringing the world's geography to life, for which I could not be more satisfied. Professional help goes a long way. My parents, my four grandparents, and my godparents all did their best to encourage my passion, but more importantly, they brought me up in this world, and for that, they should be thanked the most. Acknowledgements also go to my many other beta readers who took the time to read this book and point out all the things amiss in its unfinished form. Without them, I could not have made it this far. And finally, acknowledgements must go to Evan Winter, author of The Rage of Dragons, whose work was a huge inspiration to me. He seems like a great guy.

www.ingramcontent.com/pod-product-compliance
Lightning Source LLC
Chambersburg PA
CBHW060356260626
47160CB00006B/2330